A BRIDGE HOME

A World War II Family Saga

GREG CARSON

PROMISES BOOK THREE

ILLUMIFY MEDIA GLOBAL
Littleton, Colorado

A BRIDGE HOME

Copyright © 2019 by Greg Carson

The views and opinions expressed in this book are those of the author and do not necessarily reflect the official policy or position of Illumify Media Global.

Published by
Illumify Media Global
www.IllumifyMedia.com
"Write. Publish. Market. *SELL!*"

Library of Congress Control Number: 2019911106

Paperback ISBN: 978-1-949021-58-5
eBook ISBN: 978-1-949021-59-2

Typeset by Art Innovations (http://artinnovations.in/)
Cover design by Debbie Lewis

Printed in the United States of America

CONTENTS

Acknowledgments

I would like to thank two people for their invaluable assistance in completing this book. My wife, Vivian, proofread chapters and gave me feedback from the beginning. She also accepted graciously that my work on the novel would take me away from her for long periods of time. My neighbor and friend, Paula Pitchford, spent considerable time editing my manuscript and offering valuable suggestions. Both were always encouraging and supportive. But most of all, I would like to thank God for His inspiration and guidance from start to finish.

THE BEHRMANN FAMILY

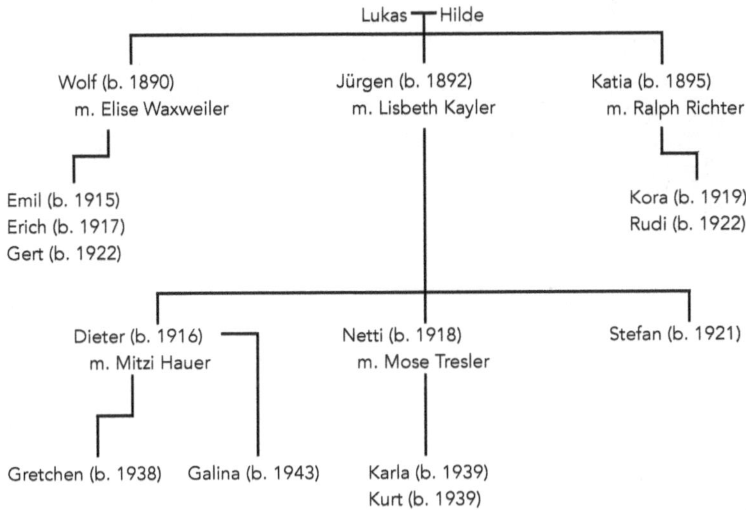

THE MENDEL FAMILY

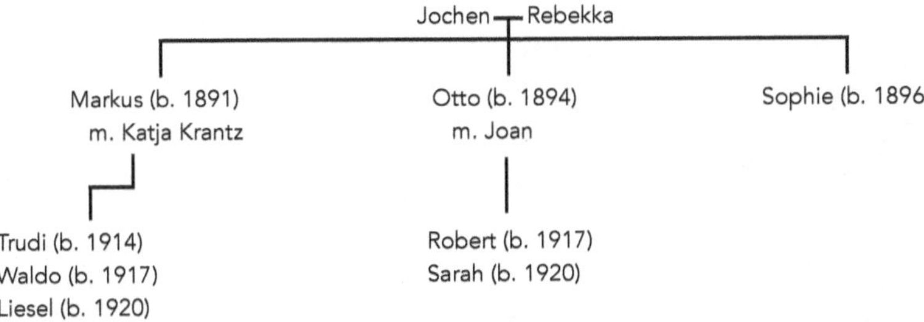

INTRODUCTION

Book two, *A Bridge Across the Chasm*, opened with Jürgen Behrmann and Lili Strobel narrowly escaping death and then making the decision to work in a Russian field hospital instead of going to a prisoner of war camp. The tense Promises series continued on two paths: the war and the backstory.

The War

Colonel Dobrynin, commander of the Sixty-Fifth Army Surgical Hospital, used Jürgen and Lili in his field hospital due to a shortage of Russian doctors and nurses. Later they barely escaped disaster at the hands of a brutal man and a scorned woman. The attack shook Lili's faith, but she survived the life-changing incident with the support of Jürgen and a young Russian lieutenant. They all moved west with the Russian Army, arriving at a field hospital near Germany in January 1945.

Didi woke from a coma to see the beautiful face of Klara Kovalik. His memories of recent events were either muddled or gone. Something prompted Klara to take care of Didi, and they soon fell in love. The following spring, the Wehrmacht attacked the farmhouse where Didi and Klara lived. They escaped with the others in the house and went to Belorussia to join a resistance detachment. Klara gave birth to their daughter in January 1943. Several months later she was blackmailed into doing the unthinkable. With the act committed, Didi no longer recognized the Klara he knew. Was she gone forever? Klara, with murder in her heart, decided on how to protect her family as book two concluded.

The Gestapo abducted Lisbeth, Trudi, and Sophie and sent them to a Polish ghetto. The three adapted to the horrible living conditions there. Lisbeth bonded with two young Polish girls, Trudi married and returned to the religion of her heritage, and Sophie's ingenuity saved the residents in their Dolna street apartment.

The Backstory

The Behrmann and Mendel children made a pact of the heart, patterned after the one made by their fathers years before. Kora's drowning in the Werra River resulted in the breaking of close bonds, endless guilt, and unforgiveness. Elise adopted Gisela after a tragedy, though the Wolf Behrmann family continued to divide and crumble.

Jürgen and Sophie, with the aid of Evert Heinz, devised a dangerous plan to save Markus' children and allow Jürgen to honor his promise. They successfully implemented the scheme, sending the Jürgen Behrmanns' and the Mendel children to their new, hidden life in Cologne. Jürgen and Wolf met unexpectedly, entwining their families in the 1930s. Wolf made discoveries that aroused suspicion concerning his brother's family. After finally bringing down the Hohe Strasse Bank, Wolf had the Gestapo investigate Jürgen's family, hoping to confirm his suspicions. He also arranged for his associate, Max Neumann, to romance Trudi to uncover information about his brother's family. Trudi and Max married in 1936.

Netti met Conrad Bauer. She joined his church, and they eventually fell in love. Netti was devastated when the Gestapo abducted Conrad and his brother.

Didi suffered bitter disappointment at the 1936 Olympic games. He commiserated with Mitzi Hauer who also endured a devastating injury at the games. Mitzi, head of the women's Hitler Youth in Cologne, successfully broke up Didi and Gisela's romance, so she could sweep in and take him for herself.

A Bridge Home

And now the *Bridge Home* offers miraculous twists and turns in dangerous times as Jürgen, Lisbeth, and Didi fight heavy odds in their struggle to get home. The saga continues to a conclusion.

1

Leaving the Marshes

As Klara Kovalik's hand came down something unexplainable deflected her arm slightly. The knife plunged to the hilt into Victor's pillow, only a finger's width from his head. He stirred briefly, being in a drunken stupor, but didn't wake up. Klara heard a voice in her head saying, "Put Victor's finger next to the knife and go back to bed. Everything will be alright." At that moment she knew in her heart that everything would be okay, and Victor would say nothing to Didi.

Klara returned to her bed, and for the first time since her devastation, she found restful sleep. The following morning, Didi and Klara packed their belongings and prepared Galina for their trip to the new volunteer detachment. They hoped it would be a trip to a safer life, if that were even possible. But mainly Didi hoped the new beginning would lift Klara's spirits out of the malaise that had been haunting her for many weeks.

When Victor woke, he opened his eyes and saw the knife hilt sticking out of the pillow, inches from his face and with the tip of his finger lying next to it. A shiver ran down his spine. He instantly knew his miserable life could have ended at the hand of the woman he ruined. "Why did she spare my life?" he thought. Victor could never understand why, but he purposed in his mind not to tell Didi what happened weeks ago in their hideaway. "For sparing my life, I at least owe Klara that," Victor thought.

At midmorning on September 29, 1943, Didi, Klara, who was carrying Galina, Igor, and Anton followed their escorts out of the marshes for the last time. All of their lives were about to change again. They could only hope those changes would be for the better. Peter Gulin and Vladimir Zharkov of the Forty-fifth Belorussian Resistance Detachment took them up the Pripyat River to an abandoned farmhouse where they stopped to rest and eat a lunch of potatoes and apples. They stayed there till nightfall and then continued their journey northward.

The Forty-fifth was building its numbers to more effectively counter the harsh German reprisals against small, defenseless towns, which were alarmingly on the increase. The two young members of the detachment came to the marshes to bring the new volunteers to their home base northwest of Baranovichi. Didi and Klara's new home would be 150 kilometers north of the marshes they gladly left behind.

Peter Gulin hid an old panel truck behind the ruins of an abandoned barn, four kilometers north of the farmhouse. After midnight, under the cover of darkness the seven travelers left the farmhouse and made their way to the truck. They traveled cautiously over back roads, reaching a safe house near Ivatsevichy, halfway to their destination, before dawn.

Partisans there fed them and provided soft beds for the day. By midnight they were on the road again, hidden in the back of a produce truck. They stopped short of the German guard station south of Baranovichi and abandoned the truck. The last fifteen kilometers of their journey, they traveled by foot. It was near ten in the morning when they reached their final destination: four bordering farms, with barns, sheds, and other outbuildings. These working farms were safe houses for the women and children of the Forty-fifth.

As they came out of a stand of trees near one of the farmhouses, Anna Gulin ran to her husband Peter, jumping into his welcoming arms. Then she turned to Klara, who held Galina. With a big smile, she hugged them both. "Welcome to our home, Klara. Please consider it your home too. Klara never forgot the warmth she felt. Anna immediately took Klara and Galina under her wing and a fast friendship developed.

Peter and Anna had married at age eighteen in Minsk, the city of their births. It was 1936, and no one was thinking of the war to come. Peter's father employed over forty people in his large bakery. After marrying, Peter abandoned plans for continuing his education and fulfilling his dream to design marvelous buildings, bridges, and stadiums. Instead, he went to work in his father's bakery. It was depressing for a time, but he took his responsibility as a new husband seriously. His priority was to take care of his young bride, whom he treasured more than anything else in the world.

With much difficulty, Anna gave birth to their daughter, Elana, in 1937. The breech birth was nearly fatal for Anna. Peter had never been so terrified in his life as when the doctor told him his wife might not survive the ordeal. But she did, and two years later she gave birth to their son, Oleg, without complication.

The Russian Army conscripted Peter two months before the Germans launched their Operation Barbarossa blitzkrieg in June 1941. He received minimal training with the Sixth Cavalry Training Corps, enough to be ready for assignment when the blitzkrieg started. The army told Peter and five other trainees to wait in Minsk until they received assignment orders. But, the Second and Third Panzer Groups captured Minsk on June 28. The Wehrmacht encircled the entire western front of the Russian Army in two pockets, one west of Minsk and one near Bialystok. They eventually captured more than three hundred thousand Soviet troops and thousands of tanks and artillery pieces in the onslaught.

At that point, the six trainees from Minsk abandoned their military uniforms and hid their weapons, in fear of capture. They all knew the consequences of their actions could be fatal. On July 1, Peter picked up a directive issued by the Russian army, warning soldiers and civilians alike that cowardice or inciting fear would be severely punished. Army commanders and the secret police would be watching possible escape routes for military deserters.

Peter and the others laid low for a month. They stayed far away from their families in order to protect them. But as the war moved east and the Germans set up their provisional government in Minsk, they decided to leave the city and join partisans forming groups northwest of the city. Peter hugged Anna and the children one last time before escaping Minsk. He promised to return when it was safe to have them join the partisans.

True to his word, Peter returned in October and took Anna, Elana, and Oleg to a newly settled safe farm near Baranovichi. Forty-five men, women, and children occupied and worked the four bordering farms. Other members of the Forty-fifth Belorussian Resistance Detachment moved clandestinely in and out of the farms on their way to and from attacks on the Germans. In the beginning, suspicious Germans visited the farms often, looking for any sign of an underground insurgency. But the permanent members of the small farming community quickly learned how to prepare for unexpected visits to allay German suspicion. As time passed, the Nazi surprise visits decreased to once every three or four months.

For a week, the five newcomers from the Pripyat Marshes received critical training as they settled into their new home base. Not by chance, Peter and Anna's bedroom was next to Didi, Klara, and Galina's room.

Oksana Pushkin, an undercover resistance operative within the Baranovichi Police Registration Office, got eight blank, officially stamped identification cards for Igor, Anton, Klara, and Didi, who was still going by Alexey Pashkin. She took pictures of them and properly attached them to the cards with their fingerprints and signatures. Then she typed in the correct personal data on the blue cards, which notated Belorussian citizenship. They made two copies for each person, one set that Oksana would file at the police station and one set to carry with them. They also completed two copies of official work permits: one to put on file at the police station and one for them to keep on their person. All four had farmworker classifications.

* * *

Through the fall and winter of 1943–44, Didi went on eleven missions, each lasting from three to seven days. Either Igor or Anton always accompanied him on each mission to keep up the ruse that Alexey Pashkin had been deaf and dumb since early childhood, and Klara had helped him for the past dozen years. No one was injured on the missions, though two of the insurgency teams had close calls.

One evening when Didi, Klara, Igor, and Anton were alone at the kitchen table, Igor said, "It still puzzles me, Didi. You're

German. You fought with the Wehrmacht. Now you're willing to kill them. Why?"

"My answer hasn't changed since the last time you asked, Igor. I don't know why."

"It's that you don't remember why," Anton said.

"You know I don't. But something happened that made me turn on them. I don't remember what it was. But somehow it feels right. I can't explain it beyond that."

"Leave him alone!" Klara cautioned. He's in misery enough trying to remember. Stop making it worse by pressing him further."

"Thanks, darling. Believe me, Igor, I want the answer to your question more than anyone."

Igor patted Didi on the back, as he and Anton left the kitchen.

When winter came, Didi's nightmares increased in number and intensity. He would wake up screaming, wet with sweat. Sometimes those in the adjoining bedroom heard his screams in German. Anna first heard the screams in late November, but she wasn't sure he was speaking German until the end of December. Peter was away much of the time, so he only heard Didi scream a few times and never recognized that he was speaking German.

Anna kept what she heard to herself until January when she discreetly approached Klara. "I'm so thankful that you and your family have joined us here, Klara."

"So am I, Anna. This is like being on holiday compared to the marshes."

"I think we've become close—close friends, don't you think?"

"Yes, we have a lot in common. And I so appreciate your warmth toward us."

"Do you trust me, Klara?"

"Of course I do."

"Then can I ask you something about Alexey?"

Klara was almost sure of what might be coming, but she played along. "Sure, what is it, Anna?"

"I hear Alexey's outbursts in the middle of the night. Sometimes they're so loud I think everyone in the house will hear him."

"I'm sorry that he disturbs your sleep. His horrible dreams had gone away, but now they've come back stronger than ever. They're very frightening, but he doesn't know what they mean. Now he's almost afraid to go to sleep."

"How does he speak in his dreams, but can't speak when he's awake? And why does he speak German?"

Klara paused, trying to quell her fear and think of what to say. Could she really trust this woman who was so loving toward her? After all, she saw the brutality of the German occupation up close and, even though she was a loving person, likely could harbor nothing but hatred toward them.

"He's always been able to speak audibly in his dreams, which not only puzzled us but the doctors we've taken him to. I wish we knew why, but no one can answer that question. As for speaking German, my mother is half German. When she separated from my father, Alexey and I went with her to stay with my Aunt in Hamburg for five years. We know that Alexey learned to understand German during that time, though he couldn't speak it. It must seem strange to you because it still does to me."

Anna didn't say anything for a minute, looking down at the floor, weighing what Klara said. "Yes, it's strange. It must be hard for you to deal with. He's terrified and the distress of not knowing why must be frustrating for both of you."

"It is. I hope we get to the bottom of it soon, so he can find peace, and we can all get a decent night's sleep. I'm so sorry that it's disturbing you and Peter."

"Peter's been away so much that it hasn't affected him, and the children have never said anything about it."

"That's good to hear, Anna. Thanks so much for your understanding."

* * *

The chores on the farm in winter centered on feeding and protecting the livestock. Between the four farms, they had fourteen head of cattle plus three milking cows, ten pigs, and several hundred chickens, thirty that laid eggs. As much as possible, they hid livestock from view. Grains and cured meats were also cleverly tucked away in places where the Germans never thought to look. They also hid hay for the livestock, along with potatoes and sugar beets harvested in the summer and fall.

However, the Germans continued their random raids to search out and confiscate booty. They loved taking the choicest cows and pigs. There was no preventing the theft; it was the cost of having the Germans leave them alone. But the losses were acceptable, and the farms continued supporting those who lived there. In fact, the residents of the small farming commune were eating better than most in Belorussia.

In February, Didi and Klara came under suspicion when a Wehrmacht major and three soldiers paid a surprise visit to the farm. They were suspicious of Didi's Aryan appearance and his muteness. The major wrote down all the information from their identification and work cards. After they left, Anna told them they would undoubtedly verify their credentials at the Baranovichi Police Registration Office. She said they shouldn't worry. Everything would check out—and it did.

2

Discovery and Retribution

As Jürgen sipped his morning coffee and took a drag on his cigarette, he opened the *Cologne Review* to find a disturbing headline: "New Hitler Youth Law." He quickly read the article. All German youth would be organized under one government entity on December 1, 1936. For the health of the Reich, it was important that all able youth gladly join. The article said that all necessary rules about the new law would follow. Currently, both boys and girls from ten through eighteen were encouraged to serve in the Hitler Youth, so Jürgen assumed those ages would still apply.

His girls immediately came to mind. Trudi was safe, now married and well past the age of eighteen. Netti would be nineteen in two months, so she might not be pressured to join. But Liesel wouldn't turn nineteen for two and a half years.

"How in the world can I keep her out of this mess?" Jürgen thought, as he nervously lit another cigarette. He pondered the matter for several minutes and then put on his jacket and headed out the front door.

Didi was sitting on the front porch swing with a cup of coffee. Jürgen wished him a good day as he went down the steps, but his son didn't look up or say a word. It didn't surprise him, as Didi hadn't been saying much to anyone but Lisbeth. As he walked to his auto, recurring thoughts vexed Jürgen. Didi talked to him only when he needed something, and the only time he and Netti conversed was during an argument. Didi tried to avoid Trudi, and now he was pulling away from Waldo and Stefan, the brothers who were never a problem. But Didi and his mother were closer than ever. Their conversations were longer and more frequent. Jürgen wished his wife would spend that much time talking to him. Lisbeth was distancing herself from him and her relationship with Netti and Trudi was strained at best. She was even pulling away from Waldo because of his support for Netti in every family dispute. Communication in the family had broken down. Lisbeth was even drinking openly, defying Jürgen or anyone else to challenge her about it.

Jürgen turned his mind to other things as he got in his auto and pulled onto the road toward the hospital. The Weiners were standing in their front yard as he passed, scowling at him with fixed eyes. Five years ago they were Lisbeth and Jürgen's closest friends on the block. But they, like everyone else on the block, except the Straubs, had emphatically joined the herd that was willingly accepting the Nazi propaganda. The Weiners quickly went from not speaking to the Behrmanns to basically threatening them unless they fell in line. The other neighbors too insisted they hail the Fuhrer and honor what he was doing to create the great thousand-year Reich. Jürgen and the family no longer spoke to anyone except the Straubs and tried not to make a scene, even when provoked, when just passing their neighbors. Of course, Didi made everything worse, as he paraded through the neighborhood in his Hitler Youth uniform, gleefully speaking to everyone but the Straubs. Being shunned by their neighbors was a major reason for Lisbeth's return to the bottle.

Jürgen sensed the unique mixture of forces coming together in his country, which was dragging it down to the pits of hell. It was strange to see fear, joy, hatred, pride, and anger all come together with expectations of both triumph and doom. But that was Jürgen's assessment of 1936 Germany. The masses had bought the cleverly crafted propaganda foisted on them by Adolph Hitler. After all, they believed, the Allies were unjust in their harsh requirements of the Versailles Treaty. And the Germans suffered the devastating effects of long-term economic hardship caused by the greedy Jews, Bolsheviks, and capitalists. Why shouldn't the purest and most worthy people on earth now ascend to what was rightfully theirs? Most citizens were willing to follow Hitler's mandates even though they clearly would eventually lead to the nation's destruction. To Jürgen it was like they were drugged into believing the lies.

The Nazis strictly warned those who voiced their opposition and then took them away if they persisted. Some went underground. It was a depressing world for Jürgen, who was trying to keep his family together and ensuring their survival in such ominous times.

* * *

A couple months later, on a cold February evening, Didi sat at the dining room table rehearsing how he would break the bad news to his family. Suddenly Netti stormed into the room.

"You can't do it, Didi, you just can't."

"News travels fast, sister. I certainly can and will marry Mitzi next month, and nothing you, father, or anyone else says will stop me."

"Have you lost your mind? You're going to marry someone who's on a first-name basis with Heinrich Himmler?"

"That can only be a plus where we're going."

"And you'll be going straight to hell, Didi. God have mercy on your poor lost soul."

"God's the only one who would have mercy; no one in the family does."

"What are you talking about?"

"You know exactly what I mean, Netti. I saw it every time I looked in Aunt Katia's eyes. I see it in father's eyes and hear it in his voice. And what hurts me most is I still see it in your eyes, Netti. You're the one who started our promises of the heart pact. You vowed to love and support me, but you haven't and it hurts."

Netti put her arms around Didi's shoulders and pulled him to her chest saying, "That's not true, Didi. I'm the one who used two of my special requests to have Trudi and Liesel forgive you of anything they held in their heart against you about Kora's death. And I forgave you right away. In fact, you know that I never thought you were responsible."

"Oh, I know you and everyone else always say the right words, but you can't hide what your eyes are saying. I see that, Netti, and it's been gnawing at me for ten years."

"That's just not the case, Didi," Netti said with tears in her eyes. "We've all forgiven you for any part you might have played in Kora's death. Most of us never held you responsible, anyway."

"I can't accept that," Didi replied, getting emotional too. "That's why I need a different life with different people and different beliefs."

"Please don't throw your life away. You can't blame us anymore; you need to face yourself and what happened. It's been ten years, and that's too long to carry such a heavy burden of guilt. Listen to me, Didi, you didn't do anything wrong. You are not responsible for Kora's death. So just stop it and forgive yourself and come to your senses before it's too late."

"I would if I could, Netti, but I can't." Didi released his sister and immediately ran upstairs to his room. Netti sat at the table for a long time, crying and interceding with God for her brother who was on the brink of disaster.

Three nights later, Didi was again sitting alone at the kitchen table when he heard his mother's voice calling. "Didi, are you in the kitchen?"

"Yes, mother, I'm here."

"Why are you sitting here in the dark, darling; can't you sleep?"

"No, I have too much on my mind."

"Can I warm some milk, and then you can tell me all about it?"

"That always helps, mother, thanks. You always make me feel better."

Lisbeth put her arm around Didi's shoulder. "I love you very much, son."

Lisbeth poured milk in a pan and started warming it on the stove, and then she sat down beside her son.

"Is it the same problem that's bothering you, Didi?"

"It always is. Netti, father, or anyone else but you, will never approve of anything I do. They think I'll be throwing my life away if I marry Mitzi. They pretty much think I already have, since I joined the Hitler Youth and started voicing my support for the Reich."

Lisbeth got up and poured warm milk into a glass and gave it to Didi. "You have to do what you feel is right, darling, and do not listen to anyone else. After all, it's not their life; it's yours." As Lisbeth lovingly stroked Didi's hair, she said, "Just between you and me, I think you're making the right choice to marry Mitzi, but please don't ever tell your father or Netti."

"Do you mean that, mother, or are you just trying to make me feel good?"

"I always want you to feel good, Didi, but I do believe you'll be much safer in the world that's coming if you're married to Mitzi."

"I think I'll be much better off too."

Didi moved close to his mother and put his head on her breast. Lisbeth put her arms around her son and again stroked his hair gently.

"Thanks, mother; your words always lift me up."

"I'm your mother, darling, that's what I'm supposed to do. I'm afraid all the time, Didi, and I worry about the family with the craziness going on and what we're hiding. At least I know you'll be safe with Mitzi's protection."

* * *

March 14, 1937—the day of Dieter Behrmann's and Mitzi Hauer's wedding—arrived. Neither wanted a church wedding nor to have a religious person officiate, so they wed in the ballroom of the Grand Duchess Hotel along the banks of the Rhine. Mitzi's parents, Phillip and Anna, wanted a grand wedding in Berlin but Mitzi talked them into having the ceremony along the Rhine and a close family friend officiated the ceremony.

General Alfred Von Koenig managed clandestine operations for Heinrich Himmler. He was ruthless in his dealings and loyal to his superior. Von Koenig was skillful in all he did, having a sharp eye for detail. One thing that was of particular interest to him was the maturing of young Mitzi Hauer into a goddess. It would have shocked her parents to know their good friend was following Mitzi's growth with lustful expectation. Von Koenig, a handsome forty-one-year-old, lived the single life of indulging in the finest liquor and women. And now, with his position, almost anything he wanted was attainable.

The groom wasn't the only one who kissed the bride after the nuptials. Shortly after Didi kissed his bride, the general also kissed her hard on the lips. The kiss surprised everyone. It peeved Didi and shocked Mitzi, though Von Koenig's lips pressing against hers aroused her.

It was a large wedding, reflecting Mitzi's notoriety. Many Nazi dignitaries from Berlin, Cologne, and western Germany attended to show respect and commiserate her agonizing disappointment experienced at the Olympics. The bride and groom's friends at the wedding were mostly from the ranks of the Hitler Youth. And the Nazis ensured that many propaganda pictures were taken.

The Behrmann family was almost lost in the crowd. It was a sad day for Jürgen, Netti, and Trudi and a gleeful day for Wolf, Erich, and Lisbeth. Gisela refused to attend, while Didi told everyone that he barred her from the wedding.

Erich was still deciding if he loved Trudi or hated her. He regretted his decision to join the cousins' pact of the heart two years before. The only reasons he joined were his love for Trudi and his gratitude for her heroics in saving his life. But Max dashed his dream of having her and now anger and jealousy ruled Erich's emotions. He disdained the promise.

It was unfortunate for Erich that he was now closer to Didi. With Mitzi's influence, Didi secured a Hitler Youth training position for him in December. The appointment brought the three closer together on the job and they also spent more time together off duty. The more time Erich spent with Mitzi, the more he was infatuated with her. Romantic feelings he once had for Trudi were now transferred to Mitzi Hauer. He respected Didi and knew his chance for a romance with Mitzi was hopeless. But his feelings for her were real, and struggle as he may, he was ensnared .

A month after the wedding, fortunes changed for Erich. It happened on a Sunday afternoon, as Erich waited in the Behrmanns' living room for Didi to return so they could go hiking. Netti was in the study, writing a letter at her father's desk. She purposely paid no attention to Erich. He also wouldn't look her way.

"Netti, can you come up and help me?" came a shout from upstairs. It was Waldo calling for his sister's help.

"What is it, Waldo?" Netti shouted back as she came into the living room.

"Just come up here, I need your help for a minute!"

"Okay," Netti sighed.

As Netti reached the second floor, Erich, walked into the study to have a look at Netti's letter. He skimmed it and quickly determined it contained only useless information that she was telling Rudi. But then his eye caught an envelope mostly hidden under two books. He pulled it out and saw it was from Aunt Katia to Jürgen. "This could be interesting," he thought. Erich pulled out the letter and started scanning it. It was boring tripe until he reached page five:

You know how hard it was for Mother and Father to learn that you hadn't emigrated to America as you pretended. They still can't understand why you didn't trust them enough to tell them you were honoring your vow to save Markus' children from what he feared would be their destruction at the hands of the Nazis. And now they fear for all of your lives, knowing that someone might find out that Trudi, Waldo, and Liesel aren't your children but the Jewish children of your best friend.

Erich slammed the letter down on the desk. "Sonofabitch! Filthy bastards! I can't believe it!" He quickly looked around to make sure no one heard him. He slipped the letter back into the envelope and put it under the books. He was steaming mad and wanted to tear each of his cousins and aunt and uncle to pieces. He walked back to the living room—pacing up and down—trying to figure out what to do about his shocking discovery. As Netti came down the stairs, he had the impulse to tear into her but then thought better of it. Instead, Erich determined that he would say nothing to anyone until he had thought the matter through.

Nearly two weeks passed before Erich found himself in the position where he could confront the issue. It happened on a mild Saturday afternoon in April, as he finished his run in the park. He saw Trudi and Netti sitting on a bench near the entrance to the park. Erich walked over to them. "I know what you bitches did with the rest of your filthy family!"

"Are you drunk? What the hell are you talking about?" Trudi yelled.

"Oh, you know, you Jew whore!"

Netti's jaw dropped. "Somehow he's learned our secret," she thought. Netti got up from the park bench as Trudi slapped Erich across the face with all her strength. Netti got between them to prevent Erich from striking Trudi back. "Settle down, settle down—both of you! What are you talking about, Erich? Why would you say that?"

"I said it, Netti, because I read it in a letter from Aunt Katia to your father."

"What letter? When would you ever see father's mail?"

"The day I was waiting for Didi, two weeks ago. Remember that Waldo called you upstairs?"

"Oh God! I was in the study writing to Rudi."

"When you went upstairs, I went into the study to look at your letter. Then I saw another letter, the letter to your father, under some books. Katia talked about our grandparents worrying about someone finding out that Trudi, Waldo, and Liesel were the Jewish children of your father's best friend. There's more, but that's how I learned the truth about your family. Do either of you deny it?"

Trudi spoke first. "No, we can't deny it, Erich. But do you remember saying over and over how much you loved me? It wasn't that long ago."

"I remember, and I meant every word of it at the time, but you never gave me a chance."

"You were still a boy, and I loved Max. But how could you now call someone you loved a whore?"

"What are you going to do, Erich?" Netti asked.

"I'm not sure yet. But I'll enjoy watching both of you squirm while I think about it."

"I'm officially asking you, Erich, as my one request from our vow of the heart, which you swore to, to never tell anyone what you've learned," Netti said.

"You have no choice but to promise, Erich, if you're now a man with any character. My God, I saved your life!" Trudi said. "Isn't that worth something? Isn't it worth everything to you?"

"Okay, dammit! You've got me on that. I promise never to tell anyone in your family what I learned about you Jews and Jew lovers. I should have never joined your damned club."

"You swear to it, Erich," Trudi insisted.

"I said it! I won't tell. But don't ever ask anything else from me. In fact, I'd just as soon never see either of you or any of your family ever again. And that goes for that sonofabitch Didi too. How could he be a loyal Nazi and hide Jews, even live with them?"

With that, Erich turned and jogged out of the park, leaving Trudi and Netti stunned. They both frantically mulled over the possible impact of what they'd just learned and what they could do about it.

Over the next few weeks, Netti and Trudi thought long and hard about their dilemma. They wanted to tell the whole family, or at least their father, but decided to wait and see if Erich would keep his word and not tell anyone. Meanwhile, Erich also thought about what he should do with the valuable information he uncovered. He knew the so-called sisters would be stewing about the matter, and for now, that was enough retribution.

As June came, Erich decided to make the boldest move of his young life. He had been seeing more of Mitzi and Didi, despising him for the secret he kept and desiring her more each day. He determined to set in motion a plan that would allow him to enjoy Mitzi's ripe fruit.

One night when Didi was at the Nazi Party training Erich took action. Just as Mitzi got out of the bathtub, she heard a loud knock on the door. She quickly put on her robe and went to see who it was. "What are you doing here, Erich? You know Didi has his leader's group training tonight."

"That's why I'm here now, because he won't be."

"What the hell are you talking about? You've been drinking again!"

"No, I'm sober—haven't had a drink all day."

"Why are you here, Erich? You can see I'm ready for bed."

"I have a proposition for you, Mitzi, one I think you'll gladly agree to."

"Can't it wait till tomorrow?"

"No it can't. When I tell you, you'll understand."

"Dammit! Come in and make it quick."

They both sat on the couch, as Mitzi clutched her short robe to hold it together and pulled it down to try to cover her bare legs.

"Go ahead, what's so damn important?" Mitzi huffed.

"I clearly recall the Saturday morning last fall when Hermann Martz came over to walk Gisela and me to the park. He seemed eager to get us there; I couldn't understand what the hurry was. Then when he got there, it seemed strange that all of a sudden he wanted to talk with Gisela alone and get rid of me."

"Hold on! Wait a minute! Why should I care about any of this?"

"I'll get to it, just listen, Mitzi. Anyway, they walked south into the park. I was going to wait there, but was curious so I followed them. I kept out of sight behind bushes and trees. As they were nearing the big shade tree that everyone likes, I saw a woman in a brown coat, wearing sunglasses and a hat. She slowly raised her right hand as if she were signaling someone. I hid behind a bush and overheard Hermann and Gisela and saw how tenderly they kissed. Then Hermann left quickly, going north. A few seconds later, Didi walked up, mad as hell at Gisela. I heard all of their pathetic conversation."

"So why are you telling me this, Erich? Didi told me the whole sad story a few days after it happened."

"Not everything; he never knew the whole story."

"What are you saying?"

"I wanted to follow Hermann to find out what was going on, but when Didi showed up I stayed behind the bush. After Didi stormed off, I waited for Gisela to leave. Once she passed out of sight, I started to come out from behind the bush but ducked back when I saw the woman in the brown coat come from behind the bushes across the sidewalk. It puzzled me, so I decided to follow her.

"I kept out of sight so she wouldn't see me. After leaving the park, she went to a small café across the street from your apartment. I solved the mystery when I crossed the street and looked in the café window. There you were, Mitzi, sitting next to Hermann and still wearing your brown coat."

"You sneaky sonofabitch! How dare you spy on me like that!"

"Sneaky!? If I am sneaky what does that make you, Mitzi?"

"Go to hell, you slimy bastard!"

"I'm sure I will, but first I need to tell you the rest of the sordid story."

"What rest of the story?"

"I waited until you left the café. Both of you went into the building where you live. I waited all afternoon but neither of you ever came out. Finally, near dark, I went home. I still wondered what was going on, so the next morning I went back and waited in the alley across the street from your apartment. Around ten, Hermann came out with a broad smile on his face. He was almost walking with a skip, and then I knew for sure what put the smile on his face."

"So you have it all figured out. Is that what you're telling me?"

"That's what I'm telling you. You bribed innocent Hermann to help you break up Didi and Gisela. Then you paid him off with favors you knew he couldn't resist."

"So you know. Now what are you going to do?"

"I have options, as my father would say. I could tell Didi and see if it ruins your marriage, which it would. After all, he blew up at Gisela and ditched her over a couple kisses. What would he do if he found out you set the whole thing up, and then you went to bed with Hermann as his reward?"

"Okay, Erich, you want something. What is it?"

"I'll come right to the point; I want you, Mitzi. You freely gave yourself to Hermann for a lot less than you'll owe me for my silence."

"How did I somehow know that's the reason you came here when you knew Didi wouldn't be home? You'd love it, wouldn't you, if I pulled back my robe and showed you what you've been dying to see for a long time? Well, that's not going to happen so forget it; I won't be blackmailed, you bastard!"

"What about your marriage and all the aspirations you and Didi have?"

"I'm not a bit worried. Didi will never take your word over mine. I'll tell him that you're delusional, and you want to break us up because you're in love with me."

"You'll be taking a big risk."

"No, silly boy, I'm totally sure of myself and what Didi will do. There's no risk for me."

Erich squirmed on the couch as he reassessed his position. Then he proceeded with the second option of his plan to have Mitzi. "Okay, I won't blackmail you, if that's what you want to call it. But I think there's another proposition you won't refuse."

"You don't give up, do you? Alright, I'll play along; what else do you have?"

"Accidentally, I've come by some information about Didi's family that you'll want to know."

"That sounds more like it. Continue, Erich; what do you know that you think will be of interest to me?"

"Not so fast, Mitzi. You know what I want, and I won't tell you anything until you agree to my terms."

"How do I know what you'll give me will be anywhere as good as what you know I can give you?"

"You'll just have to trust me. Once you hear what I know, you'll have Didi's family by the throat as long as it suits you."

What Mitzi heard intrigued her. She said nothing for a minute, mulling over Erich's offer. "So tell me exactly what you want for this information, Erich?"

"I know Hermann had never been with a girl, let alone a woman, before that night with you. I've been around a little more than him but never with someone like you. I only want three separate nights when you can teach me what you must have taught Hermann."

Mitzi paused again to think over what Erich said. "Okay, tell me what you know, and unless it's a sham I'll do it."

Erich, now aroused, was quick to speak. "I read a letter from our Aunt Katia to Didi's father. I won't go into the details of how that came about, but what I read was a real shocker. The letter specifically said that Didi's parents weren't Trudi, Waldo, and Liesel's parents. They're the children of Jürgen's best friend, a damned Jew who died. They secretly took in the three Jews to save their asses."

"Dammit! Sneaky bastards! Come to think of it, they don't look like Didi and the others. How long have you known about this?"

"Not long, and I had to vow to Trudi and Netti that I wouldn't tell anyone in the family."

"Why would you do that?"

"I joined a stupid club of theirs a while back and made a vow that's come back to bite me. They shamed me into not telling anyone in the family."

"Didi told me about that childish vow you all made. He doesn't give it any thought or credence anymore. But why did you tell Trudi and Netti? That was stupid ."

"It enraged me. I had to confront the bitches and make them squirm."

"So they know you're the only person to learn their secret, but they think you'll never say anything. Is that the sum of it?"

"That's it."

"Here's what you do now. Don't ever open your mouth about this to anyone ever again. I'm not a part of your immediate family, so you haven't violated your oath. You just need to forget about it. Do you understand what I'm telling you, Erich?"

"I understand. I'll never talk about it again."

"This information is dynamite in my hands. It's real power that no one knows I have. I'm not sure how or when I'll use it, but when I do, it'll bring down the Jürgen Behrmann family. But to tell the truth, I don't know what to think about Didi's part in the deception. I'll have to sort it out and decide what to do."

"So this information is valuable to you?"

"I have to admit, it'll be quite useful."

"Then we have a bargain?"

"Yes, I'll do what you ask. I'll teach you the way I taught Hermann. You'll be my trainee just like he was."

Just saying those words sent shivers through Erich's body, and ignited Mitzi's sensual, lustful nature. She honestly believed the headlines, that she was a goddess and the crown of German womanhood. She was perfection for her Fuhrer and the Reich. And it was not only her ordained gift to train the young women of the BDM but also to train young Aryan men in the fine art of loving those women.

To titillate Erich, Mitzi opened her robe a little and then quickly closed it. "Not now, boy, just a peek to store in your mind until we meet again. Now get out of here before Didi comes home. I'll let you know when and where we'll meet."

Erich, pushing back his overwhelming passion, got up quickly and was out the door in seconds.

True to her word, Mitzi called Erich eight days later, asking him to meet her that night at the address where one of her training subordinates lived. Her subordinate was out of town and the apartment was empty. Erich knocked on the door of the apartment just after eight. Mitzi answered the door, wearing only a skimpy nightgown. Erich could hardly contain himself, so Mitzi had him sit down and drink two shots of whiskey.

After twenty minutes, Mitzi led Erich into the bedroom where they stayed for the next eleven hours. He was awkward and unsure, showing his inexperience and selfishness. Erich left the apartment both exhausted and exhilarated but still feeling inadequate. The experience also exhausted Mitzi. She had much work to do with such a novice. But her pride was now at stake, knowing she was the goddess of love and Germany's preeminent trainer. She couldn't deflate her ego with any failure. Therefore, she didn't have three rendezvous with Erich but seven. Their clandestine meetings continued over a six-week period until she was satisfied that the boy was now a man ready to please any woman. As for Didi, Mitzi still thought a lot about the boy she married and what to do about his poor judgment in betraying the Reich. His performance and lack of improvement as a man also disappointed her, especially after her expert tutelage.

* * *

On the advice of her father, Netti joined the BDM after Christmas to avoid negative reactions from those who knew her. However, she never took part in any events before turning nineteen in February of 1937.With Elise and Jürgen's encouragement, Gisela also joined the BDM, but she only attended a few events before turning nineteen in March. Wolf had nothing to do with Gisela's decision, still having little interest in the girl Elise had adopted more than eleven years before.

The greatest pressure was on Liesel to join the girl's arm of the Hitler Youth. The girls, friends and enemies alike, in her all-girls high school waited to see if she would obey the new Hitler Youth law. It hadn't been compulsory to join before, but the other girls made life unbearable for those who didn't. Previously, with the backing of all her family except Didi, she had made a strong stand against joining most of her classmates and friends in the BDM. Her best friend, Marta Gorman, had joined the youth group two years before, and she insisted it was a rewarding experience. She said it was like an athletic club where the girls enjoyed everything from swimming to camping to skiing trips. They also built their bodies physically while learning about the accomplishments in their country. Marta didn't emphasize the propaganda, telling Liesel that she paid no attention to it if she didn't agree.

Due to the new law and under Jürgen and Netti's guidance and watchful eyes, and with Marta's help, Liesel joined the BDM in January of 1937. She started attending the Wednesday night "home evening" meetings and Saturday physical training sessions. She hated the blatant propaganda dished out at the home meetings, but she enjoyed the competitions and physical training on Saturdays. Some of the girls from school who had been her enemies now warmed up to her. Liesel kept a low profile, though, challenging none of the vile propaganda foisted on the group. She had to bite her tongue often, but Jürgen, Netti, and Marta told her not to respond.

The skiing trip to Switzerland in February was the most fun Liesel had had in a long time. So in the beginning, her BDM experience was positive. It wasn't until summer that everything changed for Liesel. At a summer camp outing near Bonn, swimming was the girls' favorite sport. Though Liesel enjoyed the physical activity and cool water, swimming proved to be dangerous. There were 180 girls in her BDM Girl Group, and many of them were unattractive. Liesel was beautiful with a kind face and slender but curvy figure. Some of the girls had been jealous of her and seeing Liesel in a bathing suit enraged them. Marta tried to protect her friend, but she couldn't watch over her every minute.

One day some of the more influential girls complained to their troop leader, making up lies about Liesel, trying to get her in trouble and sent home. Troop Leader Imma Frank, a heavy woman with a sour face, reprimanded Liesel sternly and warned her that she would be in serious trouble if she continued to break the rules. Frank, who had taken a dislike to Liesel from the first time she saw her, was more than willing to collude with those who wanted to put her in her place.

Troop Leader Frank took the occasion to elevate herself in the eyes of those in positions of power who would be visiting the BDM camp. The following day, the top leader for the Cologne

District, Mitzi Behrmann, arrived. General Alfred Von Koenig, who officiated at Mitzi's wedding, and Wilhelm Boeddeker, Himmler's head of the *Lebensborn* initiative, accompanied Mitzi. The *Lebensborn* program, known as the "fount of life," was Himmler's pet project, which he entrusted to only a close confidant.

The fount of life program was designed to increase the declining birthrate in Germany with an infusion of genetically superior Aryan births. Young unmarried women, certified as excellent Aryan candidates, would be the major bearers of the fount of life with higher ranking SS officers providing most of the seed. The *Lebensborn* program would provide for the mothers-to-be, and then they would turn their babies over to ranking SS families or other families with the right pedigree. The program was off to a slow start, but it was now picking up steam as it spread across Germany.

Von Koenig and Boeddeker were the same age and had been friends since childhood. They had advanced together through the ranks to their lofty positions under Himmler. Boeddeker was unhappily married to a barren woman, which was the source of his harsh and lustful personality. His greatest wish was to have a *Lebensborn* child of his own.

Troop Leader Frank led Top Leader Behrmann down to the lake where the girls were swimming, to point out the young woman who was the source of trouble within the troop. She had previously briefed the top leader about the problem.

"It's that one over there, Frau." Frank was pointing at Liesel Behrmann as she came out of the water. Not being the brightest woman in the BDM, she had never associated the last names of her newly married leader and the girl she was trying to remove.

It surprised Mitzi to learn the targeted girl was her new sister-in-law. Mitzi smiled as she considered the matter and the possible opportunities it offered. "So, what is it that you want from me, Leader Frank?"

"She's a rotten apple in a barrel of fine apples, and we need to severely punish her or remove her from the troop."

"I'll consider a solution and let you know what course of action to take."

Mitzi was weighing alternatives concerning her sister-in-law when Von Koenig entered her tent. "What is it, Alfred?"

"I think you know, darling. You've known for years what I've wanted—what I've been waiting for until you were ready."

Mitzi didn't respond immediately. She was well aware of his intent and had been sensitive to his leering, lustful inspections since she was thirteen. But now Mitzi had to admit that being with a man of great experience, instead of teaching young novices, was an exciting prospect she looked forward to. But she would put off that pleasure for now, not giving Von Koenig the pleasure and satisfaction of the conquest he had anticipated these many years. No, instead, she would use him and Boeddeker to exact her first punitive action against the family that was cleverly deceiving everyone. She had no reason to punish Liesel, except that she was a Jewess making girls of pure Aryan ethnicity look bad.

"Are you and Wilhelm looking for young *Lebensborn* women?" Mitzi asked.

"Why would you ask that?"

"Because of what you said earlier about Wilhelm's great disappointment in not being able to have children with his wife."

"You're not only beautiful, darling but also perceptive. Yes, he's looking for the right young maiden to father his child."

"And his wife is okay with that?"

"Of course she is. It's the least she can do so they can finally have a child."

"And what about you, Alfred? You have no wife, but are you also looking to father children for the Reich—to improve the fount of life?"

"You know damned well I have an eye for the girls, and if I can build the pure stock of the Reich, so much the better."

"Pig is too good for this filthy sonofabitch," Mitzi thought as she prepared to set the two lechers up for a big fall. "Wonder how they'll feel after breaking their precious purity and citizenship laws by having relations with a Jew," she thought.

"Let Troop Leader Frank take you and Wilhelm down by the lake; the girls are swimming and maybe you'll find a pleasing prospect for your program."

"Trying to put me off, are you?"

"Not at all, but you'll never build the program with me."

"Okay, we'll go take a look at the stock." Mitzi knew they would undoubtedly spot Liesel right away. There was only one other girl in the troop who stood out.

Mitzi came out of her tent twenty minutes later to see the two SS officers coming up the hill from the lake. They were in their robes and had undoubtedly looked over the girls swimming near them. Leader Frank was behind them and came over to Mitzi.

"Thank you, Frau, for taking action so quickly."

"What did the Generals say?"

"In five minutes they want me to escort the little bitch to General Boeddeker's tent."

"Just as I expected. Bring her up as they told you, and don't say a word about this to anyone."

"I swear that I won't, Top Leader."

Mitzi, not wanting Liesel to know that she was on the scene, peeked out of the flap of her tent. Leader Frank led the shivering girl, wrapped in a towel, to the door of General Boeddeker's tent. She could only imagine what was running through the mind of Liesel, a pawn in the drama about to unfold, innocent except for being a Jew. She almost felt sorry for her. But then Mitzi quickly concluded that she was only a Jew, and no one could feel sorry for what they get and deserve.

Minutes later, Boeddeker let out a loud scream. Then Mitzi heard Liesel's bloodcurdling scream. An SS guard, several leaders, and three BDM girls rushed into the tent. Mitzi didn't dare go near the now brewing scandal.

A few minutes later, a BDM leader and girl led Liesel out of the tent and across the compound to the girl's camp. She was quivering, with tears running down her cheeks.

"What a damn mess these idiots have created," Mitzi thought. "How could they screw up a simple matter of convincing a teenage girl of what was good for her? Now it'll be on me to clean up the mess."

Five minutes later, Von Koenig arrived at Mitzi's tent. "We asked the girl if she knew anything about the fountain of life program. Of course, she had never heard of it. Then we asked if she, as a loyal girl of the Reich, would like to create a perfect Aryan baby for the Fuhrer. We said she was beautiful, and that Adolph Hitler would personally honor her offspring. At that point the girl broke down, saying she had never done anything like that and wanted to go back to her tent."

Mitzi was seething but held her tongue.

"She was shivering in her towel, and I was ready to send her out when Boeddeker took her in his arms and forced her to lie on his bed. He got on top of her and was kissing her neck when she kneed him hard where it hurts the most. He let out a scream and rolled onto the floor in pain. As I came over to calm the girl down, she must have thought I was going after her. She started screaming and that's when everyone rushed in."

"Real discreet and smooth, Alfred! Not one of your finest moments."

"That's for damned sure! I didn't foresee Wilhelm turning into a brutish animal like that."

"So how are you going to fix this mess with the girl and her family?"

"Don't worry about that, Mitzi, I'll smooth it over. I'll have the top leader for all of Germany write a letter of apology to the girl and her family. We'll say it was an error in judgment, and the parties involved were properly disciplined. Hell, they don't need to know the identity of the perpetrator."

"I hope that works for your sake."

"I'm sure it will, darling. But now what about you, Mitzi? That young beauty aroused me."

"Maybe some time, Alfred, but not this trip. I'm returning to Cologne right away."

The next morning the troop took down their tents and packed their gear, preparing for their return to Cologne. Liesel had settled down. She was still angry but an inner strength, something dampened by loss and sadness in her young life, bubbled up.

When she got home, she said nothing to Jürgen, knowing he might do something out of anger that could hurt the family. For weeks, she told only Sophie, Trudi, and Netti. The news shocked and upset them. Sophie wanted to find the bastards and castrate them. But they finally agreed it would be best only to try to reduce Liesel's risk in the future.

She never went on another camp outing. Marta was displeased about that, however, she felt horrible about what happened and vowed to protect her friend. It was weeks later, after he received an official letter of apology from the head of the BDM in Germany, that Jürgen first learned of the incident. But Liesel smoothed it over, minimizing what happened, so her father wouldn't overreact or feel responsible.

Several weeks later, Netti said to Trudi, "I'm so moved by the character and wisdom shown by Liesel through this entire incident." It would be several years before Jürgen and the rest of the family knew the details of what happened that summer day near Bonn.

* * *

On a late Saturday afternoon in July, Netti and Pastor Mose Tresler were finishing preparations for the Sunday service at the Free Faith Church. Pastor Grobe was visiting family in Hannover, so Mose would be conducting the service.

"Sit, Netti. You're working like a trooper."

"I'll bring us some cool water from the icebox, and we can rest before finishing." In a minute Netti returned with two glasses of water and two oatmeal cookies.

Netti was finally realizing that Conrad Bauer might never be a part of her life again. But she couldn't allow herself to believe, or even think, he was dead. It had been eleven months since the Gestapo abducted Conrad and Kurt, and she hadn't heard a word. Netti and Mose tried not to let their faith waiver and constantly prayed for their safe return. Conrad was in Netti's thoughts often, but as the months passed those thoughts dwindled. During that time Mose was Netti's spiritual counselor, seeing her almost daily.

He and her father interceded with God to get her through the hardest time in her life. She was so appreciative and thankful for what Mose was doing for her. She loved him as a close brother. But, try as he may, Mose, on the other hand, couldn't help falling in love with the young woman to whom he was ministering.

"Did you go to see Trudi and the baby yesterday?" Mose asked.

"I did. She's thrilled, and even Max is crazy about Helene. She'll be three weeks old tomorrow."

"I'm so happy for them; I just wish we could impact their lives for Christ."

"That's always in the back of my mind, too. Trudi listens to what I say and even accepts it at times, but she never gets to the point of asking Jesus into her life. I'm not sure, but I still get the sense that she wants to explore the God of her heritage. She's heard so much from Sophie about her uncle Otto's brave stand for the Jewish faith, which I think inspires her to learn more about it."

"Well, that's a start; maybe we can encourage her to read the Old Testament to learn about God Jehovah."

Mose was the only one outside the family who knew that Jürgen and Lisbeth had secretly adopted the three Jewish children. In Netti's deepest time of despair, she accidentally said something that gave the secret away. She then told Mose the whole story.

"Max is off to Munich again. Trudi thinks she knows why he's making so many trips for the bank," Netti said. "She's afraid he's tied up with Wolf and his zealous support of the Nazis."

"Why does she think that?"

"She can't put her finger on it yet, but she came across several items in his desk that associate him with the Gestapo."

"Well, you know what your father and Sophie have thought all along?"

"You mean that Wolf was right in the middle of the Gestapo's taking down the Hohe Strasse Bank?"

"Sure, and it's not a stretch to assume his top assistant had a hand in it too."

"That's what Trudi fears, that her husband's a Nazi and has been deceiving her all along."

"What will she do, Netti?"

"She's in a fix. She loves Max but would hate it if he's been lying to her about who he is. And what's worse is that if he knew who she was, he would have to renounce both her and Helene."

"Could it come to that?"

"Who knows, but it concerns Trudi."

"By the way, did Sophie make any headway in convincing Katia to get away for a while?"

"Oh! That's what I forgot to tell you, Mose. Sophie's bringing Katia and Rudi to Cologne Wednesday."

"They're staying with your family?"

"Sure. Katia will sleep in Trudi's room and Rudi in Didi's. They'll stay at least until school starts and maybe longer."

"Is she doing any better?"

"Sophie thinks she's a little better, but she's still devastated."

"It must bring back the hurt you felt when they took Conrad?"

"I can't hide that it's also been hard on me, you know that all too well."

"Is she able to see him at all?"

"No, they won't allow it. The last time she saw Ralph was when the sham court sentenced him to ten years in prison. And all they could say was that he committed crimes against the Reich. Katia pleaded with Uncle Ralph for years about being so stubborn about not retooling the factory for military production."

"He's obviously a good man with high principles and great pride in the business he and his father built."

"Uncle Ralph is a wonderful man, but that doesn't help Katia and Rudi now when they need him most. Our prayer list keeps growing as the times get darker. I can't understand what so many people in our country are thinking, Mose; it scares me."

"A spirit of depravity has veiled our country, Netti. Lust of the flesh and eye is ruling the minds of millions."

"It's a new morality and purity code that's the opposite of God's righteousness. National pride and outright hatred are dragging our nation down to the pits of hell. God's the only one who can stop it, Mose. I know we both have strong convictions, but I'm so glad you're not involved with the underground anymore. I just can't lose anyone else."

"I'm torn, Netti. My calling is to preach the gospel and tend the flock, but I want to do more to fight what the Nazis are doing to our country."

"We all do. But sometimes we need to bite our tongue and pick the times carefully when we do something. We also need to be there to support our loved ones, just as you've been helping me."

In gratitude, Netti fell into Mose's arms. He gently hugged her. He felt limp as joy filled his mind. He wanted to kiss her and say how much he loved her, but he didn't. Netti quickly pulled away when she felt he might get the wrong impression.

"Do you still see Father Boesch for coffee?" Netti asked.

"At least once a week, usually Tuesday mornings."

"Does he still help the underground?"

"He does, but for my protection, he doesn't talk about it. He still speaks out privately and publicly against what he thinks is wrong, but he does it carefully."

"Even so, hasn't the Gestapo warned him to stop?"

"They have, and I worry about his safety. He's so disappointed in the Church's weak response to what the Nazis are doing. Hitler made shambles of the Pope's 1933 concordant and now every day they put new limits on what Catholics can do. He's afraid the dark history of anti-Semitism in the Church has never gone completely away and that Hitler is now feeding those feelings. Father Boesch and many other priests are trying to impact what's happening, but it's a losing battle."

"It sounds like some of the Confessing Church's weak efforts to stop the brutality of the Reich."

"It's the same, Netti, and that frustrates me. All most of them care about is preserving their precious traditions."

"That's not a surprise, Mose. I'm afraid many of them have never been to the cross of Christ, so they're still walking in darkness."

"Thankfully, there are people such as Niemoller, Gruber, and Bonhoeffer who are leading a true resistance against anti-Semitism."

"Many good people are doing all they can to stop them, but is it enough?"

"In ourselves, it falls far short, Netti, but with God, all things are possible. He's our only hope."

* * *

Wolf Behrmann eagerly entered Ricard Kluger's office at Gestapo headquarters and took a seat across from Kluger.

"It's been a year, but we finally got the full report you asked for, Behrmann. Thankfully, I won't have you badgering me about it anymore."

"I know I've been a pain in the ass, Ricard. What did they find out?"

"I almost regret telling you this, Wolf; they didn't find much that will be useful."

"Sonofabitch, is this the written report?"

"The entire report. I read it all and can give you the highlights if you want."

"Go ahead."

"About your brother's family, there are legitimate birth certificates in Leipzig for each of the six children. The names were Trudi, Dieter, Waldo, Gretel, Liesel, and Stefan. The birthdates are in the report. They searched all the records in Meiningen and Leipzig and found no records of a father named Markus Mendel. His children were probably born elsewhere. They didn't check any further. But, in snooping around Meiningen, they came up with some information about him and his family."

"At least that's something, dammit. What did they find out about the Jew?"

"The Mendel family had two markets. The one you asked about, Markus, ran one of them and his father ran the other one. Markus died in 1927, and his wife died years earlier. The paternal grandparents took the children with them when they migrated to America in 1929."

Kluger took the report and leafed through it. "Yes, here it is; they talked to a young man named Wilhelm Becker who dated one of the Mendel daughters. For some reason they didn't list her first name in the report. For a while he wrote to her in America before moving on to a new girlfriend."

"Dammit! Is that all?"

"No, they stumbled on to something else that might be of interest to you. A Sophie Mendel worked a long time for a lawyer in Meiningen named Evert Heinz. She's also worked for him in Cologne for the past five years."

"I knew it. I knew the bitch with that hairdo had to be her. So Maria Schnabel is Sophie Mendel; the little Jew girl that Jürgen adored. Thanks, Kluger, I'll read all the details and let you know if I have any questions."

"You owe me one, Behrmann. I'll let you know when it's time to pay."

Wolf went straight home to read the entire Gestapo report. But Kluger had already covered all the useful information. Little else in the report caught his eye. Now he would do some snooping on his own, with Max's help. Maybe they could find out for sure if there was something going on behind the scenes, or if he was trying to see something that was never there.

* * *

On August 23, 1937, Claus Bauer received a small package postmarked from Buchenwald. He had returned to Cologne only three weeks before when he learned the Gestapo was no longer looking for him. He opened the package to find a brief letter, wallet, and watch. He broke down in tears before he read the letter, recognizing that both the wallet and watch belonged to Conrad. The letter said that Conrad Bauer died of a stroke on July 28, while imprisoned at Buchenwald.

Claus grieved for the entire day, trying to accept the news that his youngest son was dead. He finally called Jürgen to break the bad news and decide on how they would tell Netti. Hearing how upset Claus was, Jürgen assured him that he would tell Netti when she arrived home that evening. Jürgen closed the door of his study and wept for ten minutes. He felt terrible for the young man he liked so much and thought was the perfect mate for his daughter. He ached for Netti, knowing how deeply the news would hurt her, and that nothing he could say would ease her pain.

Jürgen told Lisbeth before Netti came home. She was sad but not shocked that Conrad wouldn't be coming home. She too hurt for Netti and wondered how she would survive the blow. Jürgen feared all along that this might be Conrad and Kurt's fate. But now, how would they deal with the finality of it all?

A little past five, Netti came through the front door with Waldo. Jürgen and Lisbeth were sitting in the front room waiting for her. After greeting their children, Jürgen asked Waldo to go upstairs so they could talk with his sister.

"What is it, Father? Why can't Waldo hear it?"

"It's best that we talk with you alone, sweetheart."

Netti started to panic, dreading what she might hear, but then she quickly composed herself. "What happened, Father?"

"It's Conrad. Claus called me this afternoon after receiving a package from Buchenwald prison. They sent him Conrad's wallet and watch, with a letter saying he died of a stroke in July. I'm so very sorry, darling."

Jürgen took Netti in his arms, and Lisbeth tenderly rubbed her back. Netti said nothing for a minute, focusing with all her strength on Conrad safe at home with his Savior, waiting for her to join him. The thought mercifully comforted Netti. She could feel God's peace quieting her spirit.

Jürgen was more than a little concerned that his daughter wasn't distraught and crying. He wondered if she had heard or understood what he said. "Are you okay, sweetheart?"

"I am, father. I'm sad for Conrad's family and that I won't see him until we meet in heaven, but God has given me a special gift of peace. You might find it hard to believe, but He let me know a week ago that this day was coming. He also clearly assured me that everything would be okay, and it would be a season before I understood everything."

"I believe you, darling. We serve an incredible God."

Netti's reaction dumbfounded Lisbeth. She knew her peace must be supernatural. She wasn't reacting as Lisbeth expected; it wasn't natural. At that moment, Lisbeth felt great love for Netti and God.

Netti never fully understood how God brought her through the loss of the man she loved. She was still learning how He worked in her life and how much He loved her. She praised Him every day for His peace and strength. The great support she received from her family brought her to tears and strengthened their bonds. Waldo stayed near Netti for weeks, doing everything he could to comfort her. No one thought they could be closer, but over those weeks their love for each other deepened.

Mose Tresler was also by Netti's side in the weeks following the news of Conrad's death. He loved her so much and only wanted to comfort her and be available for anything she needed. Netti recognized what Mose was doing for her, and she loved how God moved through him. She was well aware that he loved her and at some point would ask for her hand in marriage. The last thing she wanted to do was hurt him or deny what he wanted so much. But she wasn't ready to love Mose in the way a wife should love her husband.

As the weeks turned to months and 1938 arrived, Netti relied more and more on Mose and his loving support. After Netti and Gisela finished nurses' training and started working at Cologne University hospital, she saw firsthand how brutal and dangerous life was becoming under the Nazi regime.

Gisela, Trudi, and Waldo encouraged Netti to consider Mose. With their encouragement, she started seriously thinking he might be God's protection for her in the dark days ahead. Some in her family didn't agree with Mose's strong Christian stand, but they all liked and respected him. It was obvious to everyone how much he cherished Netti, and they thought it would be wonderful if Netti responded to his love.

As March came, Netti seriously prayed for God's guidance. She felt He was leading her to marry Mose, even though she didn't love him the way she loved Conrad. So when he proposed in April, Netti accepted without hesitation, though she wasn't sure down deep if she was doing the right thing. It was then that Mose kissed his bride to be for the first time. He kissed her with the passion he so wanted to show her. Netti didn't feel the same excitement, but she gave in to his need and tried to show the same passion.

In late May of 1938, Netti Behrmann became Netti Tresler, to the delight of all present at the Free Faith Church ceremony. Mose's superior, Pastor Grobe, officiated the wedding. All the Behrmann family and close friends were there except for Sophie, Didi, Mitzi, and Erich. Mose's parents and sister came from Frankfurt, with other relatives from the east. It was a low-key occasion compared to Trudi and Max's nuptials at the magnificent Cologne Cathedral. The reception was again at the Jürgen Behrmann home, where everyone joyously celebrated the newlyweds.

Didi and Netti had had another loud argument a week before the wedding. Didi still couldn't shake his guilt over Kora's death, and he continued to accuse Netti and his father of blaming him for the tragedy. He stormed out of the house, vowing not to come to the wedding or anywhere else for a long time. Erich wanted no part of Pastor Tresler or the Free Faith Church, so he made up a convenient excuse for being out of town the weekend of the wedding. And all agreed that Sophie shouldn't attend because of Wolf's suspicions. And Wolf did indeed inquire about the absence of Jürgen's neighbor, Maria Schnabel.

3

THE MIRACLE NIGHT

In early June of 1938, Sophie Mendel looked up as the door to the offices of Heinz Enterprises opened and Wolf Behrmann entered. She tried to lower her head and hide, but it was too late. Wolf spotted her immediately and approached her desk. "If it isn't Maria—Maria Schnabel, isn't it?"

Sophie had to throw off the shock of Wolf tracking her down and think fast about what she should say. "Don't play your damn games with me, Wolf. You obviously know who I am, and now I want to know why you went to the trouble of finding me."

"You always did think you were so smart—and so damned cute and cuddly as a girl. I remember that swirl of hair flowing down over your eyebrow those many years ago when I overheard all of your lies. I wanted to grab you by that crop of hair and sling you as far as I could. You never changed that proud hairdo, just like you never changed being a smart-assed Jew. That's what gave you away, Sophie Mendel. The picture in Jürgen's study just happens to show that girl with the unique hair. I'm surprised he put it up."

"So you know who I am! So what?"

"I just find it curious that you would be here with Jürgen and not still in Meiningen."

"My work brought me to Cologne, as I'm sure you already know."

"No, I didn't know that, but it looks like your wit and charm have taken you a long way."

"What the hell do you want with me?"

"I was sorry to hear about your brother. Markus, wasn't it?"

"How would you know about my brother?"

"It shouldn't surprise you. With the Gestapo's help, I can find out anything. So his children went to America with your parents?"

"You already know that, so why are you asking me?"

"What are the children's names?" Wolf snapped.

Sophie hesitated. Should she refuse to answer or make up names? "Wilbur, Anna, and Jutta."

"You know every day is getting darker for Jews, and it won't be long until you're all disposed of, one way or the other."

"I'm not stupid, but what does that have to do with you being here now?"

"I'm here to give you a stern warning. Do you think I'm a fool? I know you're all hiding something. I don't know what it is now, but I'll do everything in my power to find out."

"You're mad! No one's hiding anything; you're wasting your time."

"No, I'm not wasting my time, and soon I'll learn what you're hiding. But you also need to know that I can protect you, Sophie Mendel."

"How can you protect me, and even if you could, why do you think I would want your protection?"

"I would simply protect you by not telling the Gestapo that you're a Jew with evil intentions."

"Since you hate me so much, why would you do that?"

"I'd do it in exchange for two favors."

"Oh yes, now here it comes, as if I couldn't guess what favors you want."

"As feisty as you are, you're still a desirable woman who looks frustrated and lonely. And I can do a damn fine job of easing both."

"The hell you can! Your filthy hands will never touch me, so get that foolishness out of your mind."

"You can't blame me for trying, though you don't know what you're missing. Let's forget that for now. If you do the other favor, I'll still give you a pass on living as a Jew in secret."

"Okay, let's hear what else you want me to do."

"From what I understand, this one will suit your skills and be easy to do."

Wolf took papers out of his briefcase and handed them to Sophie. "See the woman's signature on this document? I want you to practice forging it until it's perfect. And yes, I know you're an excellent forger. Then the day after tomorrow, I want you to complete this blank check for 300,000 Reichsmarks. Bring it to the Hohe Strasse Bank precisely at eleven and ask the teller at the far right end to cash it. She is tall and slender, with blond hair. The woman will take it to one of my confidants for approval. Put the money in this briefcase and hold it until I pick it up here at three that afternoon. Do you understand exactly what to do?"

"Of course I do, but tell me why you think you can rob this woman so easily?"

"Because she's a Jew, just like you. But this is a rich Jew who unfortunately got out of the country with her family and most of their money—all but 308,000 Reichsmarks still left in her bank account. She's done everything to get that money, but we've frozen all transactions that aren't in person."

"So you'll just take her money for yourself."

"Exactly! She has plenty of money and they're all safe, so she has no complaint. In fact, she should be thankful that she got her ass out of the country."

"What's my cut?"

"You're cut, dearie, is my silence—nothing more, nothing less."

"But you're forgetting one little thing, Wolf."

"No, Sophie; I'm way ahead of you. If you try to blackmail me, I'll have you picked up by the Gestapo."

Sophie pondered the offer for a minute. "Okay, I'll do it. But you'll be damned sorry if you cross me because I've got ways you know nothing about."

"So the tough little Jewess comes out again. Don't worry; I'll keep my part of the bargain; make sure you handle your part."

With that, Wolf Behrmann turned and walked out the door. Sophie immediately picked up the telephone, called the Hohe Strasse Bank, and asked to speak with Trudi. After waiting a few minutes Tudi came on the line. "Listen carefully to me, Trudi," Sophie said quickly and forcible, "and do exactly as I say. I'll fill in the details later. Feign that you're suddenly ill and have to go home and probably won't be better by tomorrow."

"But why, Sophie! What's happened?"

"It's serious, sweetie. Please do what I say, and I'll meet you at your place in twenty minutes."

Sophie made two other phone calls and then she put the papers from Wolf in her briefcase. After taking a deep breath, she picked up her purse and headed out the door for Trudi's apartment. Within twenty-five minutes, Sophie arrived at Trudi's building. There was no response when she knocked on the door, so she paced up and down until Trudi came up the stairs five minutes later.

"What the hell's going on, Sophie? I don't think my boss believed that I was suddenly ill, especially that I might not be in tomorrow."

"I'm sorry, Trudi, but we don't have a minute to waste. Max won't be home until Sunday, right?"

"Yes, but what's that have to do with anything?"

"We're taking a trip to Meiningen tonight. We need to pick up Helene at the babysitter and take her to Netti until we return tomorrow."

"But Netti has to work tomorrow."

"She can make up a story and stay home."

"My God! You're disrupting all our lives, and I don't know why."

"I think Wolf could expose you, Waldo, and Liesel as soon as tomorrow if we don't act now. He threatened me less than an hour ago. And by what he said, if they ask the right person the right question it might doom us all."

"What question, and who are you talking about?"

"Wolf knows that Markus' children emigrated to America with my parents. He even asked me what their names were. I couldn't play dumb, so I made up three names."

"Dammit! If he finds someone to contradict what you told him, we'll be in big trouble."

"That's what worries me. After I gave Wolf the names, I started thinking of people in Meiningen who could tell the Gestapo your real names. I called Lukas and Katia before I left my office. No one contacted them about Markus and his children. I told them the three names to use if anyone ever questions them, the names I gave to Wolf. If Wolf wasn't so stubborn and angry with his father, they would have been the first ones he went to for the information he wants."

"Thankfully, Katia and her parents were let in on our secret and would never say that we were the children of Markus Mendel. And both sets of my grandparents and Otto are no longer in Germany. Others who might have known us in Meiningen probably don't remember that much."

"You're right, Trudi, but I got the clear impression from Wolf that someone in Meiningen told the Gestapo about you emigrating to America."

"Oh my God! Are you thinking what I'm thinking?"

"I think I am. Your first love, Wilhelm Becker is the most logical person I can think of."

"But if they talked to Wilhelm, he had no reason not to give them our real names."

"Unless they never asked him."

"Wouldn't that be sloppy?"

"Sloppy, yes, but Wolf is anything but stupid. He must have information from the Gestapo that he's probably reviewing now. And if that sloppy oversight is in their report, you can bet he'll have them follow up with Wilhelm, maybe as early as tomorrow."

"Oh, crap, Sophie! We need to get to Wilhelm before they do."

"That's why I'm pushing you. Get what you need and let's get Helene to Netti's and then get on the road to Meiningen."

Trudi quickly gathered what she needed for herself and Helene, and they were out the door. Netti was upset about Sophie's news and the possible danger to the family. She committed to covering Sophie and Trudi in prayer as they tried to prevent disaster.

By eleven that night, Sophie and Trudi checked into a Meiningen hotel. The first thing they did was search the telephone directory for Wilhelm Becker. Fortunately, they found his name, address, and telephone number. On the trip to Meiningen, they had discussed what they should do. They agreed that Trudi should call Wilhelm immediately, even if she woke him up.

"What am I going to tell him, Sophie? It's been nine years since I received his last letter. He thinks I'm in America and now all the sudden I call him at midnight."

"It'll be a shocker for him. We don't know how he'll react, but we have no choice."

"What if he's a Nazi and has no feelings for me?"

"It's a chance we'll have to take. Go ahead and make the call, Trudi."

A drowsy and angry voice said, "Hello, who is it?"

"Is this Wilhelm?"

"Of course it is! Why are you calling this time of night?"

"It's Trudi."

"Trudi Mendel?"

"Yes, it's me, Wilhelm. I'm sorry about calling so late, but it's important that I see you as soon as possible."

Trudi heard a woman's voice yelling in the background, but she couldn't make out what she was saying.

"Tonight, Trudi? You woke us up."

"Can I see you early tomorrow, perhaps before you go to work?"

"I guess, but what's so important that you need to see me right away? And why are you back in Germany?"

"I'll tell you everything when I see you. What time should I come to your place?"

"My wife, Frieda, is leaving to visit her parents at six, and I leave for work at seven-thirty. Around seven is okay."

"I'll see you then. Thanks, Wilhelm."

That evening, Wolf Behrmann did reread the Gestapo report, and he did notice the Gestapo didn't ask Wilhelm Becker the first name of the Mendel girl he wrote to in America. It was sloppy investigative work but was it worth following up on he wondered. "What the hell," Wolf thought, "nothing to lose by giving Kluger a call."

Kluger chewed out Wolf for disturbing him at dinner and for bothering him about the same ridiculous investigation. But after settling down, he told Wolf that he'd make a phone call to see if the Gestapo in Meiningen would follow up with Becker the next morning. He made no promises and told Wolf never to bother him again about the matter. Wolf thanked Kluger profusely and hung up.

Sophie circled the block where Wilhelm lived, slowing down in front of his house. She circled the block again, parking several houses down the street from his home. "Good luck, sweetie."

"Thanks, Auntie. I hope Netti's praying for us now."

"Knowing Netti, I'm sure she is."

It was just after seven when Wilhelm Becker opened his front door. He remembered Trudi as a cute fifteen-year-old who was full of life but just starting to blossom. But now a woman of twenty-four stood in his doorway; someone he didn't know, attractive but sad and anxious. Also, Trudi didn't see the boy with the big smile that she loved, but rather a young man that was haggard and gloomy.

"Wilhelm, it's so good to see you," Trudi said as she embraced him.

"I'm glad to see you again, Trudi. I think about you often. And look at you, you're all grown up. I must say, you look beautiful to me."

"Thanks, Wilhelm. You look so sad, are you okay?"

"I'm not, Trudi, but that's not why you're here."

"I'm sorry to hear that. Wilhelm, I need you to do a big favor for me that you probably won't understand, but it's very important. Someone from the Gestapo or police might be asking you the first name of the girl you were writing to in America, back in 1929."

"They've already talked with me about your family. But they didn't ask about you. Why would anyone care about your name?"

"All I can tell you is the Nazis are secretly active in America, and for reasons we don't know, they're trying to track down my family. We think it probably has to do with some holdings we still have here. Anyway, it's critical to our well-being that they never find us.

"I'm back in Germany to do several things that will ensure our safety. One of them is to have you give the authorities a false name when or if they ask. So please tell them you were writing to Anna Mendel. Anna was the first name of the girl you were writing to. Can you do that for me, Wilhelm?"

"Anna. Sure, I can do that."

"Oh, thanks! I have a feeling they'll be coming soon."

"You look scared."

"I am scared, and tired and frustrated."

Wilhelm took Trudi in his arms, stroking her hair as he did nine years before. She perked up as she felt his lips gently kissing her right ear. Trudi knew this wasn't the time to spark an old romance. But that tingly feeling she first felt with Wilhelm was now radiating through her body.

"No, Wilhelm—please!"

He said nothing, as he moved his head down and covered her lips with his.

"Oh, crap," Sophie whispered, as a black auto stopped in front of Wilhelm's house. A man in a dark suit and a swastika armband got out and walked quickly to the front door. "Dear Lord, if you're there, help Trudi now," Sophie breathed.

A loud knock on the front screen door separated Trudi and Wilhelm's lips. They turned to look toward the door. "It's him," whispered Wilhelm as he walked to the door. Trudi was well aware who it was. It scared her to death, but since he saw her there was nothing she could do.

"So we meet again, Becker. Sorry for interrupting you and your wife, but the door was open."

"It's okay. Is there something else I can help you with?"

"Yes, there is. Maybe the Frau would excuse us for a minute."

"Please finish in the kitchen, darling, and let the man conduct his business."

Trudi went to the kitchen and shut the door, leaving it cracked so she could hear the conversation in the living room.

"Just one more question about our previous conversation; do you remember?"

"I do."

"Then all I need is the first name of the Mendel girl you were writing to in America."

"Anna—Anna Mendel was her name."

"Anna Mendel, is that correct?"

"Yes, that's what I said."

"Good. That's all I need. Say goodbye to the wife for me." With that, the Gestapo agent was out the door.

Sophie's tension intensified as she saw the auto drive off. Meanwhile, Trudi thanked Wilhelm with all her heart, as she started for the front door. But Wilhelm took her arm and pulled her to himself.

"No, Wilhelm! I'm married, and it's been too many years to go back."

"I'm also married, Trudi, and it was the biggest mistake of my life. I wish you'd never left me."

"I didn't want to. I had no choice."

"When we kissed, I felt the same passion for you I had nine years ago, Trudi. And I believe that you're not happy in your marriage either."

"It doesn't matter, Wilhelm. It's all too complicated; it just won't work."

Wilhelm pulled Trudi close again, and he kissed her more passionately. She couldn't resist, matching his passion and even more. He told Trudi that he never stopped loving her, and she told him that she wished everything could be different.

"Will you write to me when you're back in America?"

"I'll think about it, but I can't make any promises, Wilhelm. Goodbye."

Then Trudi left the house and walked down to the street and up the block to Sophie's auto. Tears filled her eyes. She had never expected the embers of young love to rekindle. Over the years Trudi had diminished the relationship to only the crush of a young and innocent girl. But now she knew it was a lot more.

"Is everything alright, Trudi?"

"It went well. Wilhelm gave him the name of Anna as I asked. The agent didn't question him further."

"Thank God. You don't know how worried I was when the Gestapo pulled up. Was there a problem with you being there?"

"No, he thought I was Wilhelm's wife."

"Good. Did you give Wilhelm the story we rehearsed?"

"Yes, just as we said, but the story has holes in it. I'm surprised he didn't press me further."

"Is something wrong, sweetie? You've been crying."

Trudi started crying again, shaking her fist in the air. "I acted stupidly, Auntie."

"What did you do?"

"Wilhelm kissed me, and I kissed him back. We kissed so passionately. I haven't had such feelings for a long time. I feel terrible, not just for Max but that I had to leave Wilhelm in the first place."

"I wouldn't feel bad for that sonofabitch you're married to."

"Sophie! That's my husband you're talking about."

"He doesn't know what being a husband is. Hell, he's never home long enough to be any damn good to you."

"You don't even know the worst, Sophie."

"What do you mean, sweetie?"

"Items I've found in the house confirm that Max is with a woman when he makes those trips to Munich."

"I can guess what items you're talking about."

"That's not all. He's left different clues around that I would obviously see, which proves he's conducting Nazi business on those trips."

"Why won't the bastard just come out and confess his true beliefs and where he stands with you?"

"I don't know. I've hinted about those things, but he never comes clean."

"Do you think he loves you or ever did?"

"I thought he did, but now I'm not sure if he ever loved me."

"I know you were madly in love with Max when you married him, but what about now? Do you still love him, Trudi?"

"Yes, I loved him very much, but now it's all gone; there's nothing left. That tingling through my body that I just felt with Wilhelm vanished long ago with Max."

"Then maybe it's time to leave him—get a divorce?"

"I'm to the point where I've been thinking about it, but now there are complications."

"In what way, sweetie? What else don't I know?"

"Last week I verified with Doctor Von Lowe that I'm pregnant. The baby is due in January."

"Well, that does complicate everything. Does he know?"

"No, but I'm sure that's the last news he'd want to hear."

"I shouldn't, but I'll give you some advice. You need to tell Max everything you know about him and that you're pregnant. Have it out with him, and then see where you go from there. You know you'll have all your family's support through whatever happens."

"That's good advice, Auntie; thanks. But right now, I'm not sure what I'll do."

"It's your decision. Let's get out of here, Trudi. I need to be home by mid-afternoon."

Sophie quickly put her auto in gear, and they headed back to Cologne. Both women said little on the trip home. But each thought deeply about the implications of Wolf's endless obsession to learn the truth and what Trudi would do about her failing marriage.

* * *

Jürgen looked up from his journal entry of August 8, 1938, as Netti and Waldo came through the front door.

"Hi, darling, I didn't know you were bringing Waldo home this evening."

"I called her because I stayed over for late rehearsals, and as always she was good enough to bring me home," Waldo said.

"Can you stay for supper, Netti?"

"Sure. Mose has his elders' meeting tonight and won't be home till nine."

Waldo slipped upstairs, as Netti went into the living room to sit by her father. Lisbeth was sitting in the stuffed chair across from Jürgen. She had a near empty glass of wine in her right hand. She only nodded to recognize Netti's presence.

"What's wrong with her?" Netti whispered.

"I got news from Leipzig that upset her."

"It should upset you too, Jürgen. It puts us all in danger again!"

"Danger? What do you mean, Mother? Is it something about our secret?"

"No. Ask your father; he thinks we don't have anything to worry about."

"Worry about what, Father?"

"I don't know how much you remember about it, sweetheart, but we learned the courts recently released Heinz Wagner from prison."

"I don't remember that name. Who is he?"

"You were only four, Netti, on that Sunday afternoon in Leipzig when a man came out of the bushes and started shooting at me."

"Oh, God! That does bring back memories. I don't remember much, but I can still hear the loud shots and see you rolling on the pavement in pain."

"I'm sorry that you have to remember any of it, Netti."

"Mother said you weren't too upset about this."

"I think we need to be vigilant, but the man doesn't know where we are and probably never will."

"Will he try to find us, Father?"

"He probably will. Apparently, he's still making threats against me."

"I don't like the sound of that. Can't we do something?"

"There's not much we can do, sweetheart. But no one in Leipzig knows I'm in Cologne, so I think the odds of him ever finding me are slim, and I'm not going to worry about it. Like I said, we need to be watchful but not fearful. We'll trust God to watch over us."

"You're right, Father; that's what we'll do. I don't remember if I ever knew, but why did this man want to kill you?"

"He was distraught about the death of his wife in the hospital where I worked. And to be truthful with you, sweetheart, my inaction might have contributed to her death. I left her to treat a man who had a heart attack. My oversight led to a series of errors, which prevented the woman from being diagnosed quickly so she could get the proper treatment. It was the biggest mistake of my career."

"Mother, do you hear what Father's saying? This man will never find us."

"I'd like to slough it off like your father, but I can't. You know I can't, so don't ask me to, Netti."

"Why not? So you can have another excuse to ply yourself with alcohol and make the world go away?"

"Dammit, Netti, that's not fair. We're already under tension from hiding our secret and trying to deal with life crumbling all around us. And now this. It's too much for me to handle."

Lisbeth started sobbing as she emptied her glass of wine. Jürgen was ready to intercede when Waldo came down the stairs with his violin. As he reached the living room, he started playing Netti's Song. As always, a soft tear appeared in Netti's eye.

"Thanks, Waldo, but it's well past the four o'clock time you usually play the piece for me."

"I know, Netti, but I thought everyone needed to hear it tonight."

Netti stood and hugged her brother. "You're so sweet and sensitive, Waldo."

As Waldo put his violin down, Liesel and Stefan came down for supper and sat on the couch next to Jürgen.

"How's your new job going, Sis?"

"I'm almost through the training, Netti, and next week they'll put me on the line of operators."

"The telephone company's a good and stable place to work, Liesel."

"That's the only reason I went to work there, so I could go to night rehearsals and meetings at the theater."

"Your sister aspires to be an actress, not a telephone operator. Correct, darling?"

"Yes, Father. I'd go crazy if I had to sit at that switchboard eight hours a day for the rest of my life. But acting, I could do that twelve hours a day."

"Father said you met a fine young man in the theater group that you like a lot," Netti said with a smile.

"Oh, Father, why did you have to blab that all around?"

"I didn't know it was a secret, sweetheart. You seemed quite thrilled with Felix."

"Felix, huh? Tell me about this blooming romance, Sis."

"It's not a romance," Liesel responded as she blushed. "His name is Felix Leitner, and he's from here in Cologne. He wants to be an actor more than anything in the world, so we have a lot in common."

"And I'll bet he's cute as can be."

"Stop it now, Netti! I'm already blushing, and you're still teasing me."

"I couldn't resist, I'm sorry. I miss being around you every day, Liesel—you too, Stefan."

"Me, too?" Waldo asked.

"Of course, darling Waldo. Every day I miss seeing you is a day that's missing something special."

"Thanks, Netti. I treasure every moment with you."

"Liesel, Stefan, come out to the kitchen and help me get supper on the table," Lisbeth yelled.

"Go help your mother and try not to say anything to upset her. She's having a bad day."

"Yes, Father," Stefan said as he and Liesel headed for the kitchen.

"Is Theodor going to be on time, Jürgen?" Lisbeth shouted.

"He should be here soon," Jürgen yelled back.

"As often as Theodor eats here, he should just move in; it would save him time coming and going."

"He's only here for supper three or four times a week, Netti."

"It's okay with me, Father, if he eats here every meal. I like him a lot, and I know he's your dearest friend."

"I'm glad you approve, sweetheart, and indeed he's my closest friend."

"And Aunt Sophie's your closest female friend."

"Well, there's your mother and Aunt Katia, too."

"Of course, Father. Can I ask you something? Is Liesel doing as well as it appears, or is she doing a good acting job?"

"I think your sister's doing well. How she's worked through the horrible incident in Bonn is incredible to me. She's resilient like you, Netti. And she has so much love to give, just like you do."

"So you don't think it'll permanently scar her and make her resent and fear men?"

"From what I've seen, and how she feels about this young man in the theater group, I think she'll do fine with the right man."

"You don't know how good that makes me feel. Every day I intercede for her."

"I know you do, sweetie, and I also mention Liesel to the Lord every time I think of her."

"Does she only go to the Wednesday night home meetings now?" Netti asked.

"Yes. She no longer takes part in the weekends and doesn't take trips with the BDM."

"And no one harasses her about it?"

"No—no real problems. Some of the girls that gave her a hard time felt bad about what happened in Bonn. And Marta Gorman is a good friend and support for your sister."

Shortly after Theodor arrived, dinner was served. As they finished the meal, Theodor expressed his usual gratitude. "Thank you for another delicious meal, Lisbeth. I love the flavor of your marinated beef. The berries and cake were tasty, too."

"Thanks, Theodor, you're always too kind. It was only a simple meal and easy to fix."

"It was good eating, mother, and we enjoy that the most."

"You're easy to please, Stefan."

"So, Stefan, you're joining Waldo and Isaac next week at the music college?" Theodor asked.

"Yes, enrollment is next Wednesday."

"You're majoring in piano, of course."

"Also in the masters' works."

Jürgen pulled out his small Bible and cigarette case and laid them on the table. He lit a cigarette and gave it to Lisbeth, then lit one for himself. Netti gave him one of her "please, father, stop" looks that always amused him. She knew her scowl was useless, but she had purposed never to give up the campaign to rid her family of the filthy habit of smoking cigarettes.

"I saw your journal on the coffee table, Jürgen," Theodor said. "You certainly have plenty of fodder for updates."

"I do. But like I've said many times, there's no way a journal can contain everything the Nazis are doing."

"Are you still only hitting the highlights?"

"That's all I can possibly do. But what I'm more interested in doing is using the journal as a tool for telling the family about what's happening in our country and the world."

"That's right, Theodor," Stefan said. "Father talks with us every week about what he's writing down and how it could affect our lives. Then we ask him questions if we don't understand why—especially, why people hate the way they do and what we should do."

"Sounds like it's valuable time for you, Stefan. What's the topic of discussion now, Jürgen?"

"We've been talking about the Anschluss. I've tried to explain to the children that it wasn't just a matter of German soldiers marching into Austria and taking over. That it had a lot more to do with the history of the ethnic German people and their location in Austria because of the changing borders."

"Father taught us that people of German heritage live in many countries outside of Germany," Waldo said. "We never knew that."

"It sounds like you're getting a school lesson at home, Waldo."

"It's good for us to know, Theodor. It makes us think and brings up questions Father can usually answer."

"What did you learn about the Anschluss, Liesel?"

"Hitler wanted to bring all Germans that live outside our borders back home where they belong. And to do that he had to take over the countries where they live. But he knew he couldn't just march in and take over, so he had to make it look like it was a mutual agreement between Germany and those countries. And propaganda is always the way Nazis try to influence people and change minds. Father told us that Austria has been bombarded for several years with propaganda coming from the powerful radio station in Munich. He also told us that many people in both countries, who aren't Nazis, also wanted the Germans to come home."

"Excellent point, Liesel," Theodor said. "I suppose you heard similar propaganda in the home meetings?"

"Oh, yes. They pushed that a lot."

"What about you, Stefan? What have you learned?"

"Germany was putting pressure on Austria so they would willingly come into the Reich. And the Austrian Nazi Party, though small in number, was raising hell and creating turmoil. So to quell the matter, their chancellor called a referendum vote of all Austrians to decide if they wanted to remain independent or join Germany. He felt safe, assuming the people would vote to remain independent. But Hitler also knew how the vote would come out, so he threatened to invade Austria if the chancellor didn't resign. Then, to legitimize the takeover, Hitler thought he could appoint one of his Austrian stooges as chancellor and have him ask that German troops come in and restore order. Hitler didn't expect Austria's president would balk at the idea of appointing his stooge as chancellor. The whole mess frustrated Hitler, so he invaded Austria on March 12. Then they appointed Hitler's stooge as chancellor. After his appointment, he sent Hitler the request for German troops to invade. But it was too late; everyone with a brain knew it was only propaganda to legitimize the invasion. And unfortunately for the Austrian people, the referendum vote for independence from Germany never took place."

"Excellent job, Jürgen. Not many people in Germany, let alone the world, are as knowledgeable as your children."

"It's my responsibility, as a parent to tell them the whole truth. I only wish all parents in Germany would do the same."

"The Anschluss happened almost five months ago. What are you discussing now?"

"We're talking about many issues, Theodor," Liesel said. "One of them is what will Hitler do next."

"There are many Germans in Poland and western Czechoslovakia as well as other countries to the east, even some in the Nederland's. So what do you think about that, Liesel?" Theodor asked.

"We think Hitler will do something similar to the Austrian Anschluss in western Czechoslovakia. They call that territory the Sudetenland."

"So perceptive. I couldn't disagree with that assumption, Liesel."

Lisbeth stood up in anger, with a full glass of wine in one hand and a cigarette in the other. "Would you just stop talking about this? I can't take what's happening, and I sure as hell don't want to hear any more about it!" She turned and went quickly into the kitchen.

"I'm sorry, Jürgen. I should have known this kind of talk would upset her," Theodor said.

"It's not your fault, Theodor. Lisbeth needs to face the truth the way the rest of us have. We're all trying to help her, but she doesn't make it easy."

"Let me see if I can smooth it over." Theodor got up and went to the kitchen.

Lisbeth was standing in front of the sink, staring out the window. Theodor walked over and put his hand on her shoulder. "I'm sorry for bringing all that stuff up, Lisbeth. Here you have me over for a wonderful meal with the best family in Cologne, and what do I do but offend the lovely hostess."

"Oh, Theodor, it's not you. You didn't do anything wrong. It's me—it's always me. I just can't find peace. I've tried, but I'm always full of fear, and it's only getting worse."

"You know that Jürgen's the greatest husband in the world, and all your children are precious. They all love you, Lisbeth. They'd do anything to help you through these hard times."

"I know that, but why do I always push them away instead of accepting their help?"

"I'm not smart enough to know that, Lisbeth. Maybe Netti's God is the way to get the peace you need."

"I've asked God so many times, Theodor. If He's there, He doesn't hear me."

"I don't want to overstep my boundaries, but if you make amends with Netti and come to know her God, I think you'll find what you want."

"Thanks, Theodor, I know you're right, and I'm going to try again with her."

"We all love you, Lisbeth." Theodor took his hand off Lisbeth's shoulder and went back to the dining room.

"How's she doing, Theodor?"

"She's calmed down some, Stefan. Like I told Lisbeth, I don't want to cross my boundaries, but I think you could help your mother now, Netti."

"You don't know how much I want to. It seems like every time we try to work things out something goes wrong, and we have another blowup."

"I know how that can happen; just try when you get the chance, Netti. So, what's the discussion for this week, Jürgen?" Theodor asked as he turned from Netti to Jürgen.

"I've just finished my notes about the Evian Conference last month."

"What's that, father?"

"Well, Waldo, for nine days in July, thirty-two countries and twenty-eight help organizations met in Evian-les-Bains, France, to discuss the Jewish refugee problem in Germany and Europe. Almost half of the million German Jews emigrated when the Reichstag passed the Nuremberg Laws. Many of them went to Palestine. With the Anschluss in Austria, another two hundred thousand Jews became refugees. Also, the governments of Poland, Hungary, and Romania are now much more anti-Semitic, which is adding hundreds of thousands of additional Jews who want to leave Europe. And with the increasing harassment of Jews here, it's a critical issue that many countries are trying to solve."

"Did they find a solution for the Jews, Father?"

"I wish they had, Stefan. Sadly the conference was mostly a failure."

"In what way did it fail?"

"They found no solution for most of the Jews who wanted to emigrate, Liesel. Oh, they came up with a lot of platitudes and had good intentions. But when the conference ended, no one had relaxed their immigration quotas or had done anything to solve the problem. I had high hopes that America would take the lead in finding a way to ease the problem, but anti-Semitism is even strong there. President Roosevelt, who helped to initiate the conference, only sent a personal friend instead of a government official. It's like everyone made a pretense, but they had no real interest in doing the work required to resolve the problem. No one wanted to get their hands dirty, and frankly, I'm disappointed in them all."

"They didn't help the Jews, did they, Father?"

"No, Waldo, not much. But the British said they would try to take up to ten thousand children if it could be arranged. However, they wouldn't up their quota for emigration to Palestine."

"It's all such a mess, Father. What's going to happen?"

"We don't know, Liesel," Theodor replied. "But we have to be honest about what could happen and prepare for the worst. At least we're all sure now that your father was right in going to extreme measures to protect you, Trudi, and Waldo."

"Father!" Netti shouted. "Does Theodor know?"

"He's known for a while, darling. It just came out, but as close as we are, he had to be in on it."

"It's alright, I'm just surprised. Does anyone else know, that we're not aware of?"

"No, Netti. He's the only one outside the family who knows our secret."

Netti looked away and closed her eyes, knowing she and Trudi were the only ones who knew Erich was also in on the family secret.

"Not to switch from one distressing topic to another, but how is everything with Didi and Mitzi?" Theodor asked.

"You'd have to ask Lisbeth or Stefan," Jürgen replied. "They're the only ones who've seen them for months."

"We never talk about them, so I guess I've been hesitant to bring up the subject—sorry."

"It's okay, Theodor. It's as sad as the situation we've been discussing."

"Lisbeth and Didi are still close, though?"

"Still very close. They have an unbreakable bond, Theodor. What's strange though, is that Lisbeth is now close to Mitzi, when I'm certain she's only manipulating Lisbeth."

"The baby's coming soon?"

"From what I've heard, in several weeks."

"Damn, that's got to be hard for all of you."

"You'll never know, Theodor. A broken family hurts everyone deeply."

* * *

On August 19, 1938, Mitzi gave birth to Gretchen Marie Behrmann. Only the grandmothers accompanied Didi to the city hospital to welcome the addition to the family. Mitzi and baby were fine, and Didi was a proud father.

Didi had been subject to intense Nazi propaganda over the past year, and he was now denouncing his whole family, except his mother. Mitzi was the primary instigator of both the indoctrination and separation from the family. It was what she planned all along. The only issue that concerned Mitzi was that Didi might not be Gretchen's father, as she continued to fulfill her role as Germany's love goddess with more than a few men. Didi never knew, remaining loyal to the woman he loved. However, Mitzi's concerns about Gretchen lessened when everyone, including herself, saw how the baby strongly favored Didi.

* * *

As September ended, the Behrmann family prediction about the Sudetenland came to pass. Through internal agitation by the local Nazis and Hitler's fear-mongering bluffs, no one could prevent the annexation of the Sudetenland. It supposedly freed three and a half million Germans while making refugees of another 120,000 Jews.

On September 29, the Germans made an agreement with Italy, France, and Britain. The deal ceded the Sudeten territory to Germany, and the Czech government—which was not involved in the negotiations—gave in the following day. Within two weeks, Germany completed its occupation of the Sudetenland. It was all an embarrassing show of weakness and capitulation, as Britain and France crumbled under the fear of war. Neville Chamberlain, British Prime Minister, was the weakest link in stopping the spread of the Third Reich.

But the Sudetenland wasn't the only prize left for Hitler to secure. By the following spring, all Czechoslovakia was under German control, resulting in another 180,000 Jewish refugees. This takeover laid the foundation for the attack on Poland later in the year. Now it was clear to all that the clouds of war—world war—were quickly forming.

As November approached, Jürgen and Theodor often discussed how they were seeing an increase in violence toward Jews. Jürgen witnessed an unprovoked beating of an elderly man that he couldn't get out of his mind. It felt like all hell was ready to break loose if something ignited the spark.

Unfortunately, that spark came in November. The Reich had taken over Poland and expelled twelve thousand Polish Jews back to their native land in what they called the *Polenaktion*. They took the Jews by train and dropped them over the Polish border. However, neither country wanted them, so most went back and forth, living under horrible conditions in refugee camps along the border. But when the son of an expelled Polish couple received a postcard, detailing the conditions his parents were enduring in the refugee camp, he vowed to take action that would draw the world's attention to the crisis.

On November 7, Herschel Grynszpan bought a handgun in Paris, and he shot Ernst vom Rath. The German diplomat serving in Paris died two days later. Ironically, vom Rath was under investigation by the Gestapo for anti-Nazi leanings related to mistreating Jews.

The Nazis reacted on November 8 by barring Jewish children from state schools, halting most Jewish cultural events, and shutting down all Jewish publications. Then Hitler and Goebbels organized what appeared to be spontaneous demonstrations against the murder in Paris and against all Jews. It was really a call to incite an organized pogrom. Instructions went out to the security police and the Sturmabteilung (SA) that rioters could destroy Jewish property as long as they didn't harm non-Jews and non-Jewish businesses. The authorities were also allowed to arrest healthy Jewish men and take them to concentration camps. By late night on the ninth, the bowels of hell spewed out on Jews across Germany. The *night of broken glass* struck terror in the hearts of not only Jews but also many others witnessing what they never thought was possible in their country.

* * *

"Father! You're still here."

"I had emergency surgery with complications, Netti. Then the emergency room started filling with victims of whatever's going on out there."

"Gisela and I tried to leave the hospital, but everyone said we might have trouble getting home with violence breaking out all over the city."

"Some of those coming in say violent mobs attacked them. They said they were Jews. We've already had two deaths and many assaults."

"I don't think I've ever been this scared, Father. What we feared is happening, and I don't know what we should do."

"All we can do now is stay here and help the injured and hope it quiets down."

"But I'm afraid for Liesel!"

"Why, Netti? She should be home with the rest of the family."

"No, she isn't. Their rehearsal was running late tonight, maybe until midnight."

"Dammit! I hope she stays put."

"I'm afraid that might not be enough."

"What do you mean?"

"Do you know where their theater is?"

"I'm not sure, why?"

"It's across the street from the Orthodox synagogue on Breite Strasse, next door to a Jewish market. They're in a Jewish neighborhood, Father!"

"It's what, three kilometers east of here? I'll go down and get her."

"It's too dangerous now, Father. We saw fires and smoke in that area."

"Hopefully, they'll be safe in the theater."

"I'm not sure about that either."

"Why, Netti?"

"A Jew owns the building, and it's well-known that both Jews and Gentiles are part of the theater group."

"How in the world does that even happen now, sweetheart?"

"Because actors are generally liberal in their views."

"Then I am going down to get your sister. I want you and Gisela to stay here until I get back."

"If you go, I'm going too, Father."

"And I'm also going," Gisela emphatically stated as she walked up.

"It's too dangerous, girls. I can't risk your safety."

"It's no more dangerous for us than it is for you, Father. There's safety in numbers, even if we're women. We can help get Liesel—we're going."

"My God, you're stubborn, Netti. Okay, get a couple of sacks and fill them with bandages, medications, and basic supplies for injuries. I'm taking my medical bag, there's no telling what we'll face."

Within fifteen minutes, Netti and Gisela gathered medical supplies and met Jürgen at the hospital entrance. Ten minutes later, Jürgen's auto was nearing the old Orthodox synagogue.

"The street is filling with people. We can't go any further by auto," Jürgen said.

"Turn right here, Jürgen."

Not familiar with that part of the city, Jürgen obeyed Gisela's command and swerved onto a side street.

"I'm sure there's a small parking lot, half a block down on the left," Gisela said.

Sure enough, Jürgen saw the lot Gisela referred to, and there was one vacant parking spot.

Only a few people milled around on the side street as the three got out of the auto with their medical supplies. The red glow of the fires reflected off the buildings along Breite Strasse. They heard screaming and crying as they reached the corner.

"It's over three blocks to the theater, father."

"You're shivering, Netti. Are you sure about doing this?"

"I'm terrified, but I won't let them hurt my sister. I am going no matter what!"

"My knees are knocking, but I'm going, too, Jürgen. If this is it, at least I'll go down trying to save Liesel."

"Keep close to me girls. Obey everything I say. Don't look directly at anyone, and don't answer anyone, no matter what they say or do. We're going directly to the theater to get Liesel. Once we safely have her, we can think about helping the injured."

Jürgen led the girls for two blocks through crowds of people watching the few who were breaking windows and looting small shops. Young men and boys, with a few *brownshirts,* also harassed people they believed to be Jews. There was yelling and cursing, some directed at Jürgen and the girls, as they got closer to the theater. Netti was terrified and on the verge of vomiting but continued to call out to God with every step she took. Gisela thought this was her last night on earth; somehow it made her bolder. She bowed her back as she marched down the street, weaving in and out as they passed the crowds. Jürgen, like Netti, was praying every step of the way. He feared for Netti, Gisela, and Liesel.

As they passed the final corner, the violence intensified. The *brownshirts* were hauling people out of the synagogue and market. Horrible beatings were taking place all around them. People were lying everywhere on the street, crying, moaning, and pleading for help. Army trucks were taking men out of the area in droves.

The large buildings on either side of the street were ablaze. Glass was all over the street as the mob had broken all the windows. As the *brownshirts* and others filled with unquenchable rage eagerly destroyed property and brutalized the innocent, many others watched from a safe distance, cheering them on.

"Don't look, girls. Keep your eyes forward and let's get to the theater."

Blood was everywhere, and the carnage only got worse as they approached the theater entrance. The building had no windows, and a small fire was burning inside. As they started to enter the theater, a voice from behind said, "You can't go in there."

"Go in, girls—hurry!" They all ran through the opening where the door should have been and moved quickly to the small auditorium of the theater. They looked around through the smoke to see if anyone was there.

"Liesel, are you here?" Jürgen yelled out. "Liesel, are…"

A storage room door next to the stage opened and through the hazy smoke came Liesel, Felix, and two young women.

"Thank God you're here, Father!" Liesel yelled as she ran to Jürgen's arms. "We saw people killed! It was awful, and they took two of our friends."

"You'll all be safe now, darling. I'll see to it."

"I can't believe you came down here," Liesel said as she hugged Netti and Gisela. "It's too dangerous to stay here any longer."

"We're leaving now," Jürgen said. "Stay close to me and don't look at people, say a word, or give anyone reason to stop us."

"Wait a minute, Father. All of this has made me sick as a dog." Netti went to her knees and started retching. Liesel and Gisela knelt beside her, stroking her back, trying to comfort her. Netti put her head in Liesel's lap for a few minutes, while the others looked around nervously to ensure no one was coming in.

Then, as fast as Netti went to the floor, she got up and proclaimed, "I feel much better now, and my fear has lifted. God has replaced it with His peace."

Jürgen had a look of amazement on his face, the one he often had in response to his daughter's special relationship with God.

"Father, this is Felix Leitner, Hilda Stern, and Kerstin Burgstaller," Liesel said.

"Good to meet all of you. Now let's get out of here!" Jürgen replied. As the seven went into the vestibule they saw a tall Wehrmacht soldier standing in the doorway, blocking their path to the street. His back was facing them as they approached.

"We need to get these young people home, sir," Jürgen said.

The behemoth turned slightly and softly said, "You have to stay here." He turned back, saying nothing more. The seven hastily retreated to the vestibule.

"Did you see it, Father?"

"See what, Netti?"

"I didn't see anything, Netti," Liesel said.

"Me neither," added Gisela.

"I know I saw it," Netti said as her voice broke. "I'm surprised no one else noticed. Didn't you see his face in the dim light? It was nothing like the angry faces out on the street. His eyes were kind, and he was smiling. And where they usually hang the iron cross, there was a Christian cross on his chest. I swear it was there!"

"I must have missed it," Gisela said with a puzzled look on her face.

"I know he turned around quickly, Gisela, but I'm telling the truth. It was just as I said."

"You've been so upset and sick with fear, Netti, how can you be so sure?" Jürgen asked. He was now concerned that the stress of the night was taking its toll on his daughter.

"I'm sure, Father. I only wish I knew what it means."

"But he said we couldn't leave. Why?" Liesel asked.

"I don't know," Jürgen said. "But I have to get all of you to a safe place."

They all questioned what they could do to get past the soldier blocking the doorway. They could still hear the mayhem on the street. Everyone was terrified but Netti. Felix went to see if they could go out the back door, but there was also a large soldier blocking that exit.

Twenty minutes later, the large soldier guarding the front door turned aside, motioning for someone to enter. Two men helping a young woman entered, followed by a man carrying a badly injured boy. Jürgen told them to lay the injured woman and boy on the floor and told Netti and Gisela to get the medical supplies. With his bag and supplies, Jürgen started working on the wounded.

It was nearing midnight. Netti and Gisela helped Jürgen as he worked feverishly over one and then the other. As he stabilized them, men from the street brought three other victims in. Jürgen, Netti, and Gisela, with help from the others, stabilized them also, making them as comfortable as possible using prop blankets laid on the floor. Then people brought four more victims in to receive lifesaving medical treatment from the team of seven.

Time was a blur as the team treated and bedded forty-seven victims of the horribly long *night of broken glass*. It was nearing six in the morning when the flow of wounded stopped. Netti looked up and said, "He's gone; the large soldier guarding the door is gone."

"Stay here; let me look outside and see what's happening." Jürgen slowly looked both ways from the opening where the door was. "I don't see anyone or hear anything now."

"What do we do now, father?" Liesel asked.

"Felix, escort the women to your auto and get to the hospital. Netti, if they can, have the hospital send a dozen ambulances as soon as possible. If they can't send that many, have them bring autos to get these people to the hospital. Gisela will stay with me to watch the injured. Most of them are resting comfortably, so we should be able to handle what's needed until you get back."

Within ninety minutes, ambulances and autos arrived at the theater. As emergency personnel took care of the wounded, Jürgen gathered the women and Felix, and they cautiously walked to their autos. Jürgen took Netti, Gisela, and Liesel to his house. Evidence of the atrocities was everywhere on their winding trip home: burned-out shops, broken glass, and blood. They were still afraid and hoped they wouldn't face more problems on the still dangerous streets. No one had much to say as exhaustion set in, but they all knew something miraculous had occurred before their eyes in the small theater on Breite Strasse.

It was almost nine when they got to the Behrmann house. At times during the night they had thought about what Lisbeth and the others might have been thinking, not knowing why Jürgen and Liesel didn't come home. Fortunately, the violence hadn't spread to their neighborhood, but they had seen the red glow of destruction in nearby sections of the city and heard the radio reports about what was happening.

When the four walked up to the front of the house Lisbeth, Waldo, and Stefan came running down the walk to meet them. Lisbeth rushed to Jürgen's embrace, while Netti hugged Waldo and Liesel hugged Stefan.

"Thank God you're all safe!" shouted Lisbeth as she grabbed Netti with one arm and Liesel with the other. "We knew you should be safe at the hospital, but they didn't say you'd be there all night."

"Who didn't say, mother?" Netti asked.

"The man who called around nine and said you wouldn't be home for a long time because you were helping the injured."

"Are you sure he called at nine, darling?"

"Yes Jürgen, it was a little after nine. Oh, and he said something else that didn't make sense. He didn't just say you'd be helping the injured but that you would be helping the injured from Breite Strasse. What did he mean?"

"We'll fill you in on the details later, but now a cup of coffee and hot breakfast is what we need," Jürgen said.

"Followed by eight hours of peaceful sleep," added Liesel.

Lisbeth led Gisela and Liesel into the kitchen with Waldo and Stefan while Netti made it a point to stay with her father as he put his coat and hat in the front closet.

"Now I'm really puzzled, sweetie. What's happening here?"

"I wish I could say for sure, Father. I think it's God—God's happening."

"You must be right. I hadn't seen you or Gisela yet, and I wasn't out of surgery when your mother received that call."

"They wouldn't have expected you to stay at the hospital any later and couldn't have known we'd be going to Breite Strasse an hour and a half later."

"It's all beyond my comprehension, Netti. You're sure that you saw a Christian cross on the soldier guarding the door?"

"Absolutely! And I'm even surer about his kind face with a knowing smile."

"I know we saved lives and helped innocent Jews, but what do you make of it all, sweetheart?"

"That God was with us in everything we did. He protected us with the two soldiers. I think we know who they were. He used us to answer many prayers, Father."

4

Revenge and Betrayal

"We should be on the aisle. Go on in," Mose said, motioning to Liesel and Felix. Netti followed, and they all sat down just minutes before the concert was to begin. Not knowing why, Netti had been anxious all day. She had felt a heavy burden about the concert and was in constant prayer.

It was July 16, 1941, another big night for Waldo. It was the fourth time he was the featured soloist with the Gürzenich Orchestra at the Grand Hall. Maestro Papst would again be conducting. Waldo would present his forceful but sensitive interpretation of Beethoven's Violin Concerto in D Major. It was his third favorite concerto, and he was maturing each time he played it.

At twenty-four, Waldo was considered the third most accomplished violinist in Germany. The concert hall always had a full house when he performed, making tickets hard to come by. Many dignitaries, Cologne society, and high-ranking Nazis, including Gestapo Chief Walter Hartmann, the Gauleiter of Cologne, and several high-ranking officials from Berlin were present. Felix, Liesel, Netti, and Mose had prime floor seats.

The concert began with an expanded rendition of Wagner's "Ride of the Valkyries." The next piece would be Bruckner's *Seventh Symphony*, followed by a twenty-minute intermission. The second half of the concert would begin with orchestral excerpts from Wagner's *Parsifal*. Then Waldo would finish the concert with the Beethoven violin concerto.

As the music began, Netti looked at her program. She was amazed at how the Nazis had taken over every part of German society. Only composers favored by the Reich Music Chamber would ever have their works performed at concerts such as this. The three composers that night were at the top of the chamber's list, with Wagner, Hitler's personal favorite because of the composer's Teutonic hailing of the Germanic peoples, being at the very top. Sadly, the Reich did not allow many composers' works to be played. They disallowed the works of Jewish composers and those who went against the basic tenets of the Reich. And they banned gross music, such as jazz, started by the American Negro, and swing or big band, which was dominated by Jews.

Still feeling uneasy, Netti let her mind drift back to happier days. She went back over two years to the birth of her beautiful twins, Kurt and Karla. Thank God it was a normal pregnancy, and the brief pain she suffered was well worth the joy she and Mose felt every day since. The twins were healthy and favored their father much more than their mother, something Netti was grateful for.

She never regretted resigning her nursing position at University Hospital to stay home with the twins full time, though it required Mose to take on part-time jobs to get by. Fortunately, many at the Full Faith Church helped out, which allowed Mose to support his growing family.

But there were also scary times. Netti recalled the time when scarlet fever raised its ugly head and struck Kurt at thirteen months. Thankfully, she recognized the symptoms, and under her father's care, he recovered with no permanent damage. Then there was the nasty fall Karla suffered four months ago. She hit her head, opening a deep cut that bled profusely. Netti recalled how it scared her to death. It looked a lot worse than it was, but it did require five stitches to close the wound. It made her more than a little nervous as she tried to protect her darlings every minute of every day. Jürgen and Mose tried to calm her anxiety over the normal trials of motherhood and growing children, but she still held them tightly every day, treasuring the gifts God gave her.

Netti's mind went from happy thoughts of Kurt and Karla to sad ones over Didi and Mitzi. She was happy for them when Gretchen arrived almost three years ago but sad that Didi didn't want his father to attend her birth. In fact, relations with his father were so bad that Mitzi wouldn't have the baby at University Hospital. But the saddest part for Netti was not seeing her niece in two years. And now she wasn't sure if she would see any of them again.

While thinking about her brother and his family, Netti discreetly took out a handkerchief and dabbed the tears in her eyes. She recalled Erich saying how shocked and upset Didi was when he received his conscription letter. He was so sure he would always remain in his important position of preparing German boys to take up the fight for Germany rather than be called to active duty. Erich said that he protested his conscription fiercely, contending he was assured he would remain in his Hitler Youth training position. But his protests were of no use, and he left Cologne for basic Wehrmacht training in March. No one in the family had heard anything more about Didi since he was called up, and if Mitzi did, she wasn't about to share it with anyone.

It had been well over a year since Netti or her father had seen her brother. But Mitzi's infidelity was the saddest news she had heard through Erich.

Erich, on leave from the Wehrmacht, came home late one evening and heard his parents arguing loudly in the kitchen, even screaming at each other. He heard his father say that their marriage ended years ago, and she couldn't tell him who he could see or what he could do. His mother yelled back that she didn't care about their marriage but couldn't believe he'd stoop to having relations with his nephew's wife. With that, Erich crept closer to the kitchen door to hear the rest of the sordid story. He learned that Wolf and Mitzi had been meeting secretly for weeks. Elise knew her husband had been unfaithful with many women over the years. But when she found out her aging fifty-year-old husband had seduced the twenty-five-year-old wife of his brother's son, who had recently left for military service, it was too much for her to even tacitly accept. She told him their marriage was over.

Erich was enraged. He had confessed his deep feelings for Mitzi to his father. How could he betray him with her? He felt like confronting both his father and Mitzi but didn't have the nerve. Instead, he stewed about it and let the anger and frustration build.

Without a word to anyone, Mitzi and Gretchen moved back to Berlin in mid-June. She lived with her parents while getting settled in a high-ranking BDM administrative position arranged by none other than General Alfred Von Koenig. Before Mitzi left for Berlin, Erich finally confronted her about the affair she had with his father. She told Erich that he needed to grow up and face the real world. Then, as if throwing him a bone, she offered him the opportunity to enjoy her one last time. He spit in her face and quickly left, regretting the day he met the twisted bitch from Berlin and that he let his emotions get so entangled in her web.

As the Wagner piece continued, Netti's mind continued to wander. She thought of the good that came out of sadness. She liked Gisela's mother from the first time they met. They weren't close, and she didn't see her often. But when she did see her, Elise was always kind, and Netti enjoyed her company. Netti understood early on that, except for Gisela, Elise was alone in the Wolf Behrmann family. Everyone knew she was trapped in a loveless marriage. In fact, no love existed in the family except that between mother and daughter.

Netti talked with both Elise and Gisela on several occasions about their faith in God. Although kind about it, each thought it was great for her but not what they needed. However, when Elise lost her mother to cancer in late February of 1941 and later saw her marriage ending, she sought out Netti, thinking maybe God could provide comfort. Netti showed her Scriptures that revealed He was the only one who could. Elise not only gave her life to God, but she also started attending services and studying the Bible at the Full Faith Church.

Elise and her mother had grown closer in her final years. Her mother was always in her corner. She spoiled her as a child and was a rock of support when Elise's family was dissolving. With her newfound faith and strength, Elise finally decided to separate from Wolf and go to her father's country home twenty kilometers northeast of Cologne. The relationship she had with her father had been stormy to say the least. Since her teen years they were at odds most of the time. But Elise felt it was now time to mend the broken bond with the proud, successful industrialist who provided well for his family and had long since retired to the country.

Netti's mind drifted back to Didi and Gisela. Gisela wanted to locate Didi and tell him about Mitzi's indiscretion with Wolf. Netti and Trudi thought telling him was a bad idea, if they ever located him, which they didn't think was possible. They finally convinced her to drop the idea. After all, Didi had chosen his life, and they felt strongly that it wouldn't go well with anyone who blew it up for him. He would have to learn about his wife's lusting in a different way, at a later time.

As the second movement of Bruckner's *Seventh Symphony* rang through the hall, Netti bemoaned the conscription into military service of so many of her loved ones. The hardest loss for her was seeing her father leave for training two weeks ago, on July 2, 1941. For the twenty-three years of her young life, her father was always close by, providing his love, guidance, and support when needed. He was always there to laugh with her, cry with her, and give her a hug of reassurance. But now she didn't know when he would return and couldn't entertain the thought that he might never be a part of her life again. They hoped the Wehrmacht wouldn't conscript him at forty-nine. But as Operation Barbarossa started, it was clear that casualties would increase significantly, creating a need for more doctors and field hospitals.

Lisbeth was devastated when her prized son went off to war in the spring and then her husband followed a few months later. She struggled emotionally, while still trying to blunt her fears with alcohol. Netti purposed in her heart to put aside the differences she had with her mother, including the anger she felt, so she could support her through this bitter period of adjustment.

The Wehrmacht conscripted Stefan, Erich, and Gert in 1940. Wolf used his influence with the Gestapo to allow

Erich and Gert to stay together in their unit assignments. The Wehrmacht assigned them to an infantry division that was part of the occupying force in France. Thankfully, they assigned Stefan to a small concentration camp near Hinzert, not far south of Bonn. It didn't take the Wehrmacht long to find his gentle demeanor unsuitable for combat. They sent him to an out-of-the-way place where he would be a cook and part-time valet. The family, especially Waldo, felt good that he was close and as safe as he could be.

Waldo registered with his 1935 muster class and went to training once before his trainers considered him unfit for active military service. It was apparent to the review board, and his trainers eventually, that he was mentally slow in actions critical to military service. Those who knew and loved him considered Waldo slow in completing some tasks. But they knew he was a genius in achieving others. After all, he received his degree in music and was becoming Germany's most popular violinist.

When Jürgen was conscripted Waldo became the head of the house, though Theodor stepped into the role of watcher and protector of the family. Theodor's love and loyalty to the family were never in question, and he had promised Netti he would always be there for whatever any of them needed. Fortunately, the military never conscripted Theodor, now over fifty, without skills critical to the war effort, and lacking the physical health for field unit duty.

The third movement of the Bruckner symphony was half over when Netti's thoughts turned to the predicament of Felix Leitner, who was sitting next to her. Felix and Liesel had been seeing each other for three years and were planning to marry soon. The problem was his imminent conscription on completing his studies at Cologne University a month ago. He had to fight desperately and was fortunate to receive a deferral until he graduated, but now it was unavoidable. Any day, he expected to receive a letter telling him when and where to report.

Liesel's exceptional performance at the telephone company had advanced her to supervisor in 1940. The shortage of men going to war made it easier for women to advance, but Liesel proved to be a quick learner with great leadership skills. She much preferred leading others rather than sitting in front of a switchboard for eight-hour shifts. But what she enjoyed more than anything was acting in the small theater group on Breite Strasse. The city made necessary repairs to the theater after the *night of broken glass* and allowed the group to continue. Jews could no longer take part of course. It was a dirty compromise that no one wanted to make, but their five Jewish friends willingly dropped out so the group could continue.

Felix became the theater's leading man, even though he had to devote more time to his studies. His family was proud that he graduated near the top of his class and earned a coveted degree in civil engineering. His father's manufacturing interests were more successful since retooling production for the military buildup. His parents' support allowed Felix to concentrate on his studies and the theater without having to work. But he felt guilty, knowing the money that supported him came from something he despised.

Felix's parents never joined the Nazi Party, but they were still silently complicit in what they were doing. On that point, Netti paused, thinking that was the story of too many Germans. They didn't like their association with the Nazis. In fact, many Germans didn't support most of what they were doing. But to survive, people had to hold their noses and look the other way, hoping everything would turn out well in the end.

Liesel told Netti that they were secretly thinking about leaving Cologne before Felix received his conscription notice. She said they had talked to Claus Bauer and Father Boesch about connecting with the underground resistance. It shocked Netti to hear they were thinking of such drastic measures, and she firmly tried to dissuade her. When they had talked a week ago, they hadn't made a final decision.

Netti shook her head, trying to shake off drowsiness and the malaise of bad news she was remembering. She tried to concentrate on the Bruckner symphony, as the crescendo of the fourth movement had patrons on the edge of their seats. But it was no use. Uneasiness permeated her mind, as her thoughts turned to Meiningen and Aunt Katia and Uncle Ralph.

She praised God for how He miraculously moved on their behalf. She often dwelled on what happened and still found it hard to believe. Six months ago, Ralph went before the chief transit officer at Buchenwald. He had heard that prison officials sent some prisoners east for reasons no one wanted to think about. So as he came before the officer's desk, he could only think it was the end, and he would never see Katia and Rudi again. Ralph was overcome with despair when the officer said, "We're releasing you, Richter. Here is the order of release, and you can pick up your belongings next door."

The news stunned Ralph. He wanted to pinch himself to see if he would wake up. His second reaction was to ask why, but he quickly thought better of it, taking his release papers and smartly moving next door. Within the hour he called home from Weimar. Because Meiningen was only seventy kilometers southeast, Katia picked up Ralph, and they were home before eight that night.

Katia and Rudi were joyous, but also as puzzled as Ralph at the strange turn of events. Katia was just thankful to have her husband home after four long years. Ralph had lost weight. His face was gaunt, and he had dark circles under his eyes. Though it was late, Katia fixed him one of his favorite meals: bratwurst and sauerkraut. It smelled so good, but when he started eating, he knew immediately that his stomach wasn't in any condition to accept more than a few bites. It would be weeks before his digestive tract was back to normal.

Ralph often dreamed of the night he would once again hold his precious Katia in his arms. He desired her so much, but again his body was in no condition for such activity.

Netti felt sad about their long period of readjustment, as it was frankly related to her and Trudi by their aunt. But then, as they were just getting back to a normal life, everything fell apart for Katia, Ralph, and Rudi. Rudi received his conscription letter. He had always vowed that he would never serve in the Wehrmacht or kill anyone. He hated the Nazis for what they did to his father, and he had openly defied having anything to do with the Hitler Youth. This brought persecution and distress into the life of the young man who only wanted to be left alone to live freely, something many in Germany wanted but few attained.

To complicate everything further, the Meiningen Gestapo sent Ralph a letter, demanding he report to them within two days. He called immediately to ask why they wanted to see him. Fortunately—most likely by an error on their part—they said Buchenwald had mistakenly released him. Panic swept over Ralph as he wondered what he could do to prevent disaster. Then, as though from heaven, Katia felt strongly impressed to call Sophie, the one she always trusted to have the right answer at the right time.

Netti remembered how Sophie told Katia to pack their auto with what they needed to live on for a week and immediately drive to her place in Cologne. Ralph was hesitant at first, but having no alternatives, he agreed to Sophie's request. As they traveled to Cologne that night, Sophie was developing an escape plan.

When the Richters arrived at Sophie's place, a sharp disagreement ensued. Katia felt strongly that she had to stay in Meiningen. However, Ralph, Rudi, and Sophie thought she should also leave the country. But Katia wasn't leaving her parents behind with no one to help them during the uncertain times ahead. She also wanted to keep the Reich from taking their family home. Sophie urged her to leave with her husband and son, promising that she and Evert would do everything they could to protect their home. Ralph insisted that Katia go with her family, but he knew that when his wife made up her mind, it was impossible to change it. Rudi begged his mother to go, but she wouldn't change her mind. She would stay in Meiningen, continue as head librarian, keep their home, and watch over her parents. She felt the war would be over in a year, two at most. Katia hated the idea of another separation from Ralph after just getting him back, but she knew she was making the right decision.

Knowing the Gestapo would question Katia in their search for Ralph, Sophie schooled her on what to tell them. She would say that her husband and son left unexpectedly in the middle of the night, without saying goodbye. She would tell them she hasn't heard from them since before they left and doesn't know where they went. They all hoped the story would protect Katia from Gestapo reprisals.

The next morning, Sophie called Evert Heinz, who was ailing in the final stages of cancer but still able to provide valuable assistance. She asked that he have his best forger prepare passports and visas to Switzerland and America for Ralph and Rudi. She said the forger should bring the documents to her place by the next day where they could affix the needed pictures and signatures. Evert agreed to Sophie's request, as he would agree to do almost anything for his longtime associate and the woman he respected and loved.

As usual with Sophie's plans, everything fell into place. A week later, Ralph and Rudi were in Switzerland, and a month after that both were safe in America. How Sophie and Evert pulled it off so quickly was still beyond Netti's understanding, but she knew that God was directing it all behind the scenes.

Sadly for Sophie, it was the last project she and Evert pulled off together; he died five weeks later at the age of ninety-three. It was a tremendous loss for Sophie, and she was still mourning his passing. However, she continued to be an essential cog in Heinz Enterprises, working closely with her close friend Gregor Heinz.

Bruckner's coda returned Netti's focus to the concert. As his Seventh finished, she was eager to not only leave her seat but to get some fresh air before the intermission ended. Netti persuaded Mose to take her outside so she could settle down and try to shake the queasy feeling that wouldn't go away. Mose, always sensitive to Netti's needs, could tell something had been bothering her all evening. He tried to help by asking why she seemed so down, but she only put him off, not wanting to admit to herself that trouble was at the door.

The fresh air had helped settle Netti. As she leaned back in her seat the music from *Parsifal* began. But within minutes, her mind started drifting again. She thought about Trudi and the turn of events in her life. Unfortunately, Netti mused, her sister was now a single mother of two girls, wondering where life would take her next. Helene was four and Hermine two. Max had walked out on his family eighteen months ago.

In 1940, Max Neumann proudly wore the uniform of an SS major for all to see, including his wife. And as Trudi related to Netti, it was no surprise to her with all her previous suspicions. She asked him, "Why now, and not years ago?"

He only said, "It wasn't the right time."

She wanted to ask him, "Wasn't the right time to ruin my life?" but she didn't. However, she did ask him if he ever loved her. He assured her that he did but admitted he was weak and never suited to be with just one woman. At that point, Trudi turned away so he wouldn't see her tears. With no love left for Max, there was no benefit in delving any further into the whys. All Max wanted was the right to see the girls as they grew up; Trudi would never deny him that. The last thing he said to Trudi was that he would take care of the divorce.

Then Max went to his permanent Gestapo assignment in Munich, moving in with the woman he had been seeing for three years. With Wolf's and Max's help over the years, Trudi advanced to a loan officer position at Hohe Strasse Bank. She could now adequately support herself and her daughters, even though Max vowed to provide financial help for the girls.

Wolf, knowing the marriage was over and that Max wasn't going to discover his brother's secret, wanted to ensure Trudi's security. He always liked the girl, who was now a mature woman of twenty-seven. But above all, he wanted an intimate affair with her. Periodically, he presented himself to Trudi, but each time she rejected him. Being sensitive to the delicacy of the situation, Trudi was always gentle in her rejections, knowing how important it was to keep her job in the uncertain times. Trudi wanted to tell him where to go, but she always checked her anger.

Netti thought back to the conversation she had with Trudi several months before.

"I need to tell you something, Netti," Trudi had said.

"About Max again?" Netti had responded.

"Only indirectly. I need to tell you something I haven't told anyone, not even Aunt Sophie."

"You're scaring me now, like it's some dark secret."

"Maybe I'm making too much of it, but I'm afraid. Afraid that you'll condemn me—look down on me."

"Have I ever done that, Trudi?"

"No. But I've never done what I'm about to tell you. So I'm using my one special promise of the heart request, for you, right now."

"Now I am worried! Is it that bad?"

"You'll have to decide, but my special request is that you won't judge or condemn me for what I've done. You have to swear to it."

"Okay, Trudi, I swear by our promise of the heart oath that I won't condemn or judge you for what you're about to tell me."

"Thanks, Netti. Do you remember what happened three years ago when Sophie and I left Helene with you so we could rush to Meiningen and tell Wilhelm Becker what to tell the Gestapo if they asked him?"

"How could I forget? Uncle Wolf was still trying to find out our secret. But Wilhelm told the Gestapo what you asked him to, so that ended it, and Wolf was none the wiser."

"Yes, we were able to save the family with Wilhelm's help. But that's not all that happened on that day in Meiningen. Wilhelm was unhappily married, and I was too. To make a long story short, when we saw each other, feelings from nine years before rushed back. We kissed passionately for a while, and I felt a tingling down my spine for the first time in ages."

"I had no idea, but I understand how that could happen under those circumstances."

"That's only the beginning, Netti. I started writing Wilhelm, sending the letters to Uncle Otto so he could postmark them from America. Otto then sent me the letters that Wilhelm mailed to America. We wrote back and forth for over a year. Then I told Wilhelm that I was coming to Germany for a visit. In February, I went to Meiningen without anyone knowing, except Sophie. I left the girls there, so I had to tell her what I was doing; she didn't try to stop me. Wilhelm had recently divorced, and I stayed with him for three nights. We fulfilled the joy we could only dream about when we were sneaking kisses as children. I know it was wrong, but I couldn't help myself when I finally admitted my love for Wilhelm had never died. When I was in his arms three years ago, I knew I couldn't resist the impulse to see him again."

"I understand, Trudi. I would never judge or condemn you for what you did. And you don't need to use your promise of the heart request."

"But you don't understand—that's not all. I slipped up in my cover story with Wilhelm, and he questioned me. Instead of trying to continue the lie, I broke down and told him the truth. I told him our secret; that we never went to America but lived in Cologne all along. I told him we were now the children of Jürgen and Lisbeth Behrmann."

Netti recalled not being able to say anything at that moment. What Trudi said stunned her. But she never condemned Trudi, only hugging her. Trudi assured her that Wilhelm would keep their secret and that she trusted him. She went to Meiningen again several months after their first meeting. And he came to Cologne a month after that. They were in love and started making plans for a future life together.

As *Parsifal* continued, Netti's thoughts went back two weeks, to the train station where they said goodbye to their father. Lisbeth, Waldo, Trudi, Liesel, Sophie, and Theodor were all there with her, as they wished him Godspeed. She noticed that he had his Bible and cigarette case, so all must be well with him.

On the boarding platform, her father pulled out his journal and handed it to Theodor. He made her and Theodor promise to keep it current, listing important events in Germany as they occurred. He made it clear that it might be the only way to catch up on what was happening while he was away. He also made them promise to discuss the entries with Waldo and Liesel, as he had been doing.

Netti remembered how she and Theodor read the journal to review what Father had included the last two years:

> *Hitler and Stalin sign nonaggression pact—8/23/39*
> *Germany invades Poland—9/1/39*
> *Britain and France declare war on Germany - 9/3/39*
> *German Army reaches the border of Poland and Soviet Union—9/17/39*
> *The Reich annexes western Poland - 11/1/39*
> *Germany invades Denmark and Norway—4/9/40*
> *Western offensive launched—5/10/40*
> *Netherlands surrender—5/14/40*
> *Cologne Rail Yards bombed by RAF: first bombing of Cologne—5/17/40 (little damage)*
> *Belgium surrenders—5/28/40*
> *France signs armistice with Germany, creating two separate zones—6/22/40*
> *Bombing of England commences—9/7/40*
> *Blitz; night bombing of London starts—10/7/40*

Hamburg bombed by England—11/16/40
War in northern Africa starts—3/24/41
Yugoslavia surrenders to Germany—4/17/41
The Luftwaffe destroys the House of Commons in England—5/10/41
England sinks the Bismarck—5/27/41

"It looks like father gave up on putting explanations with his entries," Netti had said.

"But he always filled in the details when he went over them with the children," Theodor had responded.

"Sadly, we have only Waldo and Liesel to share our entries with now."

"We'll sit down with them every time we make an entry."

"Yes, Theodor, that's what we have to do."

Parsifal ended to the thundering applause of the audience. The powerful acknowledgment of the Germanic people's superiority deeply moved them. Netti roused from her thoughts didn't stand or clap but silently waited for Waldo to come on stage.

There was a pause while the orchestra retuned their instruments. As the instruments grew quiet, Waldo came out to another raucous ovation. Then there was the usual period of silence as the conductor readied himself to cue the beginning of the Beethoven violin concerto. But to everyone's shock, Waldo started playing his violin. The conductor and many in the orchestra glared at him, not knowing what he was doing.

Waldo Behrmann was playing his solo adaptation of the Mendelssohn *Violin Concerto in E Minor* with incredible skill and emotion. He had composed the adaptation several years before. Mendelssohn was his favorite composer, and this was his favorite work. He loved playing the concerto but had no opportunities to do so with an orchestra. Therefore, he created the piece that he could play as often as he liked.

Waldo's rendition was flawless, but the audience became hostile, shouting and cursing at him for playing the outlawed music of a depraved Jew. Netti knew within seconds what Waldo was doing. All she could say was, "No, no, no, Waldo! What are you doing?"

"What is it, Netti?" Mose asked.

"He's playing Mendelssohn. It's forbidden by the Nazis. They'll tear him apart if we don't get to him first, Mose!"

The Gestapo chief, Gauleiter, and Nazi dignitaries from Berlin all rose with indignation, yelling for the SS to stop the concert and arrest the perpetrator immediately. Netti grabbed Liesel and Felix, demanding they follow her and Mose. The four were on a dead run toward backstage, weaving around and almost knocking over others as they went. Angry people were throwing various items at Waldo, and members of the orchestra were trying to stop him, but he continued to play.

As four SS Officers reached the stage near where Waldo had finally stopped playing, Netti yelled as loud as she could from the backstage wings, "Waldo, Waldo, run now!"

Somehow, through the ruckus, he heard his sister's voice and looked over to see where she was. He didn't hesitate, running through upset and confused patrons and orchestra members until he reached Netti. A close friend handed Waldo his violin case, as they all started running for the hall's rear exit to the alley. In the tumult throughout the concert hall, the SS and Gestapo weren't sure where the offender went. They looked everywhere, asking if anyone had seen him.

Mose went ahead of the others, telling them he would get their auto and meet them on the corner, a block north of the hall. He ran as fast as he could, knowing they had little time to get away. Within three minutes, Mose picked up the others, and they sped away.

"Why did you do that Waldo?" Netti asked sharply. "Why, oh, why, would you ever do something to bring the Nazis down on you? Do you know what you did?"

Waldo, still confused from the tumult in the hall and now hurt by his sister's harsh questions, could only say, "They beat Isaac. They beat him for playing the piece with me at school."

"What do you mean, sweetheart?" Netti questioned in a much calmer voice.

"Last month we were at school, and he wanted me to write a part for bass so he could play with me."

"A part for the Mendelssohn concerto?"

"Yes. So I wrote out a new part for bass in the first movement. We were playing it when two instructors and three students rushed in to stop us. They broke his bass and hit him in the face, knocking him down. He was bleeding, Netti! He looked so hurt, not because of his injuries but because of the looks of such hate and disgust. They can't stand him, just like they can't stand Mendelssohn, just because they're Jews. I can't understand it, Netti. Do you know why, Mose?"

"No, I don't understand it either," Mose said.

"So you played Mendelssohn to resist the hatred they stand for?" Netti asked.

"Yes, I didn't know how else to fight what they're doing."

"Did you understand what would happen by doing it?"

"No, I didn't know everyone would be so mad."

"It's okay, Waldo. We'll protect you."

"Should I drive home, Netti?"

"No, Mose. Drive around until we figure out what to do. Dear God, please lead us now," Netti prayed.

"I have an idea," Felix said. "We've almost determined that I'm not staying here and letting the military conscript me. So now's the time for me to leave Cologne, and I can take Waldo with me."

"Hold it, Felix! What exactly do you mean?" Netti asked sternly.

"We've already talked to Mose about a plan for Felix to leave Cologne and join the underground in the northeast," Liesel said.

"Why didn't I know anything about that, Liesel? Mose?"

"We hadn't settled anything, so I didn't want to worry you, darling."

"Thanks a lot! So what's the plan?"

"Father Boesch is working with the underground resistance, outside of Hannover."

"And how do you know that?" Netti asked. "Mose, you promised me that you would have no more dealings with the resistance or anyone else who would put you in jeopardy!"

"I don't, dear, please settle down. I just know that Boesch can help Felix if he chooses to leave Cologne."

"And if Felix takes my brother, I'm going with them, Netti," Liesel said.

"Nobody said anything about you going, Liesel," Felix said firmly.

"I'm still going, for a while at least. A third person can help, and when you're both settled in and secure, I'll come home."

"Is this really what you want to do, Felix?"

"Yes, Mose, and we need to leave tonight."

"I don't like it one bit!" Netti said. "But if you're doing this, we need to get you to Father Boesch at the Cologne Cathedral as soon as possible."

"He should be there now, and we're only five minutes away," Mose said.

Father Boesch was at the cathedral, and within two hours he arranged for Felix, Liesel, and Waldo's transportation to a safe house near Hannover. They arrived there safely and settled into their new, temporary living quarters by the following afternoon.

Mose and Netti drove around for an hour before going home. They drove by the Behrmann home and saw two black autos sitting in front of the house. The Gestapo was waiting for Waldo to come home. No one appeared to be watching their house, so they felt safe to enter.

"What would they do with Waldo? Would they send such an innocent person to prison?"

"That's the sorry truth, Netti. They would and maybe worse."

"Did we make the right decision in sending him away?"

"What else could we do, darling? At least we can be thankful that he's not alone."

"But Felix and Liesel are so young and innocent too. How can they survive what the Nazis can do?"

"They're not alone. They have savvy people to help them."

"I know, but I'll worry about them until this is over."

"We just need to cover them with prayer, Netti. Believe that God will take care of them."

Felix quickly adapted to life in the underground resistance. He believed in it wholeheartedly. Waldo, on the other hand, didn't understand the requirements of his new life in hiding. And he didn't fully know what the resistance movement was doing. But everyone there compensated for his shortcomings. They determined to take extra measures to protect the young man they soon grew fond of.

Liesel stayed with Felix and Waldo for three weeks before returning to Cologne. During the time she was gone, the Gestapo interrogated Lisbeth, Mose, and Netti. Netti had given Lisbeth a full explanation about what had happened, so she was prepared for the questioning. Of course, she was still nervous when they showed up. She used the cover story that Netti and Mose used. They all told the Gestapo that Waldo and three others had left Cologne for a fifteen-city stringed quartet tour. They all agreed on specific details so the tale would be believable. The Gestapo questioned the story but eventually accepted it.

As time passed, the Gestapo followed up occasionally but seemed to lose some of their enthusiasm for catching Waldo. Or maybe they had more serious issues to deal with. But they did drive by the Behrmann house periodically. Therefore, the family determined it wouldn't be safe for Waldo to return for a long time.

There was little the authorities could do about Felix ignoring his conscription notice. There were too many men for the Nazis to track down, men who had decided to avoid conscription by running. Liesel traveled to Hannover often to see Felix and Waldo. She did her best to ensure that no one followed her.

* * *

In late July, Wolf broke the bad news of Max's death to Trudi. He lost his life while conducting a special mission in Hungary. Wolf had no more details, but he told Trudi that his woman in Munich made off with all his money. He felt they would never recoup any of it for the girls as Max would have wanted.

Trudi was sad that it all had to end so badly and was angry she wasted so many years with Max. She was most upset that her girls wouldn't be able to share in what Max would have wanted them to have. But at least she had Helene and Hermine, and that made it all worthwhile. Everything about Max troubled Trudi for a while; then she resigned herself to the finality of that chapter in her life. She now looked forward to a life for her and her girls with Wilhelm.

* * *

No one in the family realized that Didi and Mitzi's marriage was faltering. Not seeing them, how would they ever know? In the four years they were together, Mitzi had been unfaithful with sixteen men. She always said to herself, "My exquisite beauty and special abilities should be shared with more than one man. Though I get personal satisfaction in each experience, my real exhilaration is in seeing, feeling, and knowing the pleasure and privilege each man feels in having the unmatched opportunity to enjoy me."

Didi was always a boy to her, never maturing the way she expected. And he was so easy to fool, never knowing for sure that she was unfaithful. He had reasons to doubt, but instead, he always looked the other way, choosing not to entertain negative thoughts about his wife.

In February 1941, General Alfred Von Koenig phoned Mitzi, dangling a most exciting offer before her. "Come to Berlin. I'll see that you get the high-ranking BDM position opening in June."

"You shouldn't tempt me, Alfred. I know what you want. You're just manipulating me because I've told you more than once how I'm bored with Didi and Cologne."

"Come on, Mitzi, I know you miss being close to the action in Berlin."

"Of course I do. I miss my parents too." With Alfred's offer, Mitzi saw a way to discard Didi and Cologne. "Okay, Alfred, I'll come to Berlin if you do something for me."

"Anything you want, dear."

"I need Didi out of my life before I leave Cologne. Can you arrange for his conscription?"

"Easily. Where do you want him to go?"

"Assign him to the worst place possible. He needs to grow up and be a man."

"That shocks me. Why do you want to punish him?

"The reason is my business." Mitzi wouldn't tell him that she wanted Didi punished for his part in the family cover-up scheme.

"Fine. I have several choice assignments in mind."

Mitzi and Von Koenig made the bargain, and Didi's life took an unexpected turn for the worse. He received his conscription letter in March. When he complained to Mitzi, she put on a good show, consoling him with feigned sympathy and bewilderment. She even said she would try to stop his conscription, which she had no intention of doing. Later that month, to Mitzi's hidden delight, Dieter Behrmann left Cologne for basic training. Mitzi, crying big tears, told him she would take Gretchen to Berlin where they would live with her parents until the war ended. Didi would have preferred they stay in Cologne, but he never made an issue of their moving to Berlin.

Not long after Didi left, Wolf got wind of it and came calling. Mitzi didn't care much for the man, though she admired his strong party loyalty and aggressive hatred of Jews. She had heard stories about him being a lady's man. Not surprisingly, the balding fifty-year-old who still had a muscular body intrigued Mitzi. She knew with such experience he must be skillful in pleasing his women.

When Wolf made his usual advances, Mitzi played along, amused with his straightforwardness. She teased him, putting him off on his first two attempts to seduce her. But in two weeks, Mitzi allowed him to have what he wanted. And she had to admit the experience was enjoyable for her, but certainly more enjoyable for him. After that night, the meetings were often, and the affair lasted until Mitzi and Gretchen left for Berlin in June.

But before she left, Mitzi had one more piece of business to settle in Cologne. She had to have a most important discussion with Wolf.

"Now that we're finished with that, I have something to tell you that you'll find quite interesting."

Wolf rolled over in the bed to face Mitzi. "So you think you know what I'm interested in?"

"I know you'll be interested in what I'm about to tell you."

"And I'm sure you'll tease me with it for a while first."

"Not this time. I'll be direct with you. First, you need to teach your son to be loyal to you."

"What the hell! My sons are completely loyal to me."

"You'll soon learn that Erich hasn't been. But first, I've heard all about your fanatical pursuit to learn what the big secret is that your brother's family is keeping."

"I haven't kept that a secret, so I suppose you have—so what?"

"I know what they've been hiding. I know what their deep, dark secret is."

"The hell you do!"

"Well, do you want to hear it?"

"You're damn right I do!"

"Trudi, Waldo, and Liesel are really the children of a Jew named Markus Mendel."

"Sonofabitch! I suspected it was something like that. Of course, that bastard Jew was involved. How could Jürgen ever make such a stupid mistake?"

"I only know the children's parents died, and Jürgen promised to take them and keep the fact they were Jews secret by claiming they were his own."

"Damnit! When I think of it, that sounds like something my soft-hearted brother would do. My God, they sure went to a lot of trouble to hide those Jew brats. You wouldn't believe all they did to cover their tracks. It all makes sense now."

"What makes sense, Wolf?"

"It doesn't matter. The question is, what to do about it now? How in the hell did you ever get this information?"

"Back to your son; Erich told me, or bribed me might be more accurate."

Wolf laughed to cover the shock and anger about hearing what Erich did. "That little bastard; so that's how he got to you. I guess I taught him well. I'm almost afraid to ask, Mitzi, but do you know how Elise discovered our affair?"

"You're afraid because you already know the answer. I told her about it."

"Damnit! Why would you do that?"

"I did what you wouldn't do: free yourself from that worthless woman. She's just like her daughter, Princess Gisela. Well, I took care of them both, and you're better off for it."

For weeks, Wolf thought about what he should do with Mitzi's information. He quelled his anger and plotted the best course of action. He would wait for the right time and then pounce on those in his brother's family who were still around.

Jürgen, Didi, Waldo, and Stefan were long gone, but Lisbeth, Trudi, Netti, Liesel, and Sophie were still here and would remain under his watchful eye.

* * *

After the concert fiasco, Netti and Mose frequently discussed the future security of their family.

"They drove by the house earlier today, Mose."

"Three times in the last week that we know about. Have you seen the Gestapo any other place, Netti?

"No. Only here. Are they only harassing us?"

"I'm not sure. But since they don't follow us, the Gestapo must not care where we go. And they can't be trying to track down Waldo through us."

"I suppose you're right, Mose. It still makes me nervous. I don't like it at all!"

"Then let's take a second look at the place Sophie showed us out west. With the increased bombing raids, we need to get further away from central Cologne anyway."

"We have few belongings, so we could move quickly and discretely. I know the Gestapo could trace our move if they care."

"Hopefully, they don't. It's a nice enough place that we can afford."

"I'll call Sophie and arrange with her friend to look at the house again."

Mose and Netti did look at the house on the western outskirts of the city again. And after praying about it, they felt strongly that was where they should be. They told no one outside the family about their move in August. Their new home was in a somewhat remote area and provided a clear view of anyone approaching.

There was also a heavily wooded area within fifty meters of their back door, which would provide an easy way to escape if needed.

It had been fifteen months since the first bombing of the railroad. Since that day, the citizens of Cologne were gripped with fear. When and where the next attack would come continually occupied the minds of most. They constructed air raid shelters, repositioned antiaircraft batteries, and transferred Luftwaffe planes for defensive purposes. Fortunately, the first bombing raids were sporadic and caused only moderate damage. Most bombers flew past Cologne, heading for targets to the east. But even the sound of the bombers filled the residents with dread.

Two days after Mose and Netti moved into their new home, the Royal Air Force struck again. They successfully bombed the Goldenberg Power Station in Quadrath, five kilometers to the west. Fifty bombers then flew low, just south of Netti and Mose's house, on their way to bomb the Fortuna Power Station in Knapsack. Netti ran outside to see what was happening. She could see the planes to the south in the flak-filled sky. She quickly ran back inside at Mose's command, and the family went directly to the cellar. From that day forward, those in Cologne were on edge.

* * *

In early August 1941 Wolf decided to collaborate with Kluger and the Gestapo to have Jürgen's family rounded up and sent to prison. But then he thought maybe he could try one more time with Lisbeth and Trudi. He would give each one last opportunity to yield to his demand. If either gave him the right answer, maybe he would delay the call.

On August 18, Trudi rudely rebuffed Wolf's crude request for a secret rendezvous. The rejection enraged Wolf, almost bringing him to the point of picking up the telephone and calling Ricard Kluger immediately. But he soon cooled down, purposing to see Lisbeth one last time before taking action. The episode shook up Trudi, who had not had such a scene with Wolf for years. She related the incident to Netti and Sophie, who were both upset and puzzled about why Wolf would make such a brazen proposal now.

On August 22, Wolf went to Lisbeth's house. She answered the door to find Wolf standing there.

"What do you want, Wolf?"

"I thought I would stop by and see how you're doing without Jürgen."

"How do you think I would be doing?"

"I'd suppose that you're not doing well, Lisbeth. You look lonely and sad. Maybe I can do something about that."

"What could you do to help me?"

"I know you're lonely, and I also know you're a passionate woman who still has needs, which I can take care of."

"You dirty bastard! You never give up, do you?"

"Be sensible, Lisbeth. Jürgen isn't coming back for a long time and nights can be long and lonely."

"Get the hell off my porch and out of my sight, you filthy piece of crap!"

"Think twice before you tell me to leave, Lisbeth; your family's well-being hangs on your answer."

Lisbeth paused momentarily. She pondered what Wolf meant, fearing maybe he found out. But then she gathered herself and told him to leave and never come back. Wolf bristled with anger, and his face reddened. He quickly turned and walked to his auto.

That evening, Wolf Behrmann made the call that sealed the fate of his brother's family.

"What is it this time, Wolf?" asked Kluger.

"I want to turn in three Jews who are passing as gentiles, along with those conspiring with them."

"They aren't the same bunch that we previously investigated?"

"Well, yes they are."

"What the hell, Behrmann! Do you have additional information—proof?"

"No, I don't. But I'm positive about this, Ricard. Please believe me! At least bring them in for questioning."

"Crap, Wolf, are you ever going to leave me alone about this? Okay, I'll bring them in for questioning, at least the ones you can find."

On the afternoon of August 26, Kluger met Wolf on Frobelstraße, two blocks from Lisbeth's house. He brought three autos filled with eight SS soldiers and Gestapo agents. Kluger, Wolf, and two SS soldiers stood on the corner, discussing the plan.

Just then, by God's providence, Liesel Behrmann drove by the scene. Several summers before, Netti had told her about Erich learning the family secret. She was also aware of Wolf's recent advances on her mother and sister. When she saw that one of the men across the street was Wolf and that he was talking with the SS, she knew what was about to happen. She pulled down her cap, checked for traffic, made a left turn, and sped to a parking place on Weinsbergstraße, around the corner from the Behrmann house. She jumped out and ran as fast as she could to the front door and banged loudly, yelling, "Hurry, hurry—let me in."

5

MITZI'S THEFT

Liesel's auto screeched to a stop in front of Netti and Mose's new home. It was almost nine o'clock on August 26, 1941, as she opened the passenger door, quickly helping Helene down and taking Hermine in her arms. They walked briskly to the front door. The lights were still on as Liesel knocked loudly.

Netti peeked through the living room drapes and then ran to answer the door.

"What is it, Liesel? Why are you here so late with Helene and Hermine?"

Trembling, Liesel couldn't respond right away as tears ran down her face.

"It can't be that bad sweetie," Netti said. "Try to calm down and tell me what happened." Netti took Liesel in her arms. Now Mose was in the doorway, looking as puzzled as Netti.

"Come in and sit down," Mose offered. "Then please tell us what's going on."

Netti led Liesel and the girls to the living room. Liesel wiped her eyes and looked at Netti. "Please tell me that you've heard from mother, Trudi, or Sophie this evening."

"We haven't talked with any of them today," Netti said.

"Oh, no!" Liesel said as she started crying again. "Mose, please take the girls to the kitchen for some milk and cookies?"

"Come on girls; let's see if we can find some cookies."

After Mose and the girls left the room, Netti put her hand on Liesel's shoulder. "Sister, what is it? Has something happened to them?"

Liesel breathed in deeply. "This afternoon I was driving home, and several blocks from the house I saw the SS talking with Wolf. I knew something was wrong, and they would most likely be going to the house for mother."

Netti gasped, but she didn't say a word.

"I drove to the house as quickly as possible to warn her. When I got there, Trudi, Sophie, and the girls were with mother. I told them we had to get out fast, as Wolf must have learned our secret and was coming right behind me with the SS. We gathered a few items and ran out the back door. We ran several blocks, knowing they were close behind. To protect the girls, they told us to hide in a barn, and they would lead the SS away from us. Trudi hugged her girls, saying she loved them and would be back no matter how long it took. And mother gave me her green, jade wedding ring for safekeeping. Then they said goodbye and ran out of the barn. I was hoping they were safe and had contacted you. I don't know what happened to them, Netti!"

Netti was speechless. She knew Wolf wasn't a decent person, but she couldn't believe he would turn in members of his family to the SS. She was angry with him and afraid for her mother, sister, and aunt. "You didn't see them again?"

"No, Netti."

"You and the girls were okay?"

"No! That's the rest of the story. We were afraid, so we went up in a loft and hid behind boxes. It wasn't long before the SS came and searched the barn. I thought for sure they would find us when one of them climbed up and shined a flashlight all around after Hermine accidentally knocked over a box. But then I think a miracle saved us, Netti. There was a loud racket in front of us, as a large cat chased a rat across the floor. Someone laughed and said it was only a cat chasing a rat. Then he got down, and they left. I've never been so scared in all my life, not even when that bastard tried to rape me at the BDM camp. But I prayed to Jesus, your Jesus, Netti. And he answered my prayer. The cat had to be a miracle, didn't it?"

"It sounds like it, but that's Jesus. He's always taking care of us, and sometimes in miraculous ways. Remember the night of broken glass when He miraculously saved us at the theater? But tell me what happened next, Liesel?"

"We waited till dark. When it was all clear, we drove here as fast as we could."

"You poor darlings," Netti said, wrapping Liesel in her arms for a minute. "I suspect they got away, but if they did, I doubt they'd go directly home with the SS looking for them. I'll call each of them anyway, Liesel."

Netti called her mother, Trudi, and Sophie. There was no answer at each place. Mose gave the girls milk and cookies and then put them to bed in the guest room. Then the three sat together on the couch and talked about what to do next. Netti's first question was to ask if they were in immediate danger.

"I don't think Wolf knows where we live now," Mose said. "But it wouldn't be hard for the Gestapo to track us down."

"But how do we find out what happened to mother, Trudi, and Sophie?" Liesel asked.

"If they were arrested, we won't be able to," Mose said. "Wolf and the SS or Gestapo are the only ones who know if they're in custody, and we can't call and ask them."

"At times like this, Mose, we used to call Sophie to get us out of a jam," Netti said. "And now we can't even do that. But we can call Evert Heinz's grandson, Gregor. He's running the business in Cologne with Sophie, and if anyone can find out if the SS or Gestapo has them, he can."

Liesel slipped into bed next to Helene and Hermine. She finally slowed her mind enough to fall asleep. The next morning Netti didn't have to call Gregor Heinz; he called her first, saying that Sophie didn't show up for work, and he couldn't reach her at home. Sophie had given Gregor Netti's new phone number for emergency purposes. Netti related the whole story to him, and Gregor said he would check around to see if he could find the women, especially if the Gestapo had them. He thought it would be wise if all of them laid low for a while.

Netti, who worked only emergency substitute shifts at the hospital, wasn't on call for several days. Mose phoned the church to say he wouldn't be in all day. Liesel also called the phone company and told them she was ill and wouldn't be coming to work. They all stayed in that day and the next, worrying about what happened to Lisbeth, Trudi, and Sophie.

The next day, Gregor called. "Bad news. Lisbeth, Trudi, and Sophie are in the Cologne Gestapo jail. But my informant said the Gestapo isn't looking for anyone else in the family, so you don't have to worry about them searching for you, for now."

* * *

At fifty, Wolf Behrmann was a lonely and bitter man, left to wonder if the decisions he made during his life were the right ones. Elise was gone, probably for good. Erich and Gert were in France and Gisela had moved out. Max and Trudi were gone, and

Mitzi had left him behind to live in Berlin. Whether at home or at the bank, Wolf felt deserted, knowing it was nobody's fault but his own. He had too much time on his hands and spent much of it regretting his past. Wolf missed Elise much more than he thought he would. They disagreed on almost everything and argued often, but still, he missed her.

He recalled the good times with her. The cat and mouse games each enjoyed when they first met, flirting and toying with each other. Wolf remembered the time when he loved Elise. "What happened?" he pondered. He knew the answer but couldn't face it. But as days turned into weeks, he admitted to himself that hatred had ruined his life. It made him strike out in anger against his family, Jews, and anyone or anything that got in his way. Hatred had warped his sense of right and wrong, allowing him to satisfy only his selfish, fleshly lusts at the expense of everyone who might have loved him. Wolf seldom went to the taverns and clubs. Instead he spent most nights drinking alone at home.

But even with all his doubts, when Ricard Kluger called in October, Wolf felt no remorse.

"None of the women broke, Behrmann. They didn't incriminate themselves under our intense questioning and severe beatings."

"What's next, then?"

"We can't hold them any longer without confessions or some evidence that they conspired to falsify the identity of Jews."

"Isn't my sworn testimony enough, Ricard?"

"No, Wolf. With only your assertions it would be hard to convict them, even with the courts stacked against them. And now with my overcrowded jail I only have two choices: free the women or send them east to a Polish ghetto. So what should I do with them? It's up to you, Behrmann."

Wolf thought about it for a moment and then said, "Send them east, Kluger."

Kluger caught Wolf at one of his worst moments. He had been at home for several hours, drinking heavily and feeling sorry for himself. Wolf was in no mood for generosity or mercy. However, down deep he knew his decision was a mistake he could never fix. It was several months later when the family learned from Gregor Heinz's informant that Lisbeth, Trudi, and Sophie were in Poland.

* * *

As 1942 arrived, Theodor Mueller had stepped into the gap for Jürgen. With Liesel now spending little time in Cologne, Mose and Netti were responsible for the care of four children under the age of five. Theodor was there when needed, whether babysitting, running errands, or just lending moral support. He had no family of his own and now felt in some way a part of the best family he had ever known. His love for the family grew as conditions worsened. And the special love he always had for Netti was hard to hide.

Theodor still directed the personnel department at Cologne University Hospital, which in these times was hard to do. Like Jürgen, many of the hospital's surgeons and other doctors had gone to war with many fine nurses and support staff. The hospital drastically cut services and diverted supplies and equipment to the military effort. Most days, Theodor was pulling his hair out, trying to find the staff needed to keep the hospital afloat. He stewed about it but refused to let it get him down or sap the strength needed to honor his best friend's request to watch over his family.

Cologne had escaped any major bombings at that point, but Theodor heard one was imminent. He worried because the hospital was ill-equipped to handle mass casualties. Every time he walked the streets, he looked to the sky, wondering when the bombers would come again.

On many occasions, both Netti and Jürgen had invited Theodor to begin a relationship with Christ.

"I love the way you practice your faith, Netti. It's so genuine. I don't think I have what it takes to believe the way you do. I know I'm a hard case when it comes to religion."

"You're such a fine man, Theodor. You've seen so much how God has moved in our lives."

"I have, dear. I've taken note each time. I don't know what it is. I guess I'm set in my ways."

"It's not hard. All you have to do is open your heart and receive God's gift."

"That's what you and Jürgen always say. I'm still trying to figure it out, Netti. Maybe I will someday."

"We only want you to experience what we have." Neither said anything for a minute. "I won't bring it up again, but I'm always here, though, when you're ready."

Netti was tempted to do so, but she never initiated the discussion with Theodor again.

* * *

In February 1942, after being in the safe house near Hanover for seven months, Waldo desperately missed Netti. He decided to return to Cologne without telling anyone. He slipped away early one morning and walked to the train station. He had just enough money to buy a ticket to Cologne.

Waldo had no way of knowing that Lisbeth, Trudi, and Sophie were gone and Netti had moved. When he got to Cologne, he walked and ran for over an hour from the train station to home. Waldo frantically knocked on the front door, but there was no response. After repeated tries, he realized no one was there to answer. He sat on the porch swing for over an hour, waiting for his mother or someone else to come home.

Frau Aeschelman was the only one to notice Waldo. Her front window was straight across the street from the Behrmann house. The Aeschelmans, once friends, were bitter and resentful of the Behrmanns' anti-Nazi stand. Frau Aeschelman had read about Waldo's shenanigans at the concert performance. She recalled that the Gestapo tried to arrest him, but he escaped.

At two thirty in the afternoon, Gestapo headquarters received Frau Aeschelman's call, saying Waldo Behrmann was sitting on the front porch at Frobelstraße 292. As Frau Aeschelman was calling the Gestapo to harm the Behrmann family, Mathias Bernhardt was taking his afternoon walk down Frobelstraße. The Bernhardts had moved to the area two years before and were only the second family in the neighborhood who agreed with the Behrmanns' views. Mathias got to know the family well, and he knew of Waldo's talents and deficiencies.

"Waldo! I'm surprised to see you here."

"No one's answering the door, Herr Bernhardt."

"You didn't know that the house is now vacant?"

"No. Where is Netti! I came all the way from Hannover to see her.

"Sit right here, Waldo. I'm going home to call Netti and will be right back."

Netti had previously given Mathias her phone number. She had asked him to watch the house and call if anything came up.

"Hello, Netti, Mathias Bernhardt here. Waldo's now sitting on Lisbeth's front porch."

"What! How in the world did Waldo come all the way home on his own? How did Liesel and Felix let him slip away?"

"What do you want me to do, Netti?"

"Oh, God! Go back and sit with him until I get there. I have no one to watch the children, but we'll be there as soon as possible." Netti loaded all four children into her auto and sped off toward Frobelstraße.

Frau Aeschelman was irritated seeing Mathias Bernhardt sitting on the swing with Waldo. Her husband recently had a fierce confrontation with him over his most unpopular beliefs. They almost came to blows. She couldn't contain herself and ran outside and cursed him and Waldo. Mathias said nothing, and she went back inside. At that moment, he knew Waldo wasn't safe sitting out in the open where anyone could see him. So Mathias led Waldo off the porch and down to the sidewalk. He thought about taking him to his house. Instead, Mathias led Waldo up the street away from his home. He knew the Aeschelmans were vindictive, and he wouldn't put it past her to call the authorities.

Within minutes, two black autos stopped in front of Frobelstraße 292, and six men got out. Two of them ran to the front door while the others peered up and down the street. Frau Aeschelman ran out to tell the Gestapo that a man led Waldo Behrmann south down Frobelstraße. One auto took off south and four men on foot ran in the direction she was pointing.

Just then Netti pulled onto Frobelstraße. She saw the black autos in front of the house over a block away, so pulled to the curb and stopped. Several men were running down the street toward her. She ducked down and told the girls to get on the floor. Mathias and Waldo were hiding near a garage in the alley close to where Netti had parked. Mathias could clearly see Netti in the auto.

It startled Netti to hear three knocks on the passenger side door. Then to her great surprise and relief, Waldo's face slowly rose and peered through the window. Netti reached across and unlocked the passenger's door. Waldo and Mathias slipped into the car, Waldo into the front seat and Mathias into the back with the girls. They all got down, not saying a word, waiting for the danger to pass.

Two more men ran by but never looked as they passed the auto. Fifteen minutes later, Netti finally eased herself up and peered out the windows to see that no one was around. But she could see the Gestapo's autos in front of the house. "Stay down," Netti said, as she started the engine and slowly pulled out of the parking spot. She turned left at the corner and headed west away from danger.

"Thanks so much, Mathias, for calling and taking care of Waldo."

"You're most welcome, dear. I'm just glad I happened along and saw him on the porch."

"Are you okay, Waldo?"

"Yes, Netti. Please don't be mad at me."

"I could never be mad at you, but what are you doing in Cologne?"

"I couldn't stay in that house all the time doing nothing. I had to find a way to come see you."

"You had money to take the train?"

"Yes, and then I walked home from the train station."

"Oh, Waldo, do you know how dangerous it was for you to come here, especially to the house, when the Gestapo is still looking for you? Do you understand what I'm telling you, Waldo?"

"I guess, but I want to be with you, Netti—nowhere else and not with anyone else."

"I treasure that, and love you so much, but we've talked at length about this before. You have to stay away from here until we say it's safe to come back. I'll try to come see you in Hannover more often, but you have to promise you'll never do this again."

"I promise, Netti. I'm sorry. Please come back to Hannover with me."

When they reached Netti's place, she called to tell Liesel and Felix that Waldo was safe with her. They were relieved, thinking something awful might have happened to him. It also shocked them that he made it all the way home on his own.

After allowing Waldo to stay overnight, Netti drove him back to Hannover the following day, while Mose looked after the children. She never told Waldo about his mother, Trudi, and Sophie's abduction by the Gestapo. And focusing only on Netti, and her seeming disappointment in him, he never asked.

After Waldo's trip to Cologne, Liesel and Netti decided that Liesel should live full-time with Waldo in Hannover. This required her to sever her employment with the telephone company. Knowing that Waldo didn't fully understand the consequences of his journey and might try it again, Liesel and Felix were more vigilant in protecting him.

* * *

In the summer of 1941, Mitzi Hauer took Berlin by storm. It had been five years since she was Germany's most popular Olympic athlete. Her publicity had faded during her time in Cologne. But now back in the Berlin spotlight, she quickly resurrected her popularity. The vivacious blond, now twenty-six, was stunning, even to her few detractors. She was now a mature woman. She worked out often. Her body was hard and her figure unequaled. Men from the highest Nazi official to the lowest laborer fantasized about her. She was the belle of every ball and the social headliner that summer. Mitzi eagerly soaked up the adoration like a sponge to water. "After all, I'm a special gift to the brave men of the Reich; it's my responsibility to thrill them with my talents," Mitzi often thought.

Though many men sought her, she was on the arm of General Alfred Von Koenig at every social event. He arranged for her move to Berlin and promotion to a high-level BDM position, so both were fully aware of the payment for such favors. Although he took the arrangement seriously, she only used it to further her fame and station in the social world of Berlin's Nazi elite. The aging Von Koenig's experience and skill pleased Mitzi, but she preferred the muscular, well-formed bodies of the younger officers she often enjoyed "on the side." Again, it only seemed right to her that these young and loyal servants of the Reich should get to enjoy all she provided.

Mitzi Hauer received two promotions by the summer of 1942—for merit and favors from those high up in the party. She was now second in command of the entire BDM, wielding great influence and power over the lives of millions of girls and young women across Germany. While she was charming in social settings, she was harsh and unfair with those under her authority. Her language was often foul, as she continually struck out at her underlings.

In 1943, the allied bombings of Berlin became more frequent and widespread. They were even bombing civilian buildings. The British spared Berlin in 1942, however, instead concentrating on bombing U-boat ports to win the battle of the Atlantic.

On June 7, 1940, the French launched the first air attack on the German Capitol, dropping eighty-eight bombs that did little damage. On August 25, the British made their first bombing run over Berlin, targeting Tempelhof Airport and the nearby Siemensstadt neighborhood. There was little physical damage from these first raids, but the psychological impact was great. Goering repeatedly told the four million inhabitants of the city that the anti-aircraft defenses surrounding Berlin would prevent Allied bombers from reaching their target. When they did, confidence waned, and the citizens of Berlin were frightened. Then Hitler and Goering changed their bombing targets from the British airfields to their cities, because of the Allies' boldness in bombing Berlin.

The Nazis entered the war thinking they would bomb the Allies, but no one would bomb them. From London to Warsaw their bombing raids were intense. But now it was their turn, and Berlin was under attack from the air. The people of Berlin were now dreading their fate, as the Allies breached their so-called impenetrable defenses.

The Battle of Berlin was heating up by November 1943. Late in the month, the Royal Air Force (RAF) conducted their most effective raid on the capital. It resulted in massive damage to the residential neighborhoods of Tiergarten, where Mitzi and Alfred lived, Charlottenburg, and Spandau, which were just west of downtown. The raid sparked Berlin's first firestorm, and the Berlin Zoo suffered significant damage. Everyone in Berlin was on edge day and night.

But *fear* wasn't a word that Mitzi Hauer recognized. She believed she was somehow immune from danger, and as the female expression of the Third Reich she would always be wrapped under its protective covering. She had no time for such worries and would concentrate only on serving her Fuhrer with the talents and skills that no one else had.

As 1944 arrived, Berlin's citizens were no longer confident. They were discouraged as they faced the reality that Germany could lose the war. And as the bombings increased and homes and businesses were destroyed millions of people's lives were thrown into chaos.

With such weighty, life-altering issues facing those in Berlin, her citizens no longer had the will to put anyone on a pedestal, certainly not Mitzi Hauer. Her time had quickly passed, and she could now walk the streets with hardly anyone noticing her. Though still adored by some in society, she now knew her run as Germany's darling was coming to an end.

Mitzi was angry about her decline and what was happening in Berlin. She was furious with the enemy for killing thousands of innocent civilian men, women, and children. Although, she never gave much thought to the thousands of innocent people killed by Luftwaffe bombing raids. Though it was out of character for her, Mitzi felt bad for the homeless families throughout the city. And though she still had complete loyalty to her Fuhrer, she was becoming disenchanted with many ranking members of the Nazi party who were conducting the war ineptly. She couldn't face that her Fuhrer was making the biggest mistakes. Sensing the downfall of the Reich, Mitzi decided it was time to save herself and Gretchen from the uncertain days ahead. She wasn't sure how, but she would be vigilant to keep them safe.

In March 1944, an exciting possibility presented itself to Mitzi. She had been on Alfred's arm at many Nazi bashes. Most were boring, but one night Alfred, Mitzi, and ten other guests were invited to dine at Heinrich Himmler's table. His wife, Margerete, didn't attend for unknown reasons.

Mitzi had previously met Himmler, and even had a few in-depth conversations. The pale leader, in his mid-fifties, never impressed her. He was less than average height with a slender build. His steely gray eyes peered mockingly at her through his glasses. He often sported an annoying grin as he went on about one thing or another.

Mitzi decided that Himmler wasn't exceptional in any noticeable way. He was boring, and she found it hard to believe he had reached such heights in the Third Reich. Mitzi knew that Himmler had more power than anyone except Hitler and was the ruthless architect of the Reich's most deadly programs. He was a skillful administrator and planner, but it confused her when he started babbling about his philosophies on the occult, runic history, and weird alternative medicines. Even so, the small party at Himmler's home proved to be most interesting. Mitzi met Himmler's new personal aide, Hauptmann Robert Fertig. He was tall and lean, with a handsome, clean-shaven face and wavy brown hair. Though young, he was her type of man, and she intended to strike up a friendship. "Who knows," she thought, "knowing someone so close to Himmler might be valuable."

That night, Mitzi teased the young hauptmann, who was well aware of the game she was playing and more than eager to participate. In fact, it was only two days later when he invited her to lunch at a secluded café in Wannsee. She gladly accepted, eager to pursue this useful association. The lunch in Wannsee led to another one in Spandau and then another. Then Hauptmann Fertig invited Mitzi to his private quarters in the Himmler mansion. They enjoyed each other's youthful enthusiasm to culminate the game she was playing. Mitzi was blowing her famous smoke rings as the hauptmann turned and looked into her eyes.

"How do I stack up against the general?"

"It's not a fair comparison. There's something about being young and energetic, and something about skilled maturity."

"I guess that's a compliment; at least I'll take it as one."

"To be frank, Robert, I'm more concerned about your age than your performance."

"Why? Hasn't your experience with young men been pleasant?"

"It's mostly about my husband."

"I take it he's young."

"Only twenty-one when we married, seven years ago."

"Is he in the west or east?"

"East, I think, I'm not sure. The last letter I received from him was in June 1941. I'm sure he's either dead or somewhere in a Russian gulag."

"Three years is a long time not to know."

"We were drifting apart long before he left for the war. I thought we would rise to prominence together and have a glorious life in the new Reich. But he was a boy when I met him, and he was still a boy when he left for the Wehrmacht."

"So his youthful flaws have sent you into the arms of the general and other mature men?"

"It's not just my husband; I've had other bad experiences with young men. It sounds arrogant, but I'm getting tired of training the young men of Germany to be skillful at pleasing their women."

"Yes, I'd say that's a little arrogant."

"I don't want to linger on the past anymore. I need to look to the future and what might happen to me and Gretchen."

"Your daughter?"

"Yes, my beautiful daughter who'll be six this summer. I need to plan for both of us, especially if everything doesn't go well."

"Then plan carefully, Mitzi; it's only going to get worse."

"So many people are saying that now. It's depressing. Let's talk about something else. Are some of the things Himmler says a little strange to you, Robert?"

"They are. In the two months I've been around him, he's surprised me in many ways. He's meticulous and calculating most of the time, but then he's careless and out of touch at other times."

"He does babble on about ideas that are nonsense to me. How is he careless?"

"I could tick off a list of examples, but one is the way he secures his personal treasures, which are extremely valuable."

"He has valuables here in the mansion?"

"He has incredible wealth stolen from places all over Europe. He chose the most valuable pieces of booty and left the rest for his underlings to pilfer. And the most careless example is where he keeps his most valuable pieces of jewelry."

"Where is that?"

"You know I shouldn't be telling you any of this. But, what the hell, he keeps them in a wall safe in his study, hidden in the most obvious place behind the picture of Hitler. Then, to top it off, he reminds his wife of the safe's combination when I'm within earshot like I'm not even there. And again, he uses the most obvious combination, the Fuhrer's birthdate, minus the zero."

"I wish you hadn't told me that, Robert. If he's ever robbed, you'll come looking for me first."

"I would. And you're right; I should have kept my mouth shut—too much good wine." Mitzi laughed and then said, "You don't have to worry; your secret is safe with me."

Nine days later, Alfred and Mitzi were again among Himmler's select twelve for an informal dinner party. Hauptmann Fertig was in the corner of the dining room, at Himmler's disposal if needed.

Again, the evening was tedious for Mitzi, as the host delved into his occultist beliefs, seemingly detached from reality. But then the evening took an unexpected turn, which instantly got Mitzi's attention. Himmler brought out some pieces from his prized jewelry collection to dazzle his guests. One piece in particular caught Mitzi's eye.

As Himmler explained, it was an incredibly valuable necklace taken from a gallery in Paris. It was centuries old, having great significance in French history. But the only thing Mitzi saw was the huge diamond in the center, surrounded by four large diamonds and countless smaller ones arrayed in a spectacular pattern.

The months that followed, Mitzi thought about the magnificent necklace often. Things were getting harder for all Berliners, as the Allies landed in France and started their certain push toward the border of western Germany. And now the air raids were dampening any semblance of normalcy for the city's beleaguered residents. Many had abandoned the city center for the suburbs or the countryside with its smaller and safer communities. She couldn't help but think about her and Gretchen's future.

Through the summer and fall, Hauptmann Fertig had little time for Mitzi. He was fully engaged in pleasing his boss, who with each military setback was becoming harder to deal with. Then one night the hauptmann invited Mitzi to his quarters. He said Himmler was out of town for the night, attending such a high-level meeting that only his chief of staff went with him. The rest of the family was in Munich for the week, so he had the run of the house.

At that moment, Mitzi Hauer decided to secure her and Gretchen's future, whether in a victorious or defeated Germany. She would never have another opportunity to steal Himmler's prized necklace, which had been calling her name all these months. She brought Robert's favorite bottle of Schnapps with her that night, fully intending to get him drunk to the point of passing out. And the evening went just as she had hoped.

The young hauptmann was frisky and eager to enjoy the woman who far surpassed all his other conquests. And Mitzi ensured that he was in a deep sleep by midnight. He had not only lost his battle with the alcohol, he was also physically exhausted from the strenuous activity. Mitzi quietly slithered out of bed without disturbing her drunken lover. She left his quarters, going south down the long hallway. With information from Robert, Mitzi had a good idea of where Himmler's study was. However, she made a wrong turn. "No, this is the wrong hall," she thought. "Go back and turn right—hurry!" Within seconds, she regained her bearings and found the study.

"Shine the flashlight away from the windows," Mitzi thought. "Robert said a button in the middle drawer of Himmler's desk would turn off the safe's alarm." She quietly moved to the desk and opened the middle drawer. Shining her flashlight inside, she saw a red button on the left side panel and pushed it. She then went directly to Hitler's picture. "God, it's heavy! Lean it against the desk. Good." And there it was, Himmler's private safe, holding millions of Reich marks' worth of jewelry.

The final hurdle was the safe's combination. She had last-minute doubts. "What if Robert was only kidding, or purposely lied about the combination? There's no turning back now," she thought, shining her light on the combination lock and spinning the dial. "The combination should be 4-2-8-9, alternating right and then left, going to the next number after passing zero." Almost in disbelief, as Mitzi hit nine and went back to zero, the lock clicked, and she opened the safe.

It was a large safe, containing over three dozen pieces of valuable jewelry. But Mitzi only cared about one, and there it was, brilliantly reflecting the beam from her flashlight. She lifted the necklace out of the safe and put it in her purse. Mitzi quickly closed the safe and spun the dial. She lifted the frame to put it back in place. It was heavy, and she couldn't get it hooked. Despite her strength, she was wavering. The picture was slipping from her grasp. Just as she was about to drop it, the hook caught and it was hanging in place.

Mitzi heard voices and footsteps coming from the hall. "What the hell," she thought. "That sounds like Himmler's voice." She quickly scanned the room with her light, desperately looking for a place to hide. "Not the desk, he'll use it, but where? The floor-length drapes on the west wall," she thought, as she ran to the window. She opened the drapes and slipped behind them, making sure to cover her feet.

The study door opened, and five men entered. Extremely agitated, Himmler yelled out orders to the other men. Mitzi identified Hauptmann Fertig's voice, obviously called out of his drunken stupor to aid Himmler in whatever he was doing. Mitzi heard the men speaking somewhere near Himmler's desk, only three meters from where she stood.

From what she could make out, Hitler had ordered Himmler's immediate return to Berlin. Seemingly, Hitler had gone into one of his fits over a disastrous incident in France that afternoon. Himmler had to prepare a plan to mitigate the disaster by eight the next morning when Hitler would meet with his top generals.

Mitzi started feeling light-headed and nauseous. It was partially due to the extreme tension but mostly from consuming too much food and alcohol. She sensed that someone was standing near the drapes, right next to her. "Still yourself, control your breathing. Your life depends on it," Mitzi thought. Her stomach started rumbling.

"What the hell's that grumbling, Fertig?" Himmler said. "You've been partying too damned much."

The hauptmann had been trying to clear his head and sober up after Himmler rudely woke him out of a deep sleep. He wasn't sure what happened; he thought he heard some rumbling behind the drapes but couldn't be sure. "Sorry sir, it's been a long night."

"And it will be a lot longer for you if you don't get your ass in gear!"

Then Mitzi could hear that the men had moved to the south end of the study. She took a chance and opened the drapes enough to see four men pouring over what appeared to be maps on a conference table. They were all facing away from her, focusing intensely on their business. Robert Fertig was sitting at the end of the table, still weaving a little as he fought to sober up.

"I'm going to vomit. I have to leave now!" Mitzi thought. "I'm doomed if I stay here!" She quietly opened the drapes and started tiptoeing toward the door, six meters away. It was a straight shot with nothing in her path. She went slowly to make no sound, hoping none of the men looked up. She could have sworn that Robert turned his head and looked at her, but he said nothing. Thankfully, the door was still ajar, and she only had to open it a little to slip safely into the hall.

Mitzi tiptoed down the hall and then ran as fast as she could to the bathroom next to Robert's quarters. She threw up for several minutes before being able to think about anything else. Mitzi started to clean up the toilet and mess around it but then suddenly stopped. A plan, an alibi, suddenly came to mind. She didn't know if Robert saw her in the study. Still, she needed a cover story that was good enough to save her life, which could easily be in the balance.

"Robert will surely ask why and when I left his quarters," Mitzi thought. "Once Himmler discovers that his prize necklace is gone, Robert will suspect that I took it. I'll tell Robert I woke up ill and went to his bathroom where I vomited, making a horrible mess. I was too ill and embarrassed, so I went home. The vomit all over Robert's bathroom will corroborate my story. Yes, this will work; I have the alibi I need." Mitzi left the bathroom and went down the stairs to the front door. She opened the door slightly, peering out to see if any security guards were around. Since no one expected Himmler back until the following afternoon, no guards were outside.

Mitzi drove home, sick and shaken by the night's events. Alfred was still on a field assignment. Opening Gretchen's bedroom door, she saw that her daughter was sleeping soundly with her nanny asleep in the next room. Mitzi gazed at the child for a few minutes before going to her bedroom. She was thankful to see her daughter again and vowed never to take such a risk in the future. But, hopefully, she had secured their future, no matter how the war turned out.

* * *

Mose sat down on the couch next to Netti. He glanced into her eyes, trying to hide the frustration of the day. "Netti, I've been praying about making a change."

"This sounds serious. What change, Mose?"

"You won't like it, but I think I'm being led to resign my pastorate and look for fulltime work."

"Really? You can't leave the work God's called you to unless you're sure. And yes, it upsets me even to think that you'd leave the ministry!"

"Times are hard, darling. Who has anything to drop in the offering plate? There's not enough money to support the operation of the church, let alone the pastors.

"But Theodor can arrange for me to take more shifts at the hospital. We'll have to scrape by, but it'll be enough. I can't have you abandon your calling, Mose. Walk away from what you love most in life? No, I just won't have it!"

"It's my responsibility as the head of the family, Netti. I'll keep looking for a part-time job."

"You've tried, Mose; they're too scarce. No, I'll increase my hours, and we'll somehow make it."

"I hate it! But we'll try it your way . . . for a while. When you set your mind, Netti, nothing changes it." So in the spring of 1942, Netti prodded Theodor to juggle the schedules so she could increase the number of substitute shifts she worked.

Night bombing raids increased, and the RAF had conducted at least one hundred raids so far. The air-raid sirens sounded every time there was an attack. On other nights, the sirens blared, but no planes came. Although most raids caused little damage, the cumulative effect was evident in the number of damaged homes and businesses. It was also noticeable in the faces of those living with the nightly fear of what could happen.

When late-night sirens sounded the alert, Cologne citizens had to make a choice: Should they get out of bed and go to their assigned shelter or remain under the warm covers until true danger was imminent? If worse came to worst, they could try to ride out the attack in their home. Most had buckets of sand, water, and shovels at the ready, in case of fires ignited by small incendiary bombs, which created havoc when exploding near anything flammable.

On May 30, Netti received a call from one of her close friends at the hospital, asking if she would cover her shift that night from eleven to seven. Netti felt uneasy about doing it, but she relented when hearing the circumstances requiring her friend to leave the city. Fortunately, Mose could watch the girls, even though the church was having its monthly all-night prayer meeting. She knew Elise would be driving down from the country to attend the meeting. With her help, Netti was confident the children would be secure at the church.

This was the first time the church had their all-night prayer meeting on Saturday, with the intent that participants would then go directly into the Sunday morning service. The prayer meeting was to start at ten, so it was convenient for Netti to drop Mose and the children off at the church and then drive the three kilometers to the hospital.

It was a typical Saturday night in old downtown Cologne. People packed the clubs, theaters, and restaurants, looking for a good time. Although there were rationing and shortages of food and other goods, the citizens of Cologne were still living better than most. And being a liberal and freewheeling people, they loved their weekend nights out on the town. They needed to release the stress and tension of living under wartime conditions—defying the constant threat of bombs falling from the sky that could cut their lives short.

As Netti reported to work twenty minutes early, she still had an uneasy feeling deep in the pit of her stomach. She had prayed about it several times that evening but never felt the peace that usually came. The nurse in charge assigned Netti to the second-floor children's ward where she usually spent a quiet night answering occasional calls for help.

Just before midnight, the blare of air-raid sirens got everyone's attention and woke many patients. Staff had to decide on whether to move patients to the basement shelter immediately or wait to see if the sirens stopped, signaling the end of the threat. Most warnings had resulted in little damage near the hospital. But the sirens went on for forty minutes, and then Netti heard the sound of planes over the sirens.

That's when Netti knew why she had been uneasy all day. This wasn't normal; she had never heard such a roar and knew something horrible was about to happen. And now she could also hear the sound of the anti-aircraft batteries as their 88-mm guns fired. Netti sensed that Cologne was about to be bombed like never before.

Patients and staff were yelling and scrambling around as panic and confusion set in. "Lord Jesus, please protect everyone here and in the city, especially Mose and the children," Netti quickly prayed. The air-raid marshals ordered everyone to get down to the bomb shelter immediately. Doctor Schultz asked for nursing volunteers to help in three unfinished operations and monitor four patients in critical condition.

Netti, though fearful, volunteered to aid in one of the operations. And just as she finished scrubbing and entering the operating room, everyone heard and felt the concussion of the first bombs. The room shook, lights flickered, and instrument trays crashed to the floor. The explosion couldn't have been more than a block away. Doctor Von Epps yelled for everyone to concentrate on finishing the procedure, which should take only several more minutes. Then two more explosions shook the operating room, forcing Von Epps to close the incision and wrap-up the procedure immediately.

Netti ran out of the room, stripping off her white gown, gloves, and cap. More bombs exploded nearby, and the building quaked with each blast. "It's over," Netti thought as she ran down two flights of stairs to the basement. "This is the massive attack we all dreaded and hoped would never happen." With several others, she ran through the door of a room fortified for use as a bomb shelter. Screaming people packed in well past capacity. Netti pushed her way to an inner wall and started praying.

It seemed like the bombing would never stop; fifteen minutes passed, then thirty, then an hour. Boom! Boom! Boom! The frightening concussions went on and on. Some in the shelter fainted from fear. Others passed out from the heat and lack of oxygen. Those who managed to speak were in shock, never thinking such an attack could last so long. Everyone was afraid for loved ones elsewhere in Cologne. Netti was concerned about her family and everyone at the Free Faith Church. She knew, though, that the most effective thing to do was to continue praying.

Sometime after two in the morning, the bombs stopped falling, and everyone breathed a deep sigh of relief. The attack had lasted almost ninety minutes. At that point, people trampled one another as they scrambled to get out of the shelter. Chaos reigned for several minutes until most were out of the room. Netti and several doctors and nurses stayed behind to help the sick and injured.

When Netti made her way back upstairs to the first floor, she was horrified by the enormous hole in the main entrance. Windows were shattered, glass was everywhere, and people were carrying the injured through the gaping eight-by-three-meter hole, seeking medical aid. "This can't be real," Netti thought. "It's like something out of a horror film." But it was real—the real face of war that was ugly and deadly had come to her city in its full fury.

Netti had no idea about conditions in other parts of Cologne, but she knew the section around University Hospital was walloped, with many casualties. The damage in the hospital and resulting chaos made it difficult to help anyone. Everyone painted a grim scene of the city, one that Netti never wanted to see. She heard many horrific stories over the next five hours, as she frantically worked with other medical staff to treat the injured. Spent, the head nurse told Netti to take a break.

The citizens of Cologne rallied to help each other. Everyone pitched in and did what was necessary with little regard for their own well-being. Thousands were on the streets, clearing rubble, assisting the injured, putting out fires, restoring power, and fixing broken waterlines. Incredibly, most would report to work Monday, just as they always had.

Netti made her way to the basement cafeteria, which was still intact and serving coffee, tea, and a few sweets. It was nearing seven thirty when she found a seat and sipped her hot coffee. Netti put her head down. She wanted to cry from utter exhaustion, but she didn't.

She was drifting off to asleep when she heard her name called from across the room. Netti looked up to see Theodor and Elise walking toward her. He looked fine, but bandages covered most of Elise's left arm, and she had a cut over her right eye. Seeing Elise's condition and knowing she was in church with her family sent Netti into a tailspin. She panicked. "Sweet Jesus, no, no, no," Netti said trying to catch her breath. As Netti stood, she could tell by the expression on their faces that the news was terrible.

"What is it, what is it?" Netti yelled.

"Sit, darling," Theodor said softly. The three sat quietly for a few seconds.

"Oh, God, there's no other way to say it, Netti! Mose and Kurt are gone," Elise said.

Netti stared blankly as if she didn't hear what Elise said. Then she started crying uncontrollably. Theodor and Elise tried to console her. Tears flowed from all three for over five minutes. Then Netti laid her head on the table. She said nothing, as Elise stroked her hair and Theodor held her hand.

"Where are Karla, Helene, and Hermine?" Netti asked. "Are they okay?"

"Karla hurt her arm and is at St. Mary's. Helene and Hermine are fine. One of the church members took them to her home," said Theodor.

"Do you know where they took Mose and Kurt, Theodor?"

"Saint Mary's, Netti. They're using their basement as a temporary morgue." Netti sprang to her feet. "I'm going there now."

Netti entered the large room lined with rows of covered bodies. Theodor thought there were over 150. Elise held Netti by one elbow and Theodor, the other, as a nurse led them to Mose and Kurt, lying next to each other. Theodor pulled back the blankets to reveal peaceful faces at rest. Neither had suffered head injuries.

Netti broke down again, as she touched Kurt's face and then stroked Mose's hair. "I should have listened to him, Theodor. If only I had, they would still be alive. My God, it's all my fault. I'm to blame for their deaths!"

"That's not possible, Netti; how could you be responsible?"

"He wanted to take a full-time job and resign his pastorate. But I insisted he be true to his calling. If only I had listened to him, he would have resigned weeks ago and never been in the church last night."

"Mose heard from God, and I'm sure he felt remaining at the church was His will. But also, Netti, even if Mose had resigned, don't you think he would have still been at the prayer meeting last night?"

Netti paused for a few seconds to grasp what Elise said. "I guess you're right. Knowing Mose, he would have been there. But what am I going to do now? When I lost Conrad, I had Mose and Father to help me. I depended on them. They were my comforters. But now they're gone, Elise. What do I do with three children and no husband, and maybe no home?"

"Do what you always do, Netti—what you do better than anyone I've ever known. Seek God's help and trust He'll take care of you."

"I can't, Elise. I can't do it anymore. I'm mad, damn mad at God right now! I can't understand this—how He let this war take Mose and my precious boy."

Netti pounded her fists on the table where Kurt lie. She tried, but couldn't release the pent-up anger, fear, and remorse exploding inside. There was nothing Elise and Theodor could do but stand close by her.

After a nurse cleaned and bandaged Karla's superficial wounds, she was ready to leave St Mary's hospital. Netti and Elise found her upstairs in a makeshift triage room, while Theodor went to get his auto. He drove them all to Netti's house. The trip required detours and backtracking to negotiate the congested streets, debris from damaged buildings, fires, water and gas line ruptures, and abandoned or bombed out autos.

The house had no damage, though several bombs exploded two blocks to the east. Theodor, Elise, or Gisela stayed with Netti and the children for the next four days until the service for Mose and Kurt. The Free Faith Fellowship Church was too damaged to have the service, so Netti decided to have only a graveside ceremony. The service was short, with Pastor Rudolph Grobe officiating. He was still recovering from shrapnel wounds in his left leg. Netti grieved silently, under the influence of a sedative that Theodor convinced her to take to calm her nerves.

Nothing eased Netti's broken heart. It was well into the following year before she completely forgave herself and knew that God wasn't responsible for the disaster that ravaged Germany. She could easily blame the British for intentionally bombing the civilians of Cologne, intending to kill and maim as many innocent people as possible, and she did. But down deep she knew they were only doing what the Luftwaffe did to them in the horrific bombings of London.

Netti finally got to the point where she said, "I don't know why you allowed this to happen, Lord. And if you choose never to reveal the reason to me, by faith I'll still walk with my hand in yours."

It would be weeks before the citizens of Cologne knew the full extent of the damage to their city. They learned the RAF called the raid Operation Millennium. It was the first raid that used over a thousand planes. The British dropped nearly fifteen hundred tons of destruction on Cologne. Most were incendiary bombs designed to spark thousands of fires. There were more than seventeen hundred large fires. The way the streets were designed, however, prevented a firestorm. But still, most of the damage resulted from fires, not exploding bombs. The raid destroyed or damaged more than twelve thousand buildings, including many churches, hospitals, and schools. Over thirteen thousand homes were lost, most of them apartments. Forty-five thousand people were now homeless, and within months after the attack, a quarter of Cologne's residents left the city.

Despite the substantial damage to the city, it was incredible that fewer than five hundred people died and only about five thousand were injured. Though significant damage occurred in future bombing raids, Cologne had absorbed the worst on that last day in May 1942. Needless to say, fear continued to grip the residents of the city. Even though fear was their constant companion, the citizens of Cologne were resilient. They carried on with life as best they could, never letting their morale decline.

It saddened Jürgen greatly to receive Theodor's letter concerning Netti's tragedy. He wrote to her many times, over the summer, trying his best to console her. But she didn't have it in her to respond with much more than a thank-you. No one told Jürgen about Waldo and Liesel fleeing to Hannover in 1941. And they had no more information to give him about Lisbeth, Trudi, and Sophie. Sadly, as the Sixth Army became entangled in the Battle of Stalingrad in the fall and winter of 1942, mail from Jürgen dwindled.

* * *

During the spring of 1940, Gisela met Manfred Hassenkamp at Cologne University Hospital where she and Netti worked. He was finishing his internship at the hospital and hoped for a military deferral, which would allow him to complete two years of residency by June 1942. Manfred had great potential to be an accomplished surgeon in his home city of Hannover. To his advantage, Manfred's uncle was a colonel and the director of conscription for the Hannover district. He was solely responsible for Manfred's deferral so he could complete his internship. The colonel was an ardent Nazi, as was Manfred's father, who was chief of security for the Gauleiter of Hannover.

Nazi tactics repulsed Manfred, and he saw through their grandiose propaganda. But he walked a fine line, needing the support of both his father and uncle to finish medical training and avoid certain conscription. This circumstance forced him to keep silent about his true feelings, and his silence allowed him to receive the two-year deferral extension from his uncle.

Gisela understood the predicament Manfred faced and made it clear that she would support him in whatever he did. As she grew to love him in 1941, Gisela's lingering feelings for Didi faded. Gisela loved Didi's winning ways—the way he romanced her, held and kissed her tenderly, and painted a beautiful picture of the future they would share. But she could never understand his inability to forgive her for one kiss, that one slip for which she was eternally sorry. And she could never accept his misplaced loyalty to the Nazi Party. Her feelings for Didi wavered back and forth for years until Manfred came into her life. "Now it's time to move on and finally leave Didi behind," she thought.

Gisela and Manfred talked about marriage, but they thought it best to postpone any plans until they resolved his conscription status. When he finished his residency at Cologne University Hospital, they both moved to Hannover in June 1942. They waited there for a decision, which would either send him to the Wehrmacht or allow him to be a practicing surgeon at Nordstadt Hospital.

* * *

Netti returned to work full-time at Cologne University Hospital in August 1942 to ease the pain of her loss. As personnel director, Theodor made Netti an offer that allowed her to work again. He would move into the house with her and the three children. His position allowed Theodor to be home by four in the afternoon. After he got home, Netti would leave for the hospital, working from four thirty to midnight. The hospital needed the help, so Theodor allowed the irregular work schedule.

The arrangement worked well for everyone until Theodor's emotions clouded his better judgment. Netti had touched his heart from the first day he met her as a bright eleven-year-old. But now, she was twenty-four and dealing with overwhelming sorrow. Theodor ached for Netti. He tried to help her in every way possible. It seemed natural that in time his deep concern for her would turn to love. It wasn't something he expected or wanted; it just happened, and now he had to deal with it. He knew romance was impossible, if not wrong, and he knew Netti would never feel the same way about him. It was his intent never to let her know how he felt.

But one day in October, Theodor slipped and did something he regretted. Netti arrived home after her shift just after midnight. Theodor awkwardly helped take off her coat. He pulled the arm the wrong way, and they became entangled with their faces close together. Theodor acted impulsively and pressed his lips to hers. Startled by what he did, Netti pulled back quickly. "My God, why did you do that, Theodor?"

"I'm sorry, Netti. I don't know what I was thinking. I wasn't thinking."

"No, you weren't, Theodor! You know I love you but never do that again."

"I won't. How stupid of me!"

Theodor said nothing more. There was never an encore.

Netti found it hard to sleep, often lying awake in the wee hours trying to make sense of her life and what the future might hold. She longed for her father's strength. Netti also wished her mother would come home and cuddle her, saying, "It'll be okay." She had always craved her mother's tender loving care but seldom received it. Netti also wanted Didi to come home to be her protector as a big brother should be. She longed for the strong bond they once had. Netti dreamed of the day Trudi and Sophie would be a part of her life again. She missed her big sister and best girlfriend, recalling the times they laughed and cried together. And she missed laughing as Aunt Sophie sprang one of her outrageous antics. But Netti mostly missed Sophie's quick wit, and the way she could solve any problem. And then darling Waldo came to mind. Oh, how she wanted him to come home, to be near every day. And Liesel and Stefan, she missed their warmth. God's love and presence were returning, but now Netti wanted her family to come home.

6

THE VEIL IS LIFTED

*J*ürgen caught Lili's eye as she entered the main hospital tent. He excused himself and went to talk with her. "Are you all set, Lili?"

"I'm packed and ready to go."

"Colonel Dobrynin said they'll be tearing everything down tonight except the billeting tents, which will come down early in the morning. We'll be trucking out by early afternoon."

"Did he say where we're going?"

"They haven't told him yet. But he's sure the Red Army's gearing up for a big offensive."

Midafternoon on June 12, 1944, staff from the Sixty-fifth Army Surgical Hospital headed northeast from Voronezh in a large caravan of trucks. Except for temporary moves, Jürgen and Lili spent over a year in the mobile hospital southwest of that city. The hospital had no new patients for a week and was empty when they left.

Jürgen and Lili were riding in the same jeep as Lieutenant Azarov. The eighteen-hour journey wasn't a waste of time, though, as Sergey continued to teach them Russian. After ten months, both could communicate well enough to meet their needs inside and outside the operating tent.

Over time, the Lieutenant's feelings for Lili grew, as he came to see her as a special woman not just a German nurse. They spent considerable time together with Jürgen but also had time alone. Sergey also spent time with two other nurses. Lili tried not to but had conflicted feelings about the position she found herself in. She liked Sergey and knew he had the qualities most women looked for in a man. But Lili still wasn't to the point of being close to any man other than Jürgen, her rock. She knew it would take time for her mind to heal. How much time, Lili didn't know, but she knew that first forgiveness had to come from her heart. And Lili didn't know if she could ever forgive Sergeant Anton Leonov for attempting to rape her. Lili also knew that she had to forgive God. He didn't let her down, looking the other way, but saved her.

By late afternoon, the caravan reached Kursk and headed north and then east to Bryansk. From there they went northwest for a long night's drive. Most of them tried to get comfortable enough to sleep. As morning came, they passed just west of Smolensk and then turned due west. By late morning they crossed into Belorussia, and at two that afternoon they pulled off the paved highway. They went south on a narrow dirt road for three kilometers, and then the caravan stopped.

They were twelve kilometers east of Orsha in preparation for a massive Russian offensive that would begin in a week. For the next day and a half, they raised tents, unloaded supplies and equipment, and assigned personnel billets. The new surgical hospital wasn't as substantial as it had been. Everyone now understood they were to be mobile.

Within days, they saw the tanks and soldiers of the Third Belorussian Front in the distance. They were heading west toward Orsha, a stronghold of German defenses on the main road connecting Moscow and Minsk. On June 22, they heard the faint rumblings of the first battle of Operation Bagration. Elements of the German Fourth Army put up a brave defense, but in four days the Russians secured Orsha. Casualties were high on both sides. The wounded started arriving at the Sixty-Fifth by the evening of June 22.

Jürgen and Lili were now more flexible in the operating tent, having the ability to communicate essential information in Russian. They could now work on different surgical teams, increasing the unit's effectiveness. After several days of rest, all medical staff was in for a long four days of surgery. Most worked sixteen-hour shifts with few breaks. Then on June 27, there was a lull in casualties, which allowed staff a much-needed rest.

Lili was eating in the mess tent when Jürgen walked up from behind and put his hand on her shoulder. She turned to see who it was.

"I thought you might be here, sweetie," Jürgen said.

"I'm glad to see you finally; it's been over two days."

"Three, I think."

"I'm exhausted and upset, Jürgen. The food turns my stomach. I can hardly eat a bite."

"Force yourself to eat, Lili, or you'll get sick."

"I've tried, but I'm done. I thought the carnage wouldn't bother me anymore, but it's too much, Jürgen! One in three who comes to our operating tent goes out with a blanket over his face. And now we don't have the blood to save them all. We're forced to judge some as unsalvageable, but who are we to decide? We're not

God; it's just too much for me to take!" Lili started to cry. Jürgen reached across the table and took hold of her hands.

"I know this brings back the horror of Clearing Station II, but we'll also get through this, Lili. We'll get back to our families one day, and that hope is what will keep us going."

"I only have hope, but I don't think it'll be enough for me. I'm afraid I'll lose it all—lose my mind."

"I'm praying for you a hundred times a day, Lili."

"I know you are. I'm trying to pray too, but it seems that God is so far away now. We talk about it often, but I still can't understand where God is amidst the devastation we see—not to mention the millions of casualties we don't see. The worst horror are all the bodies stacked outside the morgue tent."

"It's nauseating. They say it might be days before trucks take them to a mass burial pit. I don't pretend to understand it either, sweetie. All I can commit to is trusting Him—trusting He'll get us both home someday."

"I wish I had your faith, Jürgen, but no matter how hard I try, doubts overwhelm me."

"You've been through a lot. It's understandable. I know you're fighting hard to get through it, Lili."

"I don't know if I'm fighting or giving in. Two months have passed, and I'm still struggling with what happened to Larisa."

"I've been praying that you'll be able to let go of the whole tragedy with Lieutenant Lyasin."

"I wish I could, but it haunts me, especially when I try to sleep."

"You haven't wanted to open up about it; maybe this is the time?"

"Maybe? It's only getting worse."

Jürgen pulled out his New Testament and cigarette case, lighting a cigarette for both. "Go ahead, Lili, talk to me."

"I didn't understand anything, Jürgen. She despised me and took every opportunity to make my life miserable. Then after the attack, she changed."

"It shocked both of us when she came to your bedside with tears in her eyes."

"Then she became my protector and was kind to me."

"It turned everyone's head when you befriended her."

"I was only responding to her change, the warmth she showed me. And as my Russian got better and we could communicate, we became close."

"Do you know what happened with Lieutenant Babkin?"

"I guess. I'm not sure I ever knew the whole story. Larisa said she was so happy finally to have a man that cared about her and wanted to be with her. I think it was her first real love, Jürgen, even though she was over thirty. It was all too sad. For some reason she never attracted men, and I'm not sure why. Larisa wasn't unattractive, and she had love stored up if only a man would accept it. She was desperate, then joyous when she thought someone finally loved her."

"That's when it happened, I guess?"

"Yes. Larisa asked me more than once why Babkin wouldn't be intimate with her. She ached for a man to love her and make love to her. Then he crushed her heart—broke her spirit and will to go on."

"Did she find out or did he tell her?"

"Oh, he cruelly told her, saying he only led her on to win a bet. He said he never liked her, let alone loved her. And he couldn't imagine how horrible it would be to lie with her. It was all faked, and the joke was on her."

"Poor woman. I can't imagine how damaging that must have been to her self-worth."

"It took everything away, Jürgen. She couldn't recover from it and the guilt she carried."

"But you didn't know about that when she came to you?"

"No. I had no idea then. Larisa cried so hard for days, and we often talked into the early hours of the morning. Larisa felt so worthless, and she thought that she would never find love or a man she could trust. I tried to reassure her that it would happen sometime, but she never believed it would.

"That's when we started talking about God. She was reaching out for help, Jürgen. I think she was reaching out to God. I tried my hardest to tell her about Jesus. She listened and even hoped He was the answer to her broken heart and guilt. But Larisa never believed God would be able to put her back together. And she certainly never believed He could forgive her for the horrible act she committed. So she never came to the point of accepting God's love and forgiveness."

"I remember the times when you asked for my advice. Truthfully, I felt inadequate in trying to help you with Larisa. Of course, you didn't know about the guilt she was carrying."

"No, not until the note. I continued to ask what was really bothering her. I told Larisa that God forgave me of all my sins. But she never told me why she was so depressed. She had shared her deepest secrets and frustrations with men, so I knew it must be serious if she wouldn't tell me."

"You were in shock for days after you heard."

"It was like a bad dream. I knew Larisa was depressed but never dreamed she would shoot herself in the head. Then when they gave me the envelope with my name on it, I was shaking all over and didn't want to open it. That's why I came to you, so you'd be there when I read it. But it didn't shock me when I read the note. Though I wouldn't admit it, I suspected why she felt so guilty. She could never make it right with me, but I hope she made it right with God."

"I pray she did and that we'll see her again one day. You still have no anger or ill will toward her?"

"She did a terrible thing. But no, I forgave her, and I think I even partially understand why she set me up for Leonov. I believe she had no idea that he planned to rape me. But I'm still confused."

"What, Lili?"

"It's God again. How He works is what I don't understand."

"That's what makes Him God and all of us His creation. You'll never figure out how, why, or when, Lili; that's where faith and trust come in."

"But when bad things happen that He could prevent, how do we trust they won't happen to us?"

"First, you have to understand that God gave us free will. We're not puppets on a string. And when people make bad decisions, there are consequences for their actions. Consequences that affect innocent people."

"Like Hitler's decisions, which brought destruction to millions who were in the way?"

"Yes, that's a perfect example on a grand scale. But it's the same on a smaller scale. When Larisa Lyasin and Anton Leonov choose to do evil, their actions had severe consequences for themselves and you. But the point is, God wasn't responsible for what happened to you or Larisa, and He isn't responsible for the carnage we see all around us."

"I think I understand, Jürgen. But how can we ever feel safe and know that bad things won't happen to us? And if we can't feel safe, what do we trust God for?"

"When you asked Jesus to be the Lord of your life, He never guaranteed a perfect life without pain. The promise He gave us is that He will be with us through the pain and bring us out on the other side. And many times His method of deliverance is miraculous. But remember what we talked about before, Lili. We live in a world that's decaying under the cumulative effect of man's wrong choices—man's sin. And we have to live in that corrupt world where the rain falls on the just and unjust. But have faith and look up, sweetheart, we have a Savior that can deliver us out of all our calamities."

"Now I understand it better. But it's still hard to go on seeing what's happening around us and not be able to do anything about it. Thanks, though, talking it out helps me come to grips with it all."

"That's my girl. With God's help, time will start to work healing in your life for both the attack and the tragedy with Larisa."

"I hope so. I'm so weary of it all. Not just what's happened to me but for all the young men on both sides that either lost their lives or will never be the same."

"I am too, sweetie. I'm going to my billet now. Get some rest, Lili."

Each night when Jürgen and Lili laid their heads down, they thought of home and family. Neither had heard a word about their families for several years. The uncertainty was the worst part. Jürgen often thought about Lisbeth, knowing the horror she must be going through, just hoping she was still alive. Only the good times came to mind. He longed for her body to warm him in the chill of the night and ached to have her arms around him again.

Jürgen also thought of and prayed for Didi often. Jürgen deeply regretted the way his oldest son dealt with the disappointments in his life. Maybe if he had handled difficulties better, he wouldn't have gone down the wrong road. The rest of the children and Sophie were in his thoughts often. Each day he mentioned their names before the Lord many times, hoping they were all safe.

Lili and Jürgen yearned for the day when they would return home and see their loved ones. Lili feared for her brothers. She prayed that God would preserve them and that one day she would see each of them again. Lili also had great concern for her parents, not knowing what life in Germany held for them.

After the day shift on June 29, Colonel Dobrynin informed all hospital staff that they would be tearing down and moving at daylight. All the wounded would go east to rehabilitation hospitals, and the hundreds of corpses would stay there.

The Russians outnumbered the Germans in troops and equipment, allowing them to break through German lines all along the Belorussian front. The Operation Bagration strength of the Russians was nearly two million, twice as many as the Germans could muster. They also had many times the number of tanks, artillery pieces, mortars, and aircraft. Russian partisans, paramilitary who fought a guerrilla war against the Axis forces, were effective in damaging German rail and communication lines before the operation began.

By late afternoon, the trucks loaded with staff and equipment of the Sixty-Fifth Surgical Hospital left their temporary location east of Orsha. No one except Colonel Dobrynin and those in the lead truck knew where they were going. The caravan headed west again to follow the front as it pushed the enemy back. They entered the devastation that once was the city of Orsha. Time hadn't allowed the Russians to remove all the bodies, mostly German, from the streets.

"My God, they haven't even gathered up the bodies, or covered them!" said Lili.

"It's retribution," Sergey said. "They had to show the people that they would avenge the murder of their loved ones."

"It's not right! So many are just boys."

"How many of our young boys have you tried to save, Major Behrmann? It's the face of war."

"I think I'm getting sick," Lili said.

"Turn away, Lili. Don't torture yourself," Jürgen replied.

"I can't. What if my brothers are stacked along the road?"

As they proceeded, they saw the Russians unceremoniously marching German prisoners down the side of the road. "Are they going to their deaths; somewhere in a Russian Gulag?" asked Lili.

"Dear God, the fear in their faces," Jürgen said.

"I can almost see Rudolf or Marvin. God, please don't let them be in a gulag or grave," Lili said.

"Don't look, Lili."

"Shouldn't we be in that line, Jürgen?"

"It breaks my heart. All these men and boys are going into hell, and yet, here we are, safe."

"For a long time I thought you should both be in a gulag," Sergey said. "Now I don't think so. You've saved too many lives."

Jürgen and Lili looked at each other without saying another word. Each knew what the other was thinking: "What moral ground are we standing on?"

By sunset, the four-hour journey west ended when the caravan crossed the Berezina River and went four kilometers to a location south of Barysaw. Hundreds of soldiers and civilians unloaded the trucks and erected tents. But it would be after midnight before billets were ready so the staff of the Sixty-Fifth could settle in and try to get some rest before the next day's trials.

By early afternoon of the following day, the operating and hospital tents were up and stocked, ready to receive patients who were already on the way. By that evening, Jürgen and Lili began tending to the wounded coming from the southwest.

The Second and Fifth Guards Tank Corps, with the Sixty-Fifth Army, were pummeling Minsk, just sixty-five kilometers to the south and west. The Russians expected to liberate the city in a few days. However, they knew casualties would be high for both the Germans and Russians.

There were many mobile field hospitals near the front lines like the Sixty-Fifth and five large hospitals behind the lines ready for the wounded. Thousands of Russian soldiers lost their lives in operations around Minsk, while thousands more went to field hospitals. German casualties were even worse. One hundred thousand soldiers in the region died or went to prisoner of war camps. Few escaped Minsk, and with little medical care available the wounded were fortunate to survive.

Through eastern and central Lithuania to central Belorussia, down to west-central Ukraine, the massive Operation Bagration inflicted a humiliating defeat on the retreating German armies. With the massive loss of men and equipment, the Wehrmacht never recovered. The Russians gutted Army Group Center and weakened Army Groups North and North Ukraine. They were cut off from each other and had to divert resources to help Army Group Center. Each army group eventually retreated from occupied Russian territories. The Germans suffered over four hundred thousand casualties, while the Russians lost under two hundred thousand men. Wounded Russian soldiers topped half a million, overwhelming dozens of field hospitals.

Jürgen never wanted to face such conditions again. Each day in triage they made gut-wrenching life-and-death decisions.

Thousands died because there wasn't enough blood. Also, morphine and other essential supplies were soon scarce, intensifying the anguish and madness. For Jürgen and Lili, it seemed worse than the horrors at Clearing Station II.

But time moved on and so did the Sixty-Fifth. It continued traveling west following the Soviet Army into Poland. On July 28, they packed up and trucked southwest for two days, finally arriving at Sokol Poland, sixteen kilometers east of Bialystok. From there they moved on to Stajadla, twenty-two kilometers east of Warsaw. And then on January 18, 1945, they traveled to Ownice, sixteen kilometers southeast of Kustrin, a German town just west of the Oder River.

The Sixty-Fifth was busy at each location as thousands of soldiers passed through their operating tents. The Russians were pushing hard toward the prize of Berlin, but the Germans were countering with all their might despite their decreased capacity to do so. Fortunately for the wounded, blood supplies and stocks of medicine improved, though there never was enough.

The long hours and intense pressure were physically and mentally grueling for Jürgen and Lili. Some days they struggled to hang on. At fifty-two, Jürgen's body was wearing down quickly with the fourteen-hour days and inadequate caloric intake to bear such a rigorous schedule. The endless struggle had compromised Jürgen's immune system, and he struggled to fight a virus with the onset of winter. Lili was faring a little better, as she spent half of her twelve-hour days in the operating tent and half in the hospital.

Everyone spent most of their waking hours working. There was little time for eating and sleeping, and almost no time to relax. The only time that brought comfort and spiritual support to Lili and Jürgen was the few hours a week they could spend together. They talked, prayed, and sometimes held each other, letting the strength from one flow to the other. Their bond was stronger than that of most fathers and daughters.

On the evening of February 2, 1945, there was a much-needed lull in new arrivals at the Sixty-Fifth field hospital, finally allowing staff a few hours of relaxation. Jürgen and Lili were leaving the mess tent when Victor Dobrynin asked them to join him to discuss an important matter and have a shot of vodka.

Jürgen was coughing and wheezing as they trudged through the snow to the colonel's tent. "You have to go on sick call," Lili urged for the third time.

"No. I'll feel the same whether I'm lying in a bed or standing at an operating table. The wounded need every doctor."

"But you're going to break down completely!"

"I won't, Lili. I'll fight through it like I always do."

That didn't reassure Lili. She was genuinely concerned, and probably for selfish reasons, she thought. Nonetheless, she couldn't fathom going on without the man she not only leaned on but loved and respected more than anyone in the world except her father.

As they drew near Dobrynin's tent, they saw Sergey Azarov waiting for them. The colonel wasn't expecting him but invited him in for a drink. Dobrynin's orderly had stoked up the fire in the old wood-burning stove to make it comfortable in the commander's quarters. The tent had a small table and four chairs close to the stove. As Victor brought out four glasses and a fresh bottle of vodka, he invited his guests to have a seat.

Victor Dobrynin had grown fonder of Lili as the months passed. He couldn't help admiring her resilience and determination, and her strong desire to make it home someday. After the attack, his feelings for her intensified. It surprised him at how angry he was at the perpetrator, and how bad he felt for Lili. He believed he couldn't love a daughter any more than the young German woman who was noticeably aging before his eyes.

Young Azarov was infatuated with Lili from the first day he saw her face, even though their relationship got off to a rocky start. They both had to work through the emotional devastation of her attack. Lili was in Sergey's debt for saving her and Jürgen's lives, but she wasn't ready to consider an intimate relationship. Though, over time, she thought she might be able to get close to the handsome Lieutenant. She was no longer suppressing her feelings she started to have for him, although she still resented that he had been intimate with other nurses.

"Tell me, Jürgen, can you continue to operate?" asked Colonel Dobrynin.

"Yes, but honestly I should take a couple of days' rest to shake this bug—right Lili?"

"He needs more than that, Colonel," Lili said. "Please admit him to the hospital where someone will make him take care of himself."

"Lili, I've told you that's not necessary."

"I have to agree with Lili on this one, Jürgen," Dobrynin said. "I know you won't do it on your own, so I'm ordering that you report to admittance. Five days of rest and medical attention should get you on the road to recovery."

"Looks like everyone's ganging up on me. Are we here for that, or is there something else you wanted to talk about?"

"I called you here to discuss something requiring that you be in the best health possible."

"That sounds ominous, sir," Lili said.

"No, Lili, dangerous, but we need to do it soon. Something I know both of you are looking forward to."

"What are you driving at, Victor?" Jürgen said.

"The war is winding down, and Germany will surrender by summer, if not before. We're close enough to Germany for your service with the Sixty-Fifth Surgical Hospital to end. That's what we need to discuss. Of course what we say never goes beyond the four of us."

Everyone swore to secrecy.

"We've thought about this a lot, so tell me what you're thinking, Victor."

"The way I see it, Jürgen, the next time we get a request for medical support from a forward aid station, I'll send the three of you. But only Sergey will show up at the aid station, saying he was the only one available to make the trip. When he returns, he'll say the Germans ambushed you, and he was the only survivor."

"What will we do and where will we go?" Lili asked.

"That's what we have to decide," Victor replied. "Over the next week, I'll gather as much information as I can about troop locations and what you can expect as you go west. You still have your German identification papers, and we'll give you civilian clothes. You'll have to carefully make your way to a safe place in Germany. It won't be easy, but it's the only chance you have to make it home.

"Just so you know, I'm disgusted, even appalled at the way our soldiers have gotten completely out of hand," the colonel continued. "I know you've heard the stories: murders, rapes, and destruction of property—it's atrocious and shameful. They're reacting to the horrors we uncovered as we moved through the villages and towns in western Russian that were wiped out by Hitler's death squads. Even so, there's no excuse for becoming barbarians and killing more innocent people. You'll have to be doubly careful out there to avoid both the Russian and German armies."

"We'll have to hole up someplace until the battlefront moves further west and then cautiously find our way home," Jürgen said.

"I don't understand how we'll do that, Jürgen; where do we hide? Where will we stay?"

"I don't know yet, Lili. We'll be in our country, but it'll be too dangerous to trust anyone. We can't face questions about who we are and where we've been. We'll have to trust God each step of the way."

"I know you've both wrestled with it for two years, but how will you look back on your time serving the Russian army?" Dobrynin asked.

"You know, Colonel, I'm a doctor. I took an oath to help the sick and injured. I may have been working in a Russian army hospital, but I've only served the wounded men who needed our medical attention. That's how I'll always look at it."

"You're right, Jürgen, that's the way we'll look at it, and the way I'll present it if it comes to that," Lili said.

"We've discussed this too many times, Victor, but that's the only way we could live with the decision we made."

"But you never supported what Hitler and the Nazis were doing, Major. You passively resisted them before the war, so what's wrong with being against them during the war?" Sergey said.

"There's a big difference between passive resistance and being a traitor to your country, Sergey. And you know that's how they'll look at us."

"I suppose, but who else was ever put in your position? Probably no one," Sergey said. "Who was crazy enough to pull that escape stunt with a Russian ambulance? And then by chance, come across wounded Russian soldiers, saving the life of one of them who happened to be the son of the colonel in charge. And then because of those actions, have the choice to save Russian soldiers instead of dying with your countrymen in a faraway prisoner of war camp.

"I'm not a man of faith, Jürgen. But the circumstances that led you and Lili to this point, more than anything else might persuade me to consider the possibility."

"Someday I hope you do, Sergey. I know it's amazing, and I believe God's been with us every step of the way. He wanted us to care for those young men who needed the healing skills He gave us," Jürgen said.

"But I'm different," Lili said. "I was a devout Nazi from when I was little. My parents were in the party from the twenties, and they raised me in the girls' Hitler Youth. We gladly supported everything the Nazis did. We wholeheartedly supported the war and thought it was just to correct previous wrongs and bring all people of German heritage into the Third Reich."

"What changed you, dear?"

"I couldn't possibly understand the horror of war until I was in the middle of its brutality, and I saw the devastating results. Reality stopped me in my tracks, and I had to reconsider what everyone had taught me for years. But honestly, Colonel, the man you're looking at across the table is the one who changed the way I now look at everything. I know you don't understand, but he introduced me to God, and I soon learned our country and what they were doing was far from His will."

"That's a sincere and honest answer, Lili," Dobrynin replied. "Like Sergey, it almost brings me to the point of seeking a relationship with your God."

"I wish you both would, sir, it would be something you'd never regret," Lili said.

"Maybe someday I will. But for now, we need to get you checked into the hospital, Jürgen."

* * *

With her medical training, weapons skills, and strong-willed self-control, Klara Kovalik started going on missions with Didi and her brothers in the early spring of 1944. The Germans sensed the war was slipping away and their remaining time in Belorussia was short. Therefore, they were becoming more brutal by the week. German death squads were attacking more frequently and with more ferocity, heightening fears and increasing the need to take action to stop them.

As tensions rose on the farms, Didi and Klara drew closer to the Gulin family. The women spent much of their waking time together. Elana, just turning seven, and Oleg, now five, loved Galina, now fifteen months old. They took turns watching her when their mothers were doing chores or away for a break. Anna and Klara talked for hours at a time, about everything under the sun. They became as close as sisters—like the sister Klara never had but always wanted.

It had been almost a year since Victor violated Klara, and thoughts of that awful day still haunted her waking hours, although her nightmares were decreasing. She was more successful in suppressing the thoughts as time passed, but with Didi's struggles, sometimes she felt burdened to the breaking point. She never told anyone about that horrible day. Klara wanted to tell Anna that she felt so guilty and dirty in betraying her husband, but she never did.

As May arrived, Didi's nightmares intensified. One night Klara went into the kitchen for a drink. Didi was sitting with his head on the kitchen table. No one else was on the first floor of the large old farmhouse. "Oh! I didn't know you were here, darling. Did I wake you?"

"I can't sleep here or in our bed," Didi whispered as he always did, knowing someone might be close by. Klara stroked his hair softly. "This is driving me crazy, Klara. I have to know what's behind these damn dreams. It has to end!"

"Keep your voice down. It'll come out in time. I wish I could help somehow."

"I want to know, but the worst thing is that I'm so damned scared of what I'll find out. Does that make sense?"

"Of course it does, Didi. I'm also afraid of what the truth might reveal and do to you—to us."

"At least you know how I feel and what I fear, Klara. I'm so afraid my mind is hiding something horrible that I did, and I won't be able to handle it."

"No matter what, we need to find out soon. Not tonight though; let's go up and try to get some sleep."

On June 8, 1944, Didi, Klara, Igor, and Anton were in the kitchen eating dinner. Peter rushed in and said, "We've been assigned to conduct an emergency raid as soon as possible." He had just returned from a day trip to the north. "Yesterday, the village of Valeuka was occupied by the Germans. We need to get there before it's too late."

Peter quickly assembled a strike team, and they headed north within the hour. Fourteen men and Klara hiked forty-five kilometers through secluded woods and plains arriving in Valeuka the next day. They used their binoculars to scout the small village from a stand of trees two hundred meters to the south. As reported, there was a detachment of German soldiers milling around the village. Peter and Igor counted seven vehicles and thirty-two men. Peter knew from experience this was a death squad ready to unleash its fury on the poor folk of Valeuka.

As they discussed an attack plan, Didi glanced toward the stand of trees west of the village. And there she was. Didi closed his eyes and shook his head, and then he slowly opened his eyes again. He couldn't believe it; she was still there, standing in front of a tree, slowly waving him over with her right hand. It was the little girl who had visited his dreams for the past month. But there was something else that he sensed about her. He just couldn't remember what it was, no matter how hard he tried. Didi knew the girl wasn't real, but he also knew what he saw was. But why? What did these appearances and dreams mean? What was he missing? After a few seconds, she was gone, and Didi turned his attention to Peter who was giving instructions. He wouldn't tell Klara or her brothers about what he saw.

Toward sunset, there was an audible commotion coming from the village. As Peter looked through his binoculars, he saw the Germans rounding up the villagers. Peter and the others suspected the worst and prepared to take action to prevent a massacre. Within minutes, the German detachment was marching over a hundred men, women, and children toward the woods to the west.

The fifteen partisans sneaked to the west side of the woods, as the Germans and their prisoners entered a clearing fifty meters to their north. Didi and Klara nestled down behind logs. They could clearly see through the trees to view what was happening. After having them dig trenches, the Germans stripped the citizens of their valuables and physically abused them.

Peter quietly gave the order to stand by for his instruction to fire. They were confident in their ability to take down the German soldiers quickly, hopefully saving most of the villagers. Within seconds, the soldiers lined up a group of women and children in front of the nearest trench. The partisans waited for the command to fire, easily seeing the fearful faces of those waiting to die.

Then Didi's eyes fixed on one girl toward the left end of the line. She was a beautiful child of eight or nine, with pleading eyes. Suddenly his mind went blank, and it seemed that time stopped. Soon after that, the dam burst and all the horrible memories—long since suppressed—came exploding back. He instantly remembered everything. The young girl he was looking at wasn't unlike the one he murdered three years ago. In a flash, Didi relived every detail of the moment the girl's chest exploded when the bullets from his rifle ripped through her small body. Before he fired, he vividly remembered her pleading eyes asking, "Why, oh why are you doing this to me?"

Didi banged his forehead against the log in front of him as hard as he could, trying to dull the agonizing pain flooding his mind. He bit down hard on his cheeks to mute the frightening scream involuntarily coming from his mouth. Klara, Peter, and Igor looked around quickly to see what happened as did many of the Germans who heard Didi scream.

"Fire!" Peter yelled. Immediately the partisans, except for Didi, opened fire with their automatic weapons. The Germans quickly turned away from their victims and started returning fire toward the wooded area. But it was too late, the Germans were out in the open and easy pickings for the sharpshooting resistance force. It was over soon, and the twenty-seven Germans were all down, most of them dead. The remaining few were severely wounded and no longer a threat. As the gun battle began, the five Germans still in the village ran toward the partisans' location with rifles blazing. But the partisans also cut them down. Two partisans were hit but not badly. And thankfully, only one villager died and four were wounded.

For several minutes after the battle ended, Didi didn't lift his face out of the grass. Klara dreaded what she saw and heard, instinctively knowing what had happened to her husband, who was crying uncontrollably in the grass at her feet. It all confused Peter, Igor, and the others, not understanding how or why Didi let out such a blood-curdling scream or why he was having a total breakdown.

Didi was still in a daze as Igor and Klara finally got him to his feet. He remained in a partial fog on the trek back to the farm. His condition stunned everyone. Peter sharply rebuked Didi for putting the operation in jeopardy, demanding to know why he let out such a blood-curdling scream. Didi didn't answer Peter or anyone else questioning him, looking past them with glazed eyes. Three days later, he finally came to grips with his horrible revelation at Valeuka. That night, Didi cried in Klara's arms. "If you know, Didi, let it all come out. Free yourself from it once and for all—please!"

"After three days I still don't think I can say it. Thinking about it tears my guts out, Klara!"

"What is it, Didi?" You have to talk about it and let the healing begin."

Didi was shaking as he sat down. "How can I, Klara? There's no way you'll understand or be able to forgive me."

"I know it's bad, but I'll understand. I have to forgive anything that you did."

"I'll try." Trembling, Didi said nothing for a minute. "The memories I lost were from a period when I was assigned to a German death squad."

"Oh God! I was afraid it would be something like that. I'm sorry, Didi."

"I murdered an innocent girl, Klara! She exploded right in front of me! I'll never get that sight out of my mind. It'll haunt me the rest of my days, and it should. How can you, God, Father, or Netti ever forgive me? I'll never forgive myself. I hate myself for what I did!"

Klara pulled Didi up into her arms as he sobbed uncontrollably. "I don't understand why you were in that hellish position, but I know you're a caring person Didi. There's nothing for me to forgive."

"The awful thing is, Klara, I don't know why I was there. I don't know if I ever will."

Klara loved Didi so much, she could forgive any offense. And she ached for his forgiveness for something she would never have the courage to tell him.

The healing and restoration of Didi Behrmann began that warm June night in western Belorussia. It wouldn't be an easy journey for the deeply wounded twenty-eight-year-old, seeking absolution that might never come. But that night he surely learned one thing: Klara would always love him and stand by him, no matter what. She now knew his dark, horrible sin, but she still loved him. He would forever be thankful for that, the only healing balm to his soul.

July and August came and went as the summer crops flourished on the partisan farms near Baranovichi. In July, the Germans made one last visit to pillage what they could as they retreated. Operation Bagration was slowly pushing the Wehrmacht west; then, suddenly, the land around the farming commune was under Russian control. There was a great celebration until it became obvious the Russian Army wasn't their friend either. The farmers quickly realized they were just as brutal and ruthless as the Germans. In particular, they were looking for Russian Army deserters and locals who were complicit in helping the Germans.

Fortunately, Peter Gulin, second in command of the Forty-Fifth Belorussian Resistance Detachment, could detail his heroic actions in fighting the Germans to his uncle, a colonel in the advancing Russian army. They eventually absolved Peter of deserting the army three years before. But he had to rejoin the army as it moved west. They gave him only ten days to move his family back to Minsk, before reporting for duty.

Peter also had glowing words for Didi and Klara. And the Russian officer interrogating them bought the ruse that Didi was a deaf-mute. He approved issuing new identification cards for each.

It was September when Didi and Klara accompanied the Gulins on their return to Minsk. Igor and Anton returned to their home in Lisok to help their mother, who they hoped was still alive.

Peter settled his family with Anna's Uncle Joseph, who still had a habitable house on the outskirts of Minsk. He lived alone as his wife, Tanya, died of cancer the year before and their two sons were somewhere with the Russian army. The house was damaged but satisfactory to hold the Gulins and Didi's family.

Shortly after arriving in Minsk, Didi expressed through Klara his strong wish to find his mother who lived near Warsaw before the war. It puzzled them to hear the story about Alexey's mother for the first time. Klara said he hardly spoke of his mother, the only one left in his family, but now felt a strong urge to find her and forgive her for neglecting him. Peter and Anna had no reason to doubt Alexey's story or their need to leave Minsk, so they didn't question him or Klara further. Again, Didi and Klara had successfully put forth another ruse.

Didi still suffered under the weight of his guilt. He knew making it home would give him the best chance to unburden himself. He needed his family's forgiveness, not only for the murder he committed but for everything he did to them before the war. He had to get there as soon as he could or risk losing his mind. But Didi would never leave Klara behind, and Klara would never let Didi go alone. However, each knew it would be an impossible journey with Galina.

After expressing their concerns, Anna offered to take care of Galina until Didi and Klara returned for her after the war. Klara hated the idea of leaving her daughter for so long. But Didi, Anna, and Peter tried to convince her that it was the only sensible choice. Everyone knew it was an agonizing decision, knowing it might be many months before they saw their baby again. They finally accepted Anna's offer, having no reasonable alternative.

Peter left to join the Russian army the following day. He embraced Didi and Klara, thanking them graciously for all they did for the Forty-Fifth and for their true friendship. He tenderly hugged and kissed Anna, then kissed Elana and Oleg and said good-bye. He waved to them as he walked down the street toward Minsk.

Didi and Klara waited impatiently in Minsk until they had the assurance of getting safely into eastern Poland. From there they weren't sure how they'd get to Germany, but knew they had to try. Finally, in December, a unique opportunity arose to ride with a Russian officer and his wife to Bialystok, Poland. They immediately accepted the offer.

Saying goodbye to Galina was bitterly hard for Klara, not knowing when she would see her again. But she stiffened her resolve, believing her husband wouldn't survive to see his home and family again without her help. He wasn't ready to cope with all the potential pitfalls on the journey without her continuous love and support. Didi, too, felt the heavy burden of leaving Galina behind.

From Bialystok, the couple carefully worked their way west, arriving in Bydgoszcz in January. The journey was perilous. Both the Russian and Polish armies detained them. They were robbed, assaulted, and threatened. Both went days without food and suffered frostbite when there was no place to stay on cold nights. But somehow they made it two-thirds of the way across Poland.

They both said it was miraculous that they found a Christian family in Bydgoszcz who took them in from the cold and dangerous streets. The family fed them and kept them warm for ten days before sending them on their way with heavy coats and a knapsack full of food. And most important, they arranged for their transport to Krzeszyce in the back of a delivery truck returning there. They had a close call at one checkpoint when soldiers shined flashlights into the back of the truck, empty except for one large box that Didi and Klara had crouched behind.

January waned as the weary travelers reached the small town only thirty kilometers from the Oder River, which they hoped to cross soon. It was amazing how they kept finding people willing to help them. A pastor and two nuns from a small Catholic parish had big hearts and a dangerous ministry of helping people in dire circumstances. They stayed with the good folks at the parish for two weeks before they arranged for their transport across the Oder and down to Frankfurt an der Oder.

On February 10, 1945, Didi, Klara, and another young couple left Krzeszyce in a panel truck. They dressed as priests and nuns on a mission of mercy. When they were halfway to Kustrin,

Germany, they found themselves in the middle of a gun battle between a Polish militia unit and a trapped squad of Wehrmacht soldiers.

They couldn't stop in time before shots started hitting the truck. A bullet hit the young driver in the head and the truck skidded to a stop. The young woman next to him ducked, but it was too late. She was also mortally wounded when two bullets struck her in the chest.

Didi and Klara crouched down in the back of the truck, and for the first time in years, he prayed. He asked God to protect them and get them home safely. After five minutes, the shots stopped. They waited another five minutes and then carefully exited the truck through the rear doors. They were walking around to the passenger's door when out of the night came four German soldiers. They desperately wanted to escape in the truck, having no interest in the lives of anyone who got in their way. They started firing as they approached, and both Didi and Klara fell to the cobblestone road with multiple gunshot wounds. The German soldiers pulled the dead bodies out of the front seat, and the panel truck was soon heading into the night toward Germany.

Didi was fading as he lifted his head enough to see Klara. She was less than a meter away and not moving. He could hear her wheezing, so he knew she was still alive. Didi tried to move to her side and comfort her, but he couldn't. All he could do was lay his head back down on the road. Just before darkness overtook Didi, he heard Klara whisper, "Please forgive me, Didi—I'm sorry."

7

Rails to the End

"Run, father, hurry!" Johann said.

Jacob turned enough to see four young men pass them, running as fast as they could down Lagiewnicka.

"Don't stop! Get out of the street!" Johann yelled at his father. An automobile roared in pursuit of the men on foot. Jacob saw two boys, maybe eight or nine, were in the street as the auto bore down on them.

"Get out of the street!" Jacob pleaded.

The auto went over the curb as it swerved to miss the boys. It was heading directly for Jacob and Johann. Johann shoved his father out of the way, but in doing so he slipped to the pavement. The auto's right front wheel went over Johann's left leg, below the knee.

"Owww," screamed Johann in unbearable pain. "Help, father, help me, oh my God, make the pain stop, please!"

Jacob was soon at his son's side, as Johann rolled back and forth, yelling loudly for the pain to stop. His left leg had a compound fracture and there was blood on the sidewalk. Some men gathered to see what happened, and Jacob asked if they could help carry his son to the clinic two blocks over on Chopina.

With their aid, Jacob managed to get his son to the illicit medical clinic that he had learned about only a few days before. Jacob was now in shock and had stopped screaming. He only moaned softly as he neared unconsciousness. Fortunately, an elderly Jewish doctor and young nurse were at the clinic, and they stabilized Johann. They gave him contraband morphine for his pain, cleaned, and splinted his leg as best they could, and used nearly a bottle of antiseptic before bandaging his leg. The doctor tried to set the bones. "The tibia and fibula are badly crushed below the knee. They'll never heal properly without delicate surgery in a well-equipped hospital, something not available in the ghetto."

After monitoring Johann for two hours, the clinic transported Johann and Jacob back to 7 Dolna Street. It was dark as two men helped Jacob carry Johann up the stairs to the second floor and down the hall to apartment 228.

Trudi had been pacing the floor for two hours, wondering where her husband and Jacob were. They were always home from work on time, and she sensed that something was terribly wrong. Trudi was afraid and anxious, and it was spreading quickly to Lisbeth, Sophie, and Isabell.

They all heard muffled voices coming up the hall, but they never opened the door to anyone unless they knew who it was. Then there was a loud knock, followed by Jacob's demand to open the door.

Trudi quickly opened the door and saw Jacob and two other men holding Johann so he wouldn't fall. He was semi-conscious, muttering something that no one understood.

Trudi yelled, "God no! What happened to you, Johann?"

"An accident," Jacob said. "Let's get him to bed quickly."

The three men carried him to the bedroom and lay him carefully on his bed.

Jacob thanked the two men from the clinic as they walked out the door. Then he explained what had happened to Trudi and the others. As Jacob talked, Trudi sat on the bed next to her husband, rubbing his face gently and whispering words of encouragement. It baffled everyone that Trudi was now calm and didn't shed a tear. Having no time to think of herself, her focus was only on soothing her husband.

The next three weeks were agonizing for Johann, who was in constant pain—pain like he had never felt before. Trudi and Jacob took Johann back to the clinic three times to see what the doctor could do for him. He was able to supply morphine to help with the pain and redress and re-splint his leg. He told them the pain would gradually subside, but the leg would never heal properly, most likely leaving him with a permanent limp.

With life in the ghetto becoming harsher by the day, this unfortunate incident made everything worse, sending the normally positive Johann into an extended period of depression. However, by June 1944, twelve weeks after the accident, the pain was bearable, though his mental anguish continued to build. But with the support of Sophie, Isabell, and Jacob, Trudi stayed strong as she attended to Johann.

While Jacob and the women ministered to Johann, Syma, one of the women they shared the apartment with and who worked in the ghetto's administration office, convinced the Jewish Commission that soon he would be able to return to his job at the carpenter's shop. Because of her efforts, they didn't classify Johann as *no value* and transit him out of the ghetto. Syma's intercession, which again required that she give herself to Chaim Rumkowski's assistant, saved Johann's life.

Thanks to Syma, Trudi was also able to get extra time off from her position at the groceries and bread section of the Jewish Administration Supplies Department, so she could minister to Johann. They spent time in prayer and reading the Torah, Talmud, and Psalms, which eventually released Johann from the depression that was dragging him down. But what brought back Johann's spirit and resolve more than anything else was the exhilaration he felt in witnessing Trudi's spiritual growth in embracing the faith he loved.

In the twenty months since their wedding, Trudi had nurtured her newfound faith, which seemed strange to some but most at the Dolna Street apartment applauded it. She studied daily with Jacob and Johann to learn as much as she could about the Jewish faith. She also took part with them in their weekly Sabbath ceremonies and all holy day observances. But one issue continued to trouble Johann and Jacob.

"Why, Trudi, do you still hold on to your belief in Jesus when our teachings clearly show that we're still looking for Messiah?"

"I'm sorry, Johann. The last thing I want to do is offend you and your father. I can't get Netti's Jesus out of my mind and heart. I've seen Him move in Netti's and our family's lives too many times. How can I deny my experience, Johann? How can I change what I feel even though I believe what you and Jacob say?"

"But you've said that you never took Jesus as your Lord as Netti wanted you to—never went to church or followed the Christian religion."

"I never did, though at times I wanted to. But I just can't deny Him, Johann. What else can I say?"

"But the texts from the Nevi'im Aharonim that we've studied, Trudi—"

"I know. We've studied the prophets a lot, and it seems like Messiah hasn't come. But every year Netti read Isaiah 53 to us. And each year she gave a thorough explanation of how this depicted our suffering servant, Jesus, how we're healed and made whole by his stripes. I believe that Johann."

"No, Trudi, Isaiah refers to Israel, not Jesus."

"I honor what you and Jacob have taught me, but I can't change what I feel in my heart. I embrace the religion of my heritage, but I can't deny the Christian influence on my life either. I love you, Johann. Can we leave it at that?"

"I don't understand, Trudi, or have a choice. So yes, we'll drop it for now. I love you too much to let this come between us."

In summer 1944, the Litzmannstadt Ghetto's population was down to seventy thousand, a decrease of 75 percent since 1940. If disease and starvation didn't take the weak, the transports to Chelmno did. Most knew that the transports—supposedly to work on farms or in factories in Germany—were really one-way trips to the grave. Now there was a strong sense among many that the end was near for those remaining. All assurances of a short war had long since vanished.

Food and other essentials for survival were in scarce supply. As spring came, Sophie knew that her shoebox full of ration cards was losing its value as there was little food or anything else to exchange them for. Now it would only be Syma's position in the Jewish Administration Office, and Chaim Rumkowski's feelings of remorse for her, that would provide for the needs of those in apartment 228. But it was the close bonds formed over time that helped them most, as living conditions became harsher.

Lisbeth's love for Gela and Gesza increased over the months, and she thought of them as her own. Syma didn't understand nor care much for it, but she never said anything. Trudi and Sophie suspected it was Lisbeth's way of making up for her lack of mothering to Netti. It was also obvious that Lisbeth was trying to make everything right with Trudi, and she was also drawing closer to Sophie.

The three women from Cologne and Isabell spent hours each week teaching the girls German. Their parents thought it was a waste of time, but the girls begged them to continue. They eagerly soaked up the teaching and showed an incredible ability for picking up the new language. With six people in the apartment speaking to them in German, by the spring of 1944 they were surprisingly fluent in speaking the language and satisfactory in reading and writing it.

Teaching the girls brought them all closer, and Gela and Gesza loved them all, but especially Lisbeth, who poured her soul into both girls. They had no one their age to play with. Their entire socialization came from the adults in the apartment, and Lisbeth affected them most.

March 10 had been Gesza's ninth birthday, and Lisbeth and Trudi wanted to make it a special day. And with the misfortune of Isak Reznik, everyone needed to do something positive to lift their dampened spirits.

Lisbeth had sadly recalled Netti's ninth birthday in 1927. Didi and Waldo had painstakingly planned everything, with Jürgen's help, to make it Netti's most unforgettable birthday. Everything that went into the party helped to seal Netti and Waldo's special bond. She recalled that Netti was surprised and thrilled by everything about her party. She also recalled Netti commenting about how Kora beamed and had such a good time at the party. Lisbeth lamented that Kora never had the chance to see her eighth birthday that June. But Lisbeth's recollection of the party was only from what others had told her. She was in the midst of a month-long depression at the time and was upstairs drinking through the entire party. She regretted her absence and now, with Gesza reaching her ninth birthday, it was all coming back to her—the anger and sorrow of being so selfish and neglecting her daughter. Lisbeth vowed not to miss a second chance to bless a precious daughter on her ninth birthday.

For Trudi, Gesza's birthday party was special because she had missed the last five birthdays of her daughters. Helene was soon to be seven and Hermine was now five. Each birthday she missed broke her heart, not having any idea about how her girls were doing or what hell they might be going through in Cologne. All Trudi could do was to focus her love on the little girls who were now a part of her daily life.

All the adults pitched in to make it a special birthday for Gesza. Janas and Isabell fashioned a beautiful dress and vest for Gesza at the tailor shop. At the cobbler shop Gimpel Warski made a pair of shoes fit for a princess. Jacob and Johann made a special top at the carpenter's shop, as well as a small but adorable dollhouse. Sophie and Trudi bought a special doll for Gesza. And Lisbeth gave her the beautiful silver brooch she had managed to hide from the authorities since arriving in the ghetto. Next to the wedding ring Jürgen gave her, it was her most prized possession.

Though the party wasn't a total surprise, Gesza's excitement and joy were heartwarming. She loved each gift, as any little girl living in such harsh circumstances would. She thanked each one in their own tongue for making it the best day she ever had. As she marveled at each gift, she smoothly transitioned between speaking

Polish and German, and Isabell kept very busy translating back and forth. Gesza came to Lisbeth last and hugged her neck as the fifty-six-year-old knelt down. Gesza whispered in her ear, "I love you so much, Auntie Lisbeth."

What amazed all was that Gela showed no sign of jealousy when they showered her little sister with lavish gifts. She was almost as joyous and excited as Gesza. If they didn't already know it, they all knew now what a loving girl Gela was. As it turned out, the birthday party in March had lifted everyone's spirits until Johann's accident.

A month before the birthday party, disaster threatened Sophie and the rest at the Dolna street apartment. It was midafternoon and Sophie was posting food deliveries repetitiously when Syma swiftly entered the office. She was noticeably upset as she addressed the office staff. Hubert Bloom interpreted for the German workers.

"I'm quite upset to tell you the Gestapo arrested Manfried Braun for illegally selling goods outside the ghetto. I'm not sure, but they might have shot him on the spot. From what I've learned, he used information from our files, even though he didn't have direct access to most of the records he would have needed. He put us all in grave danger, and that's why I'm so damned mad about what he did.

"It's expected that Gestapo investigators will show up here anytime, as they suspect he had accomplices, some probably working here. I know nothing about it, but if you're one of his conspirators, consider yourself warned."

Hubert looked directly at Sophie as he finished his translation. He knew nothing but suspected that Sophie and Manfried were doing something illegal.

Sophie knew she had to act quickly. She was grateful that Syma was giving her a chance in light of the danger she and Manfried put everyone in. If not for Sophie's scheme to save her daughter, Syma might have done nothing to help her.

Sophie immediately got up from her chair and went to Manfried's desk in the special deliveries section. Staff in that office watched her closely, so she had to be careful not to do anything suspicious. She knew that everything he had detailing their racket was in his Daily Merchandise Delivery ledger, locked in the left drawer of his desk. They had keys to each other's desks. Sophie unlocked the desk drawer, as those in the office had seen her do many times before. Then she pulled out the ledger and put it on the left side of his desk where it normally was during business hours. She casually returned to her desk and set her Master Residents log on it.

Everything about Manfried's and Sophie's clandestine scheme was in the thick ledger and log. Manfried always said the safest place to hide something is in plain sight. The ledger and log aroused little attention when sitting openly on their desks. After all, they were tedious books to the employees of both offices who never had much interest in looking at them unless their job required it. Sophie and Manfried entered new participants in the scheme in the same way they made all other entries, without raising any suspicion. When Syma and other managers looked at the ledger or log, they never knew that coded information detailing the whole scheme was right in front of them.

The two slick operators listed all the information needed to carry out their scheme for obtaining goods from ghetto residents and selling them to buyers outside the ghetto. The sellers were all in Sophie's Master Residents log, and the buyers were in Manfried's Daily Merchandise Delivery ledger. They placed the sellers only on lines three, eight, thirteen, and nineteen for pages where Sophie would make an almost undetectable red mark near the bottom. The lines in Sophie's ledger listed name, sex, age, physical rating, address, work location, occupation and work status, ration status, and identification number. For those Litzmannstadt residents selling to the outside world, Sophie coded the last two digits of their identification number to show the articles they were peddling. These numbers matched the product numbers in the Merchandise Confiscation ledger that many workers in both offices used. They listed the buyers similarly in Manfried's Daily Merchandise Delivery ledger, with names, addresses for pickup points, and coded numbers to identify the items they would buy. So, unknown to anyone else, all the buyers and sellers were in plain sight for anyone to see if they only knew what they were looking at.

They only matched buyers and sellers and never documented financial or delivery information. Manfried made all the currency exchanges and then paid his accomplices in Rumkies. His two partners, working outside Baluty Marketplace, had the goods ready for pickup each day that he delivered outside the ghetto. He picked up the goods before leaving the ghetto at the time the German escort joined him. The buyers always waited outside the normal delivery locations for the Jewish Commission. The German guard never paid attention to what was happening at each stop and usually saw none of the illicit transactions. If they did, they didn't know what they were seeing and didn't care. They mostly napped and then received their usual bottle of schnapps and pack of cigarettes at the end of the trip.

Within twenty minutes of Syma's announcement, Major Rudolph Kepler, assistant chief of the Gestapo in Litzmannstadt, entered the main headquarters building of the Jewish Commission with two SS officers and three armed soldiers. Syma was close behind them, holding her breath and praying that disaster wasn't near. She and Chaim Rumkowski had dealt with Kepler before, so she knew what a sonofabitch he was.

"What the hell kind of crooked operation are you running here, Berkowicz?" Kepler yelled as he turned to face Syma. Hubert Bloom was interpreting as he quickly got between the two.

"I know nothing about the incident and assure you that we do everything honestly. Leader Rumkowski isn't here today, but he would agree with me."

"Then tell me why someone working under your nose was selling items to citizens in Lodz—items clearly made in the ghetto?"

"I have no idea, sir; we reviewed his work ledger often. There is no hint of wrongdoing. Have you questioned him about it?"

"Oh, be sure that we did, before his demise. And we know he has conspirators who work in your office."

"Did he name any of them?"

"We have our suspicions, Frau. Let me see the log you keep for all ghetto residents and the person who keeps it."

Syma told Hubert to get Sophie and have her bring the Master Resident log.

Sophie could see the fear in Hubert's eyes, as she picked up the heavy logbook and walked slowly but confidently toward Syma. She laid the logbook down on a table and turned to face Syma and the major. Kepler asked Hubert to be extremely clear in interpreting his conversation with the woman.

"She's German, sir, you can talk to her directly," Hubert said.

"So, Frau, you're German?"

"Yes, sir."

"Tell me what you know about Herr Braun's scheme. And if you lie, your fate will be the same as his. Before you speak, also know that I have already gathered a lot of information about this conspiracy."

Sophie, quivering inside, boldly lifted her chin and looked directly into Kepler's eyes. "I know nothing of what you're talking about, sir." In quickly assessing the situation, Sophie knew the major was running a bluff that he assumed would elicit a confession.

"That's the wrong answer, Frau! Mendel isn't it—Sophie Mendel?"

"Yes, that's right."

"See, we've already checked around and know about your relationship with Herr Braun—your lover, I suppose."

"No, that's not true. We knew each other in Germany and by chance reestablished our friendship here as coworkers only."

"You expect me to believe that crap? I already told you I know all about the conspiracy that you had to be a part of."

"That's just wrong, sir! What makes you think I had anything to do with it?"

Sophie was trying to force the major's hand to see what he knew. Syma hoped she wasn't involved, and if she were that she would somehow talk her way out of the mess. While they talked, one of the SS officers carefully looked over the Master Resident log while another officer examined Manfried's Daily Merchandise Delivery ledger. The major said nothing more until he conferred with the officers who examined the documents.

"My experts tell me the documents you and Braun had control of are in order. Just one question though, what do the red lines in each document mean?"

"I can't speak to his ledger, but in my log, I've underlined inactive residents in red—you know, sent away or dead."

Kepler talked with one of the officers before turning his attention back to Sophie. He looked sternly into Sophie's eyes. "I don't believe you, Frau. You're lying, and we'll soon have proof that will condemn you to death. It's only a matter of time. We know where you live and work, and one day soon we'll settle this matter." He threw Sophie's logbook on the table and abruptly exited the building with his minions.

Sophie let out a muted sigh of relief as did Syma and Hubert. Syma told everyone to get back to work and then she asked Sophie and Hubert to come to her office.

"Tell me please, Sophie, that you had nothing to do with this."

"I didn't, Syma, and there'll never be any evidence that I did. You know the bastard was bluffing all along, just fishing to see what he could uncover. Don't worry, it'll all blow over and Kepler will move on to more important business."

"For your sake, he damned well better!"

They learned later that Major Kepler also had *his* hand in the cookie jar. In May the Gestapo implicated him in a fraudulent scheme to keep looted treasure for himself. So before he could discover who conspired with Manfried, the Gestapo executed him by firing squad. And no one else pursued the delivery scheme further. Syma and Hubert reserved their judgment, but they wondered about Sophie's involvement. Meanwhile, Sophie cleaned up everything at the office that could be incriminating, and she hid all their Rumkies in a safe place.

* * *

The winter months of 1944 were hard on the forty-four year old Russian, Isak Reznik. His entire family was gone. Isak tried to be a part of the budding family in the apartment, but he never felt he fit in there or any place else. His romantic experiences were one frustration after the other. He felt doomed to go through life without the companion he desperately wanted. But then he had a glimmer of hope that raised his spirits. He even dared to think there might be someone for him after all.

Lisbeth liked Isak and treated him with kindness. She felt the pain of his losses and through Isabel's interpretation always had comforting words for him. But she never had a romantic interest in Isak, though he and some others in the apartment thought that maybe she did. He knew that Lisbeth had already turned away Jacob's romantic overtures. However, Isak falsely hoped she might have feelings for him.

One night Isak found Lisbeth alone in her bedroom. "Isak, you scared me!" Lisbeth said as she suddenly turned around. He didn't understand what she said, but he realized that she was surprised and upset.

I'm sorry!" he said, as he moved closer to Lisbeth, putting an arm around her. She also didn't understand what Isak said. Lisbeth mistook his apology as a romantic advance.

"Get the hell away from me!" Lisbeth yelled as she shoved him away. "Get out—I hate you!"

Isak felt the hate in Lisbeth's reaction and saw it on her face. It cut like a knife through his already depressed spirit. He quickly left the bedroom and ran out of the apartment.

Lisbeth came to regret the way she handled the awkward moment, realizing her strong reaction crushed Isak's fragile spirit. From then on, Isak spent most of his nonworking hours alone with a bottle of vodka or whiskey. He hardly spoke to the others, and at times he seemed far away.

In late February, Isak stumbled his way down Dworska Street, going nowhere in particular. Night and day, he couldn't make the thoughts of failure and losses go away. Depression and the effect of alcohol made Isak unaware of what he was doing. He tipped a bottle of vodka to his mouth to empty it. Then seeing two German jeeps slowly approaching, he heaved the empty bottle at them. The bottle struck an SS officer in the head. He winced and bent over, as the soldier in the back seat turned and raised his rifle. Four shots rang out and Isak Reznik fell face first onto the street. He was gone in seconds, finding relief, though perhaps not the kind he had sought most of his life.

* * *

When Syma arrived home from work on June 12, she asked everyone to sit near the small kitchen table. "The leader of the Jews told us this afternoon that they're shutting down the ghetto, and they'll send everyone to Germany to help repair damage done by the Allied air raids. They'll tell us when the evacuation starts, but I expect it will begin before the end of the month."

Everyone shivered with fear. Lisbeth clutched Gela and Gesza tightly.

"Lisbeth, please take the girls to the bedroom so they can play with their dolls," Sophie said softly. After they left the room, Sophie asked, through Isabell, "Is that really where they're sending us?"

"Rumkowski tried to be honest with us, he doesn't know for sure, but he hopes they're telling us the truth."

"What do we do now, Syma?" Jacob asked.

"We wait. That's all we can do. Our fate is no longer in our hands if it ever was."

What Chaim Rumkowski didn't know was Heinrich Himmler had recently ordered the SS to liquidate the ghetto. Going to Germany was only a ruse, to quell the fears of the ghetto inhabitants. With the continued thrust from Operation Bagration, the Russian Army had now penetrated deep into Poland, and Himmler knew it was time to dispose of the ghetto.

On June 21, 1944, notices went out to everyone who lived on three streets in the Litzmannstadt Ghetto. They were all to be at the Radegast train station at eight on the morning of June 23. They allowed each person to take one suitcase and a coat. The SS issued a stern warning that they would deal harshly with anyone not reporting as scheduled.

Syma Berkowicz, as she had done for over three years, not only protected those in apartment 228 but everyone else at 7 Dolna Street. Rumkowski allowed her to have some say in scheduling the final transits from the ghetto, so she arranged for those on Dolna Street to leave Litzmannstadt on the second to last train.

People in the ghetto were always afraid, but now they were irrational and chaos began to rule. Hopeless people scurried around, either getting ready to go or trying to do whatever they could to avoid the train. Many hid in clever spots, some successfully, but the SS caught most of them and sent them to the train station or shot them on the spot. Others—believing they were going to Germany—tried to take as much as possible with them. But most, knowing the truth deep down, resigned themselves to the fact there was nothing they could do to avoid their fate.

The first train rolled out of the Radegast train station as scheduled, around noon on June 23. Nine other trains had followed by July 15, all making the short trip to the Chelmno extermination camp. None of the seven thousand men, women, and children making the trip survived. But then the trains going north suddenly stopped. The seventy thousand souls left in the ghetto rejoiced. But no one there knew the trains had stopped because the Russians were closing in on Chelmno. Himmler decided to close the death camp and cover up the evidence of the horrible deeds done there.

All the ghetto workshops and businesses had shut down, leaving the bewildered citizens to wonder what they should do next. The number of suicides and heart attacks increased over the months as hopelessness, confusion, and fear brought many lives to a sudden end.

On August 2, Syma gathered everyone around the small kitchen table. "The transports will start again in two days, and those left in Litzmannstadt will be gone by the end of the month."

"Where in the hell are we going?" Sophie asked. "Does Rumkowski know?"

"He doesn't. But we've heard rumors that a large uprising broke out in the Warsaw Ghetto. And now the Germans need to clear Litzmannstadt before the revolt spreads here."

"We just don't know where," Jacob said.

"We know it won't be to the north. There was a reason for stopping those transports. And we have to be honest; it won't be Germany." No one had the heart to pursue the discussion further.

The residents on Dolna Street waited impatiently for information about their departure. They had to agonize for three weeks before receiving orders to report to Radegast on the morning of August 23. They had two days to prepare for their journey. On the morning of their departure most everyone was up early. No one could sleep anyway. Syma Berkowicz came into the kitchen looking somber.

"Gimpel and Perla are dead."

"What happened!" Lisbeth shrieked.

"Yesterday I took Gimpel down to see the young doctor on the second floor," Sophie said. "The doctor who gave us Gesza's sleeping powders two years ago. He was giving people a powder that would allow them to decide their fate on their terms."

"God no, they didn't—"

"They did, Trudi. At sixty-six and sixty-five, Gimpel said they had endured enough, so they agreed that their road would end here."

"Such a shame that it's all come down to this. I never thought I'd see such madness," Jacob said with watery eyes.

"None of us want to face this day. Perla and Gimpel might have made the right choice," Isabell whispered.

Trudi held Lisbeth as she wept. Then after a short pause to reflect on the Warski's act and what lay ahead, everyone got up from the table. Janas came from the bedroom with Gela still asleep in his arms. "We'll keep the door shut and tell the girls that Gimpel and Perla left early to take another train home," he said.

By seven thirty, all the residents of 7 Dolna Street were filing out to the street and heading for the train station with their suitcases and coats in hand. Janas and Syma, holding Gela's hand, were slowly leading the group from the apartment. Lisbeth, holding Gesza's hand tightly, was following closely, with Jacob, Johann, and Trudi right behind them. Johann's leg was only a little better as he limped along, struggling to keep up. Sophie and Isabell trailed the others down Dolna Street.

It was a miserable morning for all. They had to wait for the train to arrive and then endure long lines while officers crossed names off transit ladings and inspected baggage . The girls were restless, increasing Lisbeth's anxiety to near the breaking point. To help, Sophie gave her a flask of Schnapps that she sipped when the girls weren't looking. Sophie knew that not only Lisbeth, but the others would need something to bolster them before boarding the train. So Schnapps was her special gift to each.

They were all underweight, but still in better health than the thousand souls waiting with them. Trudi and Johann tried to lighten things by recalling the few good times they had during their stay in the ghetto.

"Remember the special times we had at Marysin," Trudi said, as she looked toward the park, only a block away.

"The evenings, after a hot summer day."

"Yes, Johann. Lying in the cool grass, watching the sun go down. How is it that such an oasis existed here?"

"God's blessing in the middle of hell, Trudi. And we found it."

"We did. And now we have another beautiful day. The cool breeze and fragrance of the summer flowers belie what's happening here."

"Ironic, isn't it? Beauty is surrounding such ugliness and evil."

"Bittersweet was the best we could ever hope for, Johann. Remember three years ago when we last stood on the Radegast train siding?"

"That seems like a lifetime ago."

* * *

As early afternoon arrived, Sophie and Isabell led the others up a ramp into a reddish cattle car with two small windows, covered with barbed wire. There weren't many people in the car when they entered. But the subsequent stream of souls pushed them backward toward the far side of the boxcar. When they shut and bolted the door there was hardly room to turn around. Gela and Gesza were crying as were most of the other children. Lisbeth pulled Gesza close to her while Gela's mother tried to comfort her. Sophie, bolstered by her flask of Schnapps, was mad as hell and in no mood to take crap from anyone. The alcohol had soothed Lisbeth's nerves, but it was obvious she was still nearing the edge. Johann was in great pain, standing on a leg still not fully healed. The Schnapps helped, but he knew his circumstances would only worsen. Trudi cried out to God for her husband, and she did everything else she could to help him, with little success. And now the packed cattle car was quickly getting hot. Sophie joined others in yelling, "When is this damn train leaving?" But there were still cars to fill, so it was near four in the afternoon when the wheels turned and the train labored slowly out of the station. By then a dozen of the car's 130 occupants had fainted and others were throwing up. An elderly man tried to fall to the floor after having a heart attack, but there was no room for him to die with dignity. Several who fainted never regained consciousness.

The Jewish Commission gave all the occupants a small loaf of bread before entering the train, and they allowed them to take some other food with them. There was a water barrel at either end of the car with four ladles. But there was no one to regulate consuming the warming and suspect water. And it was impossible for some people to ever get to the water barrels. But Sophie and Isabell, who kept their flasks as did the others, shoved their way to the water barrels with Sophie cursing people to move out of the way. With eight flasks of water, they could keep their body temperatures down, for a while at least.

Desperate passengers from previous trips had chiseled out small holes in the slats making up the cattle car's floor where they could relieve themselves. There was little room to squat though and people jostled and nudged each other trying to do so. After a while no one cared; dignity was an extravagance desperate people could no longer maintain. Women pulled down their underpants beneath their dresses or skirts and used coats or hats to cover themselves. Men were less hesitant in meeting their basic needs. By the time the train started to move, the latrine holes were putrid in the sweltering boxcar. Weakness had already overtaken some. The mass of humanity pushing tightly against them from all sides was all that kept them standing.

The train looped north and east from the Radegast station. Then Sophie and Jacob noticed that the train unexpectedly turned south. "If we're going south, then we're sure as hell not going to Germany," Sophie whispered in Jacob's ear.

Forty minutes later, everyone felt several jolts as the train slowed and then stopped. "Why are we stopping?" Lisbeth yelled. "Oh no! We haven't arrived already, have we?"

"Calm down, mother. I don't see any lights or hear anything. We've just stopped," Trudi said as she squeezed Lisbeth's hand.

Most of the passengers panicked at the slightest change they didn't understand. Then suddenly they heard another train passing them and realized they had only pulled onto a siding. Someone looking out the small window yelled out, "It's a Red Cross train probably carrying wounded soldiers back to Germany." It was long and took several minutes to pass. The transit train sat motionless on the sidetrack for another hour. Finally, they heard a train in the distance coming from the other direction. It zoomed by at a much higher speed, shaking their train as it passed. The man at the window yelled out, "It's a troop train. The poor bastards are on their way to the front." After the train passed, they had to wait another twenty minutes before the wheels turned and the journey resumed.

The train continued south into the night, stopping on six additional sidings. They sat at one place for three hours as four trains passed. As dawn came, they were sitting on another siding. Conditions inside the boxcar worsened. A few passengers had expired, and many were close to joining them.

Lisbeth was physically ill. She was again plagued by diarrhea. The once beautiful and proud woman was sobbing, trying to cope with the embarrassment of soiling herself and realizing the smell was gagging some around her. Jacob slipped his arm around Lisbeth and pulled her close, kissing her on the forehead. "It'll be alright, dear. They can't tell it's you and couldn't care less at this point anyway." Lisbeth continued to sob as she buried her head in Jacob's chest.

Johann's injured leg was now burning with pain, and no matter how much he and Trudi prayed it only got worse. Trudi and Janas braced him so he could take the weight off the leg, but it helped only a little. Syma and Isabell sheltered the girls as they slept on the floor between their feet. They were confused and frightened but were finally able to go to sleep.

There were more stops to endure before it was night again and the train slowed and entered a station, finally stopping. Wherever they were going, good or bad, most felt they had arrived. Everyone heard yelling and the ominous sound of barking dogs. People were frightened and started to cry out. Some prayed and others pled for those outside to open the doors so they could get out of the suffocating boxcar.

"This is crap; you know where we are, don't you?" Sophie yelled to the others.

"I think we're at the end of the line," Jacob said softly."

"I've heard stories that only the healthy survive in these places," Syma said. "Get out your lipstick and rouge and make yourself look as healthy as you can, ladies; your life depends on it."

Sophie took out a small bag from her dress pocket and quickly applied rouge to Lisbeth's cheeks and lipstick to her lips. It helped some, but she still looked old and haggard. Sophie then applied rouge and lipstick to her face. The other women, except for Syma, helped each other to look as healthy and attractive as possible. But Syma did nothing to mask the pain and exhaustion on her gaunt face.

Finally, the bolt turned, and the door opened to reveal a scene of utter chaos. As people filed out, there finally was room to move around. Lisbeth noticed Sophie pulling a dress off a lady who had died in the corner. She then reached into her pocket and pulled out a clean pair of underpants. "Take off your dress and underwear!" Sophie commanded Lisbeth, who was on the verge of fainting. Sophie held up a coat in front of Lisbeth while Trudi helped her strip off her soiled dress and underpants and cleaned her up as best they could. Then they helped her put on the clean underpants and the dress Sophie took. By then most of the car had emptied and men in striped hats, shirts, and pants were yelling at them. "Get off the train now!"

They were Jews like the conspirators in the ghetto. "Bastards!" Sophie cursed under her breath.

The ten from Dolna Street walked or stumbled down planks into a sea of desperate humanity that filled a large staging yard. They were in the midst of a thousand weak and confused souls, who had little fight left. Loudspeakers blared out instructions.

"Line up as you're ordered. You'll get your suitcases later. All families will stay together." The voice echoed across the yard.

After several minutes of confusion, the kapos, Jews who served as prisoner functionaries or supervisors, and SS officers tried to organize the throng and quiet them. "Thanks, Syma, for making us look as good as possible," Isabel said while waiting in line.

Nearing the front of the line, they realized they were being separated into groups of men, women, and children. As they reached the selection spot, an SS officer broke protocol and let Syma go to the right with Gela and Gesza. Janas, suffering from a high fever and half out of his mind, chased after them. "I won't allow it! You won't separate my family from me." An SS soldier immediately released his German Shepherd. The animal ran directly to Janas, knocked him to the ground, and latched onto his throat. It was an ugly scene. The dog had punctured his carotid artery and blood gushed from Janas's throat. It was over quickly. Syma screamed loudly as she pulled Gela and Gesza's shivering bodies close to her, pressing their faces into her dress so they couldn't see. Sophie and Trudi turned their faces away as they held the fainting Lisbeth upright. But they had no time to lose. They had to revive Lisbeth quickly.

Trudi tried to hold her husband upright so no one would know he could hardly walk. But before the guards divided them, a man in a white coat approached. His manner caught everyone's attention. He smiled as he whistled a familiar tune.

"Come out, young man, and dance." Johann stayed in place, and no one said a word. "Let him go, Frau," the man ordered as he shoved the end of his riding crop against Trudi's arm.

Trudi let go of Johann, and he tried to walk forward. After several steps he stumbled to his knees, writhing in pain. The doctor turned to three kapos and motioned for them to take him away. They rushed over and dragged Johann to a line filled with lame or old men. Trudi and Jacob sensed it was the line for those going to the gas chambers.

Without thinking, Trudi ran after her husband. She had already seen enough and was now more than willing to die with Johann. For a moment the kapos allowed Trudi to stay with Johann. But then, out of nowhere, a very tall German soldier gently pulled Trudi away from her husband. She started to resist, but his face was kind with a reassuring smile, nothing like she would have expected. "Follow me," he said. "You can't be in this line. Your girls are waiting for you to come home." He said nothing more as he led Trudi back to the others. She looked back at Johann as they led him away.

"God bless you, darling," Sophie said as the soldier brought Trudi back to her. "He'll take care of Johann." Tears flowed down Trudi's face, as Sophie and Isabell hugged her, letting their love and what strength they had left flow to her. They all sobbed deeply until it was their turn for selection.

Jacob—distraught with his son's fate—went to the left with the healthy men, most of whom were younger than him. Due to his good health and strong constitution, the women from Dolna Street felt he would be okay. At least they could comfort themselves with that hope. But now they all had to bolster Lisbeth. She was reeling from what happened to Janas and Johann and the agonizing separation from her girls and Jacob—not knowing what would become of them.

"Are Gesza and Gela safe, Sophie?" Lisbeth asked fearfully.

"Yes, Lisbeth, they're taking all the children to a compound where they'll be safe."

"Thanks, Sophie. I couldn't bear it if anything happened to them."

Lisbeth pressed her head into Trudi's chest, feeling some comfort from Sophie's assurance. Trudi put her arms around her mother, trying to shield her from the world they now faced.

An SS guard directed them to a line of other women who looked healthy. Sophie, Trudi, and Isabell rejoiced that they didn't take Lisbeth from them. They all thought it had to be a miracle. As they waited in line, Sophie had to find out what happened with Trudi and the tall German soldier who looked out of place. "I thought you'd fight him to stay with Johann."

"He could have crushed me if I tried, Sophie, but his gentleness and the brightness of his face took all the fight out of me."

"I don't understand, Trudi," Isabell whispered.

"I don't either. He smiled at me and his eyes were so kind. I didn't know what to think. But I knew he was there to help me."

"Why would anyone here help you?"

"I'm not sure, Sophie. But he said my girls were waiting for me, and I had to go home. It sent shivers of joy down my spine, unlike anything I've ever experienced. And then something happened that I can't explain."

"What was it?" Isabell asked.

"His face was so warm."

"Why does that matter?" Sophie said quietly.

"You don't understand. I mean that I felt heat coming from his face. It was hot!"

"Damn! Are you telling me he was like the soldier who saved Jürgen, Netti, and Liesel on the night of broken glass?"

"I think I am, Sophie. I don't understand it, but I felt such peace. I know I'm going home. I'll hold Helene and Hermine again. And I know Johann will be secure in God's arms. But, my God, Sophie, they're also sending Syma, Gela, and Gesza to the gas chamber."

"Shush, Trudi, don't let Lisbeth hear you," Isabell cautioned.

"Now we know why Syma refused to use rouge or lipstick to escape death; she had to stay with her girls to the end if she could," Sophie said.

A kapo standing next to them said, "They're now letting some mothers stay with their children. They all have to die, anyway. If they can't work, there's no place to house them."

After selecting life for the Dolna Street women, the SS officer in charge called out Chaim Rumkowski and his wife and sent them to the gas chamber. But the women still didn't know their fate and lived in fear of what would happen next.

SS guards and kapos marched several hundred women over a kilometer to a large barracks, telling them to enter single file. One by one, all their possessions were taken. Then kapos registered each woman, gathering required personal information. Each was then tattooed with an identification number on her arm. Then the women were ordered into a large room where they were told to take off all their clothes.

SS guards marched the naked women several hundred meters to a long building, referred to as the sauna. Each woman took their turn standing on a stool. Kapo women crudely cut and then using dull razor blades shaved the heads of each woman. For Sophie, Lisbeth, Trudi, and Isabell it was the most humiliating experience of their lives. Most of the women cried as they endured the shame. But Sophie and Isabell froze, concentrating on faraway places.

After searching their body cavities, kapo women led the prisoners to the bath area, where each was subjected to a repugnant Lysol disinfecting bath. Then they went into a large shower room, already packed with women. Some of them started screaming, as they had heard stories that such rooms were gas chambers. Panic in the room spread quickly, but then like a breath of fresh air from heaven, tepid water came from the showerheads, flowing down over the huddled women. Sophie and Isabell pulled Lisbeth and Trudi close. The four women hugged as the water tried to wash away the vile remains of an unspeakable journey.

Kapo women gave everyone leaving the shower room clean underpants and striped hats, shirts, and pants. Only by chance would anything fit. Then the guards led them some distance to a group of barracks and told them to enter the third one on the left. All along their trek from the bathhouse to the barracks, soldiers and kapos prodded and screamed at them.

The Jewish Functionary for the barracks stood on a crate and addressed the women.

"I'm in charge here. Everyone will obey my instructions if they want to survive. Now find your bunks; lights out in ten minutes."

The weary travelers wanted nothing more than to escape their plight, and sleep was the only way they could. The long brick barracks had twenty-two bays, three roosts high, with an aisle down the center. Sophie shoved women out of the way to secure a second level roost. "Get up here quickly!" she told the others. Isabell looked at Sophie in shock, noting how aggressively she took responsibility for taking care of their group, as Lisbeth and Trudi were now too distracted to care.

They were all thankful that Lisbeth had made it through the journey, but now she seemed far away. Trudi knew what was in store for Johann. She continually reminded herself that Johann would be safe in heaven, but it was hard for her to hold on to the peace she had felt earlier.

Their bed of wooden slats was deep enough for the four women to lie side by side, with their heads toward the aisle. Each was issued a thin blanket, but no pillows. And no breeze stirred on the warm summer night. Uncomfortable as it was, the four from Dolna Street were so exhausted even their sorrow and fear couldn't keep them from sleep.

"Get up now!" yelled several kapos. "Be outside in three minutes!"

"Crap! It's still dark," Sophie said.

"Help me with Lisbeth, Auntie."

After enduring the hour-long roll call and inspection, the kapos marched the women to the latrine. The woman in charge overheard Lisbeth and Sophie talking.

"Sophie, do you think our girls are safe in the children's barracks?"

"We'll see their smiling faces soon, sweetie."

"Are you crazy or just plain stupid?" the kapo said. Pointing to Sophie's hair, she said, "What the hell do you think these ashes are? Could be your girls. Wake up and face it. Children go to the gas chamber; your girls are ashes."

Lisbeth froze. A tear ran down her right cheek, and her mouth quivered. She wanted to yell, but no sound came forth. Trudi put her arms around Lisbeth, saying, "I'm sorry that you had to hear it this—"

"No, Trudi. Just hold your mother; don't say anything," Sophie said.

Then Sophie quickly turned and punched the kapo in the face. She fell to the ground. To everyone's surprise, the woman didn't get up and retaliate. Instead, she curled up, bawling like a four-year-old.

"Dammit," Sophie said under her breath. "She's as broken and desperate as the rest of us—pathetic like every damned thing in this place. I shouldn't have hit her," she thought. "What good did it do?"

Lisbeth whimpered as Trudi held her. Sophie reached down and helped the kapo to her feet. The woman said nothing, but she never bothered the Dolna Street women again. In fact, she helped them on several occasions. Trudi thought it was a miracle that none of the SS guards saw the incident, which undoubtedly saved Sophie's life.

Inside the latrine, Lisbeth started to drift away again.

"Gesza and Gela are gone?"

"I'm sorry, Lisbeth," Sophie said. "We can be thankful that Syma was there to comfort them."

"She was a good mother, not like me. Do you think Netti's alright? I didn't love her as I should have. And I don't even know why, Sophie. I want to hold her so badly. Tell her how sorry I am—how much I love her."

"I'm sure she's safe at home, sweetie." Sophie took Lisbeth in her arms as she wept. "You'll see her soon. Then you can make it all up to her."

"Thank God Netti's fine, Trudi! She's safe, Isabell. Netti's okay!"

It would take days for Lisbeth to clear the cobwebs from her mind. Some would never recover from the shock of losing their loved ones if they survived themselves, and no one would ever be the same.

A few days later, the barracks kapo asked the women if they would like to have a Rabbi come and recite the mourner's Kaddish. Some asked how it could be recited without the required minyan, quorum of ten men. She said the Rabbi was still willing to do it. So, later that day the Kaddish was said for the mourners in the barracks, as Sophie and Lisbeth looked on with reverence. Isabell had participated in Kaddishes in her early years. And Trudi was taught about it by Jacob and Johann, but she participated only once when twelve men were gathered from the apartment building.

Lisbeth, Sophie, Trudi, and Isabell endured four long weeks in the barracks, going to different labor sites most days. Life in the camp was harsh. Small rations of bread, watery soup, and tainted water were all they lived on. The latrine was putrid. Each woman had only thirty seconds to use one of the sixty holes.

In late September, SS guards ordered over half the women in the barracks, including the four from Dolna Street, to board trucks waiting outside. Everyone feared the worst when something unusual happened. Within the hour, nearly two hundred petrified women boarded twelve trucks; they had only the dirty clothes they were wearing. The motors turned over and the trucks slowly moved forward and wound their way west out of the Birkenau concentration camp. It seemed to Sophie that they traveled nearly two hours before going through a guarded gate. The trucks then went several blocks before stopping next to a three-story building. Trudi saw the name of the town on a sign: Prudnik, she thought.

SS guards quickly herded the women into the building and directed them up the stairs to the second floor. They saw a huge open room with rows and rows of beds stacked three high; beds similar to those they had used for the past four weeks. The SS guards ordered the women to find beds in an orderly manner— four women to a bed.

The four from Dolna Street soon learned that most of the women already inhabiting the second and third floors were Jews from Hungary. They also learned they would be working ten-hour days at the Schlesische Feinweberei AG Textile Mill, two blocks away.

Twenty SS guards staffed the work camp under an SS commandant. The Germans had hastily constructed a small pit latrine and bathhouse, fifty meters from the barracks. A chain-link fence topped with barbed wire surrounded the camp. The women would perform tedious work at spinning machines day in and day out. It was more grueling than they thought, but at least they could sit. The ration of food was woefully inadequate to keep the women fit as fall and winter came. Most fought illness and feared the spread of disease—especially typhus—in their filthy, rat-infested living conditions.

Each day before marching to the mill, the women of Prudnik fell in for morning formation and roll call and then went to the mess hall. The menu seldom changed: a cup of watery soup with no meat and few vegetables and a slice of dry bread. At midday they got another slice of dry bread with a chunk of margarine and a piece of dried fruit that was sometimes unrecognizable. When they returned from work after six in the evening, they usually got the same thing they had in the morning. A horrible drink, supposedly coffee, was available at each meal, but most never drank it. Even the water in the billet and mill was suspect, but the women had no choice but to drink it.

As December arrived, Sophie, Lisbeth, Trudi, and Isabell were learning to cope with their meager existence at the Auschwitz sub-camp, one of over seventy such camps. At least now there was some stability in their lives, though they were noticeably losing weight and strength. They continued to be concerned for Lisbeth as she continually fought off illness. Her stomach and bowels were worse than ever. They could only hope the war would be over soon and end their horror.

The first story of the prisoner's billet housed the mess hall, kitchen, rooms for ten SS guards, and latrine used only by the guards and kitchen personnel. There was never a thought of escape, but many feared the guards downstairs would come up one night to assault the women.

By mid-December, Lisbeth's condition worsened, and she needed help from others to get to work and the bathhouse and latrine. The bathhouse had only five showers and six sinks with trickling cold water and usually no soap. In the cold weather the water pipes burst, making it almost impossible for the women to clean up. The shallow pit toilet with only twelve holes was becoming a serious health problem. Too much groundwater was seeping into the pit. And with nearly four hundred women using the toilet daily, it was close to overflowing. The villagers charged with maintaining the latrine, refused to do it anymore, citing it was a danger to their health.

As Christmas approached, Lisbeth hadn't been able to work for three days. She was in danger of being sent out of the camp. Everyone knew what that meant, so they did what they could to protect her. Sophie steadied her each evening as she made the fifty-meter trek to the latrine. But on the evening of December 22—as they prepared to make their nightly trip—several women cautioned them not to go, as the pit toilet had overflowed and wasn't usable. But Lisbeth, feeling the severe cramps of a diarrhea attack, was desperate, so they went anyway. Many of the women had been relieving themselves behind the bathhouse and latrine building and covering it with snow. But as the ground around the building became sullied with feces, SS guards started shooting at women they saw squatting.

When Sophie and Lisbeth reached the latrine, the pungent smell almost forced them to turn around and look for a place outside. Fearing getting shot, however, they forged ahead instead. No one was in the latrine and the pit toilet had overflowed through all twelve holes. Waste floated in filthy ankle-deep water.

"We can't go any further, Lisbeth! We need to find a place outside."

But Lisbeth was desperate and stepped into the latrine anyway. She slipped. Sophie tried to catch her, but Lisbeth fell on her back. "Help me please, Sophie!" Lisbeth cried, sobbing in despair, not knowing what to do.

"Dammit, Lisbeth! I told you not to go in. Take my hands, and I'll pull you up."

Sophie braced herself and pulled Lisbeth up. As she started to stand her feet slipped out from under her again, and she fell face first, and her coat came off. Feces covered the back and front of her shirt and pants. It was in her face, hands, and hair as well.

Lisbeth screamed hysterically, and Sophie had no idea how to calm her. She was gagging at the smell and sight of feces all over Lisbeth. Sophie dragged Lisbeth to a spot near the door where it was dry and got her to her feet. Just then Lisbeth's cramping bowels released, running down both legs.

"My God, Lisbeth, you're a damned mess!"

Lisbeth just stood there shivering like a terrified child. It was frigid outside, and Sophie knew she had to get Lisbeth out of the wet clothes. In one swoop she pulled off Lisbeth's pants and underwear, pulled the shirt over her head, throwing them all to the ground. Sophie quickly cleaned Lisbeth up the best she could with the outside of her coat. She then took off her clothes and redressed Lisbeth, wrapping her coat around her. Then Sophie put on her coat before forcing Lisbeth out the door.

She yanked Lisbeth across the snowy terrain toward their barracks. Halfway there, Lisbeth slipped. As she was falling, she grabbed Sophie's coat, pulling it off, as she fell to the ground. Sophie, now only wearing a cap and clogs, lifted Lisbeth to her feet and they ran to the barracks. SS guards taunted them as they went by, even shining a spotlight on them. Sophie half-shoved Lisbeth up the stairs. The women on the second floor stared at them in disbelief. Trudi and Isabell quickly ran toward them.

"Sophie! What the hell is this?" Trudi yelled. "Where are your clothes? Are you crazy, it's a wonder you didn't freeze to death!"

"We need some water and rags to clean her up. And throw this damned coat out the window," Sophie ordered. Then Sophie put on a striped pair of pants and shirt that she had previously stolen from the first floor supply room.

It took an hour, but the women managed to clean Lisbeth up and then lift her to the bed where they slept. Lisbeth and Sophie finally stopped shivering. It was past lights out as Isabell slipped into bed beside Trudi. Lisbeth was next to Trudi with Sophie on her other side.

The warmth, one to the other, felt good as they settled in for the night. Lisbeth was calming down, to Sophie's relief. She even talked about their ill-advised trip to the latrine. Lisbeth was half-crying and half-laughing.

"What are you laughing about, mother? There's nothing funny about what happened."

"I'm sorry, Trudi, but there is." Lisbeth burst out laughing, to their surprise. "You should have seen Sophie running through the snow naked, except for those silly clogs and that damned cap. The guards were laughing and hooting it up."

Trudi and Isabell chuckled, picturing the scene and admitting it was funny.

"It wasn't that funny, Lisbeth. I'm sure my bony body didn't raise any flags," Sophie said. They all laughed again as tears started to dry. "If they would have been there, Trudi, I could just hear Jürgen or Markus saying, 'There goes Sophie again.'"

They all had another good laugh that allowed each finally to drift off to sleep.

Five nights later, the four Dolna Street women struggled to get into their bed. Each had declined in health, and they were resigned to their fate. Lisbeth had a deep cough, and they all suspected she had pneumonia. She hadn't eaten in two days and had drank very little. Sophie was now sicker than she had ever been in her life. She prayed it wasn't Typhus, which had spread through the barracks a month earlier. And Trudi and Isabell were also coming down with something; both were vomiting and had no appetite. Except for Lisbeth, the others had managed to struggle through an endless workday at their spinning machines, but each knew they had no strength to return the following morning.

"Trudi, Sophie. Trudi, Sophie!"

"We're here, Lisbeth" Sophie whispered.

"Tell Netti I'm sorry. Tell her how much I love her. Tell Jürgen too. Tell him how much I missed him, that I'm sorry, and I love him."

"We'll tell them, mother, but you can tell them yourself; you're going to make it home."

"I don't know. Please tell them—tell them both."

"We will, sweetie, but they already know that," Sophie said.

"Do you think God is waiting for us? Waiting to greet us when we die?"

"I'm sure He is, mother."

"Whose God will it be? Jürgen's, Netti's, or yours, Trudi?"

"They're the same, the same heavenly Father."

"What about you, Sophie? Do you think God is really there?"

"I'm the last one you should ask, sweetie. I wish I knew. I wish I had faith like Netti and Jürgen. There are too many questions, too much horror to understand how God would let it all happen. But I do believe what Netti and Trudi said about the tall soldiers who helped them. It had to be God."

Lisbeth labored to breathe, but she finally fell asleep. The others snuggled up close and finally went to sleep too. A short while later Lisbeth nudged Sophie. "I need to get up and go to the girls' bedroom and tuck them in for the night."

"It's okay, Lisbeth; they'll be asleep, and you don't want to wake them."

"But I told Netti, Gesza, and Gela that I'd read them a special story and then tuck them in."

"You can do it tomorrow night."

"Will I see them in the morning?"

"I'm sure you will, sweetie."

Wheezing and coughing, Lisbeth finally settled down. They were all motionless until Sophie woke up early in the morning. She was freezing and much sicker than the night before. As she got her bearings, Sophie could tell Lisbeth's body was cold. She reached over and felt her forehead. It was ice cold, and her chest was no longer rising and falling. She was no longer making those horrible wheezing sounds. Tears flooded Sophie's eyes when she admitted to herself that Lisbeth was gone, hopefully to a better place.

Sophie lay there for a few minutes, thinking about how close Lisbeth had been to her these last years and how much she would miss her. She also thought about Jürgen and Netti and how much they would miss her. She wished they could have had the opportunity to know the new Lisbeth, the Lisbeth who finally learned how to love and only wanted the opportunity to make everything right and have everyone's forgiveness.

As if someone had shaken her, Trudi suddenly woke and opened her eyes, pushing her body up. She focused on Sophie, who had her arm around Lisbeth and was sobbing. She looked into Lisbeth's face and knew she was gone. Trudi started to shake, fighting back the tears. "Is she—"

"Yes, she died sometime last night."

Trudi cried as she buried her head in the breast of the woman she had come to call mother. The commotion woke Isabell and a few other women. No one had to say a word to Isabell; she knew what had happened.

The three women laid their heads down, trying to stem their tears. Each was deathly ill. Sophie tried not to let on but believed she would soon follow Lisbeth. Her stomach and all the muscles and joints in her body ached. Trudi was starting to wheeze, and they all feared she also had pneumonia. She was burning with fever. Though feeling horrible and starting to cough from deep down in her lungs, Isabell was in the best condition of the three.

"What are we going to do, Sophie?"

Sophie labored to respond. "We'll tell them to get her but wait awhile."

"You're not in good shape, are you, Auntie?"

"No, darling."

"Will they bury her in the Jewish cemetery down the street?"

"I'm sure they will. At least she'll have a grave instead of having her ashes drift away in the wind."

"Maybe the family can come here someday and see where she's buried?"

"Yes, they should have a marker. Trudi, I'm not going to make it home either. I know it deep down inside. Sometimes you know."

"Please don't say that, Sophie! I need you. I won't make it without you. I've lost Johann and mother, and I can't lose you too. I know I have pneumonia like mother. I was so sure, Sophie, so sure I would make it home when the tall soldier told me Helene and Hermine were waiting for me. But now I have to be honest with myself. I'll never hold my girls again."

"You will, Trudi. Muster up the faith you have from Johann and Netti. Tell everyone how much I love them and how sorry I am I couldn't make it home."

Isabell started coughing up blood as she rolled over and finally went back to sleep. Trudi lay there feeling terrible that she would never hold her girls again. She finally drifted off to a restless sleep. Sophie was unconscious, life starting to slip from her body.

* * *

Mitzi Hauer fell to the floor. Pain shot across her face from the powerful blow wielded by Alfred Von Koenig.

"You ungrateful bitch!" he yelled as he kicked her in the stomach. "You could have gotten me killed, dammit, and after everything I've done for you and Gretchen."

Mitzi, now groaning, put up her arms to deflect Von Koenig's foot as he kicked at her face.

"Stop, damn it! I can explain," Mitzi pleaded, but the attack didn't stop.

Alfred shoved the Himmler necklace in her face. "They've been looking for this for weeks, and you had it all the time. I'm sorry, dear, but the only way to save my ass is to fry yours. I have no choice but to turn you and the necklace over to the Gestapo. Damn you! I've never felt more betrayed in my life," Von Koenig kicked her one more time. But this time Mitzi didn't groan. Instead she got mad—enraged as never before.

As Alfred turned to pick up the phone and report the theft, Mitzi rose to her knees and opened the middle drawer of her bedroom vanity. She pulled out the Luger she kept for security. Mitzi raised the pistol, and without giving it a second thought, fired three shots in rapid succession. They all struck Von Koenig in the back. He crumpled to the floor with only a faint whimper and the most horrible expression of shock.

As Mitzi struggled to her feet, the bedroom door swung open and Frau Freund, Von Koenig's personal housekeeper, stormed in with a look of disbelief on her face. She immediately screamed out in shock and started to yell for help. Mitzi pointed the luger at the hysterical woman, "Shut your mouth or I'll shoot." Though panicking, Frau Freund quieted down.

At first, Mitzi thought she should kill the Frau but then thought better of it. Instead, she handcuffed her to the bed frame and tightly tied a scarf around her face, shoving some of it into her mouth so she couldn't speak. The handcuffs were compliments of Alfred's gag gift several months before.

Mitzi immediately went down the hall to Gretchen's room and told Frau Goebel, her nanny, to pack clothes and toys for the six-year-old, as they were going to the country for several weeks. Fortunately, the Frau was partially deaf and didn't hear the gunshots or Frau Freund's screams. She told the nanny that she wouldn't be going with them on the trip. Then Mitzi returned to her room and packed everything she would need for a few weeks. She wrapped the diamond necklace in a large handkerchief and put it in her handbag.

Before noon on January 27, 1945, Mitzi and Gretchen left the Von Koenig estate in the Tiergarten section of Berlin. Gretchen pointed and laughed as they passed the remains of the zoo where she had many good times. It had shut down months before when the Allies bombed the zoo. The streets were a mess from the consistent pounding of the bombers, requiring Mitzi to make several detours before reaching the autobahn to Magdeburg, and the west.

Mitzi, and most rational citizens of Berlin, knew for months that it was only a matter of time until the war ended in defeat. For Mitzi and those having hopes of building a new world in the Third Reich, it was a bitter time. But the statuesque blonde had reconciled herself to the idea, making plans since fall to provide for herself and Gretchen under any conditions. She now had the necklace and a large sum of marks taken from Alfred's safe. She had to take Gretchen west to ensure the Russians would never capture them. She hated them passionately, fearing their vengeance as they moved toward Berlin. She would feel much safer in the hands of the Americans.

Mitzi planned to return to Cologne, even though the Allies had also ravaged that city. She hoped Wolf was still there and would take her and Gretchen in. She assumed he would no longer be with Elise, but if he was, she thought other family members would take them in, considering that Gretchen was their own flesh and blood.

As she drove, Mitzi wondered how Alfred discovered the necklace. "Did Robert tell him, or did he stumble on it by chance?" Mitzi thought. "But why would Alfred rummage through shoe boxes on the top shelf of my closet unless he knew there was something of value there? No, it had to be Robert. He must have told Alfred that he suspected me of lifting the necklace before Himmler had him shot. But they killed him six weeks ago. Did it take Alfred that long to find the necklace?"

In December, Mitzi had learned it was early November when Himmler discovered that his prized necklace was missing.

He had returned from a trip to Munich and wanted to show it off at the dinner party he was hosting that evening. He went into an uncontrollable rage when the necklace wasn't in his safe. He immediately commanded his best investigators to find the necklace and the person who took it. But even with a whole team of investigators on the case for a month, no one knew what happened to the necklace.

Then one evening, Himmler's wife Margerete reminded him of something he had either forgotten or wasn't aware of. She told him how he blurted out information about his safe's combination with Hauptmann Fertig in the room. Himmler didn't recall the incident, but it shocked him that he would be so careless. He immediately told his chief Gestapo investigator to bring Fertig to him.

At first, the hauptmann said he couldn't recall hearing anything about the safe's combination, as Frau Himmler had recollected. But after a beating he cracked and admitted he had foolishly related the story and the safe's combination to Mitzi Hauer. Himmler, one of Mitzi's fondest admirers, had doubts about Fertig's story, as did the Gestapo interrogator. They couldn't believe that Frau Hauer would be able to break into Himmler's safe. But the hauptmann insisted that no one else could have done it. He further disclosed how she could have accessed his study several times when she stayed in his room, and no one else was in the house. He admitted sheepishly that he was usually drunk by midnight. Then Himmler remembered the night he returned unexpectedly and had to rouse Fertig from a drunken stupor to aid him in conducting some important late-night business. According to Fertig, Mitzi was in the house that night.

With the information from the hauptmann, Himmler had Mitzi brought to his downtown headquarters. She had never been called there before, so she thought this might be the end of the line for her and Gretchen. But she gathered herself quickly—as she always managed to do—and greeted Himmler with a warm smile, as he kissed her on the cheek. He invited her to sit while two Gestapo agents and Himmler sat opposite her.

Himmler angrily related all that Hauptmann Fertig told him. "Did you steal my necklace?" he finally asked.

"No! I had nothing to do with the theft." Mitzi broke down in tears. "Though I do recall something Robert told me in his bedroom. He had had too much to drink and didn't make any sense, so I discounted it until now. He told me he had taken your necklace earlier that night. I didn't believe him, as he was rambling on and on, confused most of the time. I was violently ill that night and left the house after midnight. In fact, I recall seeing your auto pull up to the house as I drove down the street."

Himmler and the Gestapo agents believed Mitzi was telling the truth. She was so confident and forthcoming, and her story was more believable than Fertig's. And if there was any doubt, the woman Himmler often dreamed about would always come out on top. As Mitzi left SS headquarters, she smiled wryly and whispered, "That bastard's not nearly as smart as he thinks he is. I've fooled the so-called elite minds of the SS and now can go on with my life.

Himmler had Hauptmann Robert Fertig executed by firing squad later that day. Mitzi learned of his death several days later. "Too bad that such a fine specimen had to die," she thought. "It was either him or me, and for damned sure it'll never be me. After all, he blamed me first. I had no choice but to remove him."

As Mitzi passed through Magdeburg, she decided that Robert must have talked to Alfred before Himmler had him shot, telling him that she stole the necklace and probably hid it somewhere in his estate. "It's the only conclusion that makes sense; it just took Alfred a long time to find the necklace," she thought. "He must have panicked when he found it, fearing they would blame him for the theft if it came to light."

As Mitzi and Gretchen passed Helmstedt, they suddenly hit heavy snow, reducing visibility to less than fifty meters. Even so, she decided to push on to Brunswick, twenty kilometers away. Five minutes later, the road became very icy and treacherous. Gretchen was sleeping next to Mitzi. It was quickly becoming dangerous to be on the autobahn. Rarely had Mitzi felt so vulnerable. She felt as though she had to push on, as she slowed down to less than ten kilometers per hour.

Then out of the snow, with no warning, lights came directly at them. There was no time to react. There was a horrendous crash. Glass was everywhere. Mitzi felt the painful impact for a few seconds, and then she felt nothing. Gretchen didn't wake up as the auto careened into a ditch.

8

GOING HOME

On Christmas Eve 1942, Theodor drove Netti, the girls, and Elise to Hannover to spend the holiday with Waldo, Liesel, Felix, Gisela, and Manfred at their underground resistance house. The four-bedroom house, eighty meters from the nearest neighbor, was rundown. It needed a fresh coat of paint and repairs to the roof and front porch. But the two-story house was large, with a big kitchen, living room, and basement with many hiding places for weapons and other contraband, which served the resistance fighters well.

Hannover had a large rail and transportation center, significant industry, and many oil refineries, which made it a prime target for Allied bombers. By late 1942, the city had absorbed many raids and suffered massive damage downtown and in industrial locations. As they did in Cologne, the citizens lived daily with the fear of wondering when and where the bombs would fall next. And like their fellow citizens to the southwest, they were a stubborn and proud people who kept their chins up under the severest of conditions.

Since Liesel and Felix had announced their intent to marry in early 1943, they shared one of the bedrooms. Netti didn't like the sleeping arrangements, but she said nothing about it to her sister, only hoping they would marry soon. Either Liesel or Felix always stayed in the house to watch over Waldo, who shared a bedroom with three resistance fighters who lived in the house part-time. Felix heard nothing more about the authorities trying to track him down for evading conscription, so he had felt safe moving about freely.

Theodor and the girls had managed to buy some food for a traditional Christmas dinner before leaving Cologne. The residents of the safe house provided bratwurst, sauerkraut, potato salad, and vegetables for their Christmas Eve dinner. It would have been difficult for most in Germany to have such a bounty of food due to the severe shortages.

Helene, Hermine, and Karla had a fine time running merrily through the large house. They were the focus of the adults' love and joy. It had now been over a year since the Gestapo took Trudi from her girls. Helene was finally adjusting to her absence, strongly bonding with both Netti and Liesel. Hermine was only three and memories of her mother were fading. She looked to Netti to fill that role.

Under Liesel and Felix's watchful eyes, Waldo hadn't tried another trip to see Netti and was ecstatic to have her close by for three days. Liesel was usually the one who stayed with him, as Felix spent much of his time helping the underground hide Jews or smuggle them out of the country. It was a dangerous business. Twice, Felix narrowly escaped capture. And now Liesel was having second thoughts about being a part of the resistance. She tried to persuade Felix to rethink the direction their lives were taking, but he was determined.

It concerned the Behrmann children that they hadn't heard from their father for over a month. They followed the news reports telling of the glorious victories at Stalingrad, but they also heard rumors the battle was going badly. Netti spent many hours—especially when she couldn't sleep—praying for the safety of her father and brothers. Sadly, they hadn't heard from Didi since he went to the Wehrmacht, and Mitzi never contacted them after moving to Berlin.

Stefan still had his position as a cook at the Hinzert concentration camp south of Bonn. He hated the Wehrmacht assignment, especially the harsh treatment of the prisoners. But at least he was safe there and able to come home on leave often.

According to Elise, Erich and Gert were still together, stationed with a Wehrmacht artillery battery north of Paris. Periodically, they actually wrote to their mother and even to Gisela. Reading between the lines, Elise knew they were fearful, waiting for the Allies to invade France. Stefan found out that Isaac Sitz, Waldo's best friend, safely escaped to Switzerland in November.

Netti, Waldo, and Liesel sat by the fireplace reminiscing about their childhood Christmases, as the three girls snuggled up to them and went to sleep. "I remember the beautiful Christmas tree we always had with the star on top. We kept adding ornaments until the branches drooped," Waldo said.

"It was special for all of us, Waldo," Liesel said. "And then we'd set up the nativity scene with baby Jesus in His crèche."

"And I just happened to bring that crèche and the baby Jesus with me," Netti said. "Waldo, please get the sack by the window and bring it to me." Waldo brought the sack to Netti. She took out both items and set them under the Christmas tree.

"Do you remember the advent wreaths and calendars Father always made?" Liesel asked.

"I do, Liesel, and he always worked so hard to make them. Looking back on it now, I'm not sure how he ever found the time."

"I remember, too, Netti. It was exciting to see what picture he selected each day."

"Yes, Waldo. You really loved it, didn't you?" Netti said.

"I did. Christmas has always been my favorite time of year and even more so now that I can play all the carols on my violin."

"We'll have you play later so we can sing all our favorites," Netti said.

"Netti, tomorrow are we having duck with dressing, potato dumplings, and red cabbage?"

"Every one of them just for you, Waldo—stollen too."

"That's wonderful, but what I enjoy most is just being with you."

Waldo leaned over and put his head on Netti's shoulder, and she squeezed his hand gently.

"Has anyone heard from Father Boesch recently," Felix asked? "He hasn't called us in several weeks."

"Bad news, I'm afraid," Theodore responded. "The Gestapo recently seized him at the Cologne Cathedral. Two parishioners heard a commotion and saw the Gestapo take him away, and that was all anyone knew."

"That's awful," Liesel said. "We've come to appreciate the father so much over the past months."

As everyone gathered around the fireplace, Boesch's possible death saddened and frustrated them. They talked about how although they knew the Church was aiding the German resistance as much as they could through diplomatic channels, the Pope's neutrality in his official utterances disappointed them. They applauded him for speaking out against racial atrocities, but they wanted him and his Church to take an official stand against Hitler. They also lauded the works of many priests, such as Father Boesch, and thousands of other Catholics who put their lives on the line by helping Jews.

As the political and religious discussion continued, they also criticized the Protestants. In particular, the Confessing Church seemed woeful in their efforts to help the persecuted Jews. From the early thirties on, many of them continued to be more interested in resisting government interference in their religious practices than in taking a serious interest in helping the Jews. But they recognized that, like the Catholics, there were Protestants, such as Lutheran pastor Dietrich Bonhoeffer, who put their lives on the line by vocally opposing Hitler's euthanasia efforts and suspected mass murders of Jews. Elise and Netti urged everyone to continue praying for the safety and effectiveness of those brave men and women.

To resist the will of an authoritarian government took bravery and dedication. But to resist Hitler and the Third Reich—with its secret police and violent organs—took a special type of courage and love for the people the resistance was trying to help. Such was the heart of Felix and the other men at the safe house.

As they lamented the spiritual condition of Germany, they were amazed at how the masses could be so deceived for so long. Even though the war, which was supposed to be short, was bogging down, most people were still behind the Fuhrer, to the point of adoration. They could only assume the worshipers of Hitler were under his spell. It was so bad that children of the Hitler Youth were turning in their family members and neighbors to the authorities for the slightest misstep. Everyone was looking around in fear to see if someone was watching them, if someone might send them to prison or worse. And the Nazi propaganda machine was still cranking out deceptions that even a thinking child could see through, yet most people swallowed it whole. Indeed, it was a puzzling and most dangerous time to live in Germany.

By the late afternoon Waldo grew tired of the conversation around the fireplace. He went to his bedroom and returned with his violin.

"Netti, Can we sing Christmas carols now?"

All agreed it was a splendid idea. They needed cheering up after such depressing conversation.

"But first," said Waldo. Then he passionately played Netti's Song to the delight of all. One of the new men in the house said he had never heard such a beautiful melody delivered with such feeling. Waldo blushed, and then he played some carols as everyone joined in, whether they had a voice for doing so or not. For thirty minutes, they all escaped into memories of Christmases past when loving families were together and life made sense.

Then Netti remembered their family often listened to carols performed by the Munich Philharmonic Orchestra over the powerful radio station in Munich . She went over to the large radio against the wall and turned the dial until the Munich station came in clearly. Accompanied by the near-perfect voices of a large choir, the orchestra softly played "Silent Night."

"It was Father's favorite," Netti thought as she hummed along. In fact, it was the favorite carol of all the Behrmann children. The rendition lifted everyone's spirits as they thought about the birth of Christ and what it meant. A tear formed in the corner of Netti's eye as she thought about her father at that moment. No one knew that Jürgen had tuned to the same Munich radio station and heard the same performance of "Silent Night" in the mess hall at Clearing Station II.

As Theodor sat on the couch next to Netti, he looked around the room, sensing a sweet presence he couldn't identify. Then looking directly at Netti, he said, "Such is the world of Netti Behrmann. Every day I'm proud to be associated with this special family, and maybe even proud of the small part I play in it."

"Oh, Theodor! Why do you keep saying, 'Such is the world of Netti Behrmann?' It's embarrassing, and I don't know what you mean by it."

"Just my way of saying you're an amazing woman, dear; your life is unique to say the least."

"Well, stop it, please," Netti responded, as she reached out and pinched Theodor's cheek.

Soon the call came from the kitchen that supper was on the table. Everyone was ravenous, especially those making the trip from Cologne. The bratwurst, sauerkraut, potato salad, and freshly baked bread was a feast that all enjoyed. But as much as they enjoyed the food, the conversation and growing camaraderie were more satisfying.

The one troubling issue that came up in the conversation around the table was what Theodor heard at Cologne University Hospital earlier that week. "One day while I was at lunch, a man came in asking for Jürgen Behrmann. The elderly man insisted he had to find him, even though staff told him many times that Jürgen was in Russia serving as a Wehrmacht doctor. He finally walked out in disgust. As he left, one of the nurses swore he mumbled, 'I'll find that sonofabitch someday.'" Fear immediately filled Netti, as she whispered, "It had to be Heinz Wagner."

"That's what I thought too," said Theodor.

"Will that crazy man ever give up?"

"It doesn't matter right now, Netti. But when Jürgen returns, it's something we might have to deal with."

"I can't worry about it, Theodor. Let's talk about something else."

All at the safe house spent an enjoyable evening reminiscing. By nine thirty everyone was ready to retire and get a good night's rest in preparation for Christmas Day. Helene, Hermine, and Karla were bursting with excitement and expectation of Christmas morning, but they were also exhausted. Netti, Gisela, and Liesel carried them to their bed in the room where Gisela and Netti would share a bed. The girls were sound asleep as Gisela crawled into bed next to Netti. She thought Netti was praying, as she was gazing up at the ceiling.

"Can I talk or are you praying, Netti?"

"No, you can talk, Gisela. What is it?"

"We're best friends, right?"

"Of course. We've been close friends for many years; why do you ask?"

"Just something that's bothered me a long time that I don't feel comfortable talking about. And maybe I shouldn't say anything now, but you're probably the one person who'll understand."

"Go ahead, dear. What's bothering you?"

"I love Manfred, but I'm not sure I love him enough to be his wife."

"Is something wrong? Did he do something?"

"No, Netti, it's not him; it's me. I try to get him out of my mind but just can't."

"You're talking about Didi, my brother?"

"Yes, it's always Didi. I hated what he did to me for one small mistake. I hated what he did to his life, but I can't stop loving him. I want to, but I can't. I thought I put him in the past, but I was kidding myself. The saddest thing is, I love Manfred, but I don't think I'm worthy of his love while I have feelings for Didi."

"And you thought by coming to me you would be talking to the person with experience in such matters?"

"I thought so, though I don't know what your exact feelings for Conrad and Mose were."

"It wasn't the same, Gisela—Conrad died. But you're right that I married Mose without loving him the way I loved Conrad. And I certainly didn't love Mose the way he loved me. I felt torn about marrying him and probably wouldn't have under normal circumstances, but nothing was normal then, just as it isn't now."

"Do you think first loves are always stronger, and once you give your heart away it's hard to get it back so you can give it to someone else?"

"That's perceptive, Gisela. Some can do it, but it's hard. Conrad took my heart, and I knew it could never fully belong to anyone else."

"But you still married Mose even though you didn't give him your whole heart."

"I did. And he understood that he had only part of me, but it was enough for him. It's complicated if one partner doesn't love with their whole heart."

"What about Sophie? Her heart was shattered, and she could never give it to another man."

"It's sad, but there's always a choice. I only wish that Sophie would have taken a chance to love again."

"Dammit! I just wish Didi and all his problems would go away and leave me alone, so I can love Manfred the way he deserves. What should I do, Netti?"

"I know you're not a praying woman, but you need God's wisdom. I'm afraid I don't have an answer for you. But something to consider is that my brother might never come home."

"I know it's a possibility. I've thought about it for a long time."

"I love you, Gisela. I trust you'll make the right decision about Manfred."

"I just wish I had that same confidence. Thanks for understanding and helping me. Goodnight, Netti."

"Goodnight."

Christmas that year in Hannover was special for everyone at the safe house. Three days together to celebrate life, love, and family in a country where the value of all three had so quickly dwindled. Each understood the importance of the love and support of those close to them, which they needed to push on in such trying times. Netti and Theodor, with the three girls and Elise, returned to their uncertain life in Cologne, while Waldo, Liesel, Felix, Gisela, and Manfred remained in Hannover under equally uncertain and more dangerous circumstances.

In January 1943, Manfred Hassenkamp received the notice he hoped would never come. It was personally delivered to him at Nordstadt Hospital by his uncle's aide. His conscription notice ordered that he report to the Wehrmacht training center near Magdeburg on the twenty-fourth. It took two days for the shock to wear off before he could break the news to Gisela. She took the news about as well as he did. They didn't know if they should marry right away or wait. But the truth was they had little time to marry in the few days before he left Hannover. They decided to wait and not rush it, feeling they could plan their marriage for a future time when he came home on leave.

Uppermost in Manfred's mind, even more than marrying Gisela, was why his uncle, Colonel Amand Faust, chose to conscript him now. He confronted the colonel on the night he received the fateful notice. His uncle, who became an angry and brutal man under the blinding influence of Nazism, was not happy to see Manfred but expected his visit.

"To be bluntly honest, Manfred, you had nothing to do with your conscription."

"What the hell does that mean?"

"It's a sordid story that you'll not want to hear. Your father seduced my wife. It was all Marvin's fault! He corrupted her. He's a lecher and deceiver. I forgave Mary but vowed to punish Marvin."

"But why me, Uncle Amand? I had no part in it!"

"Short of killing your father, which I wouldn't do, it was the only way I could hurt him."

"Damn you!"

On January 24, Manfred hugged and kissed his fiancée at the main Hannover train station, which was showing significant air raid damage; then he turned and boarded the train. After basic military training and field hospital orientation, the Wehrmacht assigned Manfred to a field hospital attached to the Africa Corps in Tunisia. He arrived there in late March. Sadly, his military career was brief. An errant German artillery shell hit the field hospital's mess tent. It instantly killed four people, including Manfred Hassenkamp. There would be no leave, no marriage, and no joy for Gisela.

She didn't cope well with the news. Gisela had dreaded what might happen and felt partially responsible. She hadn't loved Manfred the way she should have and hadn't given him her whole heart. She just couldn't free herself from Didi's grip, or purge from her heart the love she still had for him, even though she hated it.

Gisela made several trips to Cologne seeking Netti's comfort and counsel, but time wasn't healing her wounded heart. Netti consoled Gisela as best she could, trying to absolve her of the false guilt that was overwhelming her. In May, on her second trip to Cologne, Gisela ran into Anika Lowe, their good friend from nurses' training. Anika was visiting her mother before returning to her nursing position at the municipal hospital in Brunswick. As they talked over lunch, Gisela learned the hospital was looking for several experienced nurses. After consulting with Netti, they both agreed it might be God's will for her to apply for the position in Brunswick and leave the sad memories of Hannover behind.

Gisela returned to Hannover in a quandary: should she leave the support of Liesel, Felix, and Waldo or follow a new path to heal and forget? She was so irate at Manfred's father and uncle that she could strangle them with her bare hands. She dreaded what she might do if she ever saw them on the streets of Hannover. After several weeks of contemplation, and even prayer, Gisela drove to Brunswick and applied for the nurse's position. In June the hospital hired Gisela, and she moved there in July to start her new life.

* * *

On the morning of September 12, 1943, everyone at the safe house gathered around the kitchen table for breakfast. As they started to eat, Felix thought he heard autos approach. The others paused momentarily and then continued eating, but Felix got up and briskly walked to the front window.

"They're here!" Felix yelled. "SS. Let's go now! Get your weapons and valuables; hurry, dammit!"

Everyone jumped to their feet, as Liesel tugged at Waldo to get him up.

"Get your violin and papers, Waldo. Hurry, we need to go now!"

Waldo—now shaken—nodded that he understood. He ran to the bedroom and got his violin.

All eight people in the safe house bolted out the back door with their weapons. They ran as fast as they could toward the woods 150 meters away. The uneven terrain with shrubs and bushes sloped upward. The SS made their way to the rear of the house before the resistance fighters were halfway to the cover of the woods. A dozen of them opened fire with rifles and submachine guns. Bullets whizzed over Waldo and Liesel's head as she pulled him frantically along. Felix and three others made it to the shelter of the trees while bullets hit two men, sending them to the ground. As they were nearing the tree line, Waldo released Liesel's hand. She turned to see why he pulled away and discovered he'd been hit by a bullet. Liesel cried out as she ran to him.

"Waldo, Waldo, Waldo! No, not this, dear God!"

Paying no attention to the bullets flying by, Liesel knelt beside Waldo, weeping. A bullet had hit him in the head, where exactly she couldn't tell through all the blood. She froze in shock. Within seconds, Felix grabbed her arm and yanked her up, pulling her to the safety of the trees. All the while she was yelling. "No Felix, I can't leave Waldo! Let me go back for him. Netti will never forgive me for leaving him behind."

"He's gone, darling! There's nothing more we can do for him."

The three men with them blunted the SS charge with their submachine guns as Felix and Liesel scurried to safety. After the men sprayed the hill again with gunfire, Felix, Liesel, and the others ran as fast as they could into the woods. They quickly reached the crest of a hill and went down the other side. The five came to a small stream at the bottom of the hill and decided to go upstream in the water for several hundred meters before continuing west in hopes of losing their pursuers.

After the fire from the top of the hill stopped, fifteen SS men moved cautiously up the hill to the tree line. Just to make sure they were dead—or out of pure brutality—they shot the first two resistance fighters in the head. When the officer in charge reached Waldo, he pointed his Luger at him but then pulled it down, when he saw that he was already dead.

The group soon reached a large meadow. It was about a kilometer to the forest on the other side. The grass in the meadow was only knee high, providing little cover if they didn't get across before the SS arrived.

"We need to get across the meadow fast, Liesel. Can you run across faster than the wind?" Felix said.

"I can; let's go," Liesel yelled as she burst into the open, running as fast as she could. The others lit out behind her. Exhaustion began to set in near the other side, but they pushed through the pain and dove into the shady grass sheltered by trees on the west side of the meadow.

The five rested for a few minutes. Then they took a drink from the one canteen they brought and quickly headed deep into the flat, wooded area. The SS chased their prey until they reached the stream on the other side of the hill. They weren't sure which way they went but crossed the stream heading west until they reached the open meadow. Not seeing any sign of the resistance fighters, the SS commander called off the search, and they returned to the resistance house to look for anything of value.

The group quickly walked to the west and south until nightfall. Exhausted, hungry, and thirsty, they decided to stay the night on a grassy knoll surrounded by lush trees. They hid as best they could. Each one took a turn guarding the others throughout the night. The next day they planned to walk to the safe farm on the Weser River southeast of Bad Oeynhausen.

As Liesel leaned against Felix, trying to find the sleep her exhausted body demanded, she could only think of Waldo and the horrible reality that she'd never see her precious brother again. She wept silently, trying not to disturb Felix who was now sleeping.

"This will devastate Netti," she thought. "How will we ever tell her?"

Liesel finally went to sleep only to wake up less than an hour later screaming. All, except the man on guard duty, woke out of a deep sleep, thinking the SS had overrun them.

"She just had a bad dream," Felix explained, as the others turned over and went back to sleep. Felix put his arm around Liesel to comfort her, but there was no comfort or peace for the shattered young woman. Now every time she closed her eyes, she saw Waldo's bloody head. She couldn't shake it, couldn't get it out of her mind. Liesel got little sleep that night, but she was still able to go with the others to the safe farm the following day. When they reached the farm, they were all exhausted, weak from hunger, and nearly dehydrated.

* * *

On the afternoon of September 12, Andrew, thirteen, and Adele Larenz, eleven, were taking their weekly hike into the woods northwest of their home, south of Hannover. Their mother told them not to venture far from home, especially not near where they heard gunshots that morning. But as children often do, they chose not to obey their mother. Curiosity called them to the exact spot where they heard the shots.

"That's ugly—horrible!" Adele said when they saw two bodies.

"Look away, Adele. Don't go near them."

"Believe me, I won't, Andrew. Let's go home. I'm scared someone might still be here who'll hurt us."

"No, they're all gone. But we should get out of here, anyway. Don't cry, Adele, it'll be okay."

"I've never seen a dead body—so bloody," Adele said as she started sobbing.

As the children retreated, Andrew saw another body further up by the tree line.

"Stay here, Adele. I'm going to look at the body up there."

"Do you have to? Hurry back; I want to go home!"

As Andrew reached the body he shouted, "Come quickly, Adele. This one's alive!"

She hesitantly went up the hill to where her brother stood over what looked like another dead body.

"He moved his arm, and I'm sure I heard a moan."

"His head. God, it's awful!"

"Don't look at him, Adele."

"What are you going to do?"

"There's nothing we can do but run home and get help."

The children ran down the hill and through the meadow to their house. Panting, they frantically told their mother what they saw.

By God's grace, Mary Lorenz's brother was a practicing doctor in Hannover. And she knew he was at home that morning, only a kilometer away. Within twenty minutes, Doctor Leonard Kassmeyer and a neighbor were at Waldo's side.

"It's a miracle, but somehow he's still alive. He should be dead," Doctor Kassmeyer said. "That's a horrible head wound."

As he rolled Waldo over to check his pulse and breathing, he noticed Waldo was cradling a violin case next to his stomach. The case was not damaged.

"He's alive now, but I see little hope that he'll survive if we can't get him to the hospital soon," the doctor said.

The doctor and neighbor picked Waldo up and carried him down to the doctor's auto. From there they raced twenty minutes to the hospital . To Doctor Kassmeyer's surprise, Waldo survived the trip. Under intensive care, Waldo's vital signs actually improved over the following week.

Three weeks passed, and it appeared that Waldo would survive, though he hadn't regained consciousness. His head wound started to heal, but the doctors believed he had extensive brain damage and would never be the same.

Waldo had no identification with him, so no one knew who he was. No one, that is, until Nurse Gerda Schultz recognized him. Gerda, who had worked with Gisela at another Hannover hospital, had met Waldo several times at the safe house. Being a lover of classical music, she remembered how passionately and skillfully he played the violin. When she told Doctor Kassmeyer who he was, he pointed to the violin case on the table, lamenting that he would never play again. No one opened the case or realized the violin in it was worth thousands of marks. Gerda didn't know where Gisela was, so couldn't tell her about Waldo. She heard that Gisela had moved to Brunswick but wasn't sure where. And when Gerda went to the house where Waldo lived, it was abandoned. Knowing how worried they'd be, she wanted desperately to tell Waldo's family, but she couldn't locate any of them.

A month later, while Doctor Kassmeyer was attending a training seminar in Leipzig, hospital administrators decided to send Waldo to a sanatorium for the mentally ill or unresponsive.

He could no longer stay at the hospital, as there was nothing more they could do for him and they needed his bed. Doctor Kassmeyer and Gerda Shultz were upset to find that Waldo was no longer at the hospital.

Felix and Liesel stayed at the safe farm near Bad Oeynhausen for two weeks before making plans to visit Netti in Cologne. Liesel had to tell Netti about Waldo in person. She wanted to put it off, dreading the moment Netti would learn that her best friend in the world died a gruesome death. Pushing back their fear, Liesel and Felix took the train to Cologne the last day of September. For the entire trip, Liesel begged God for strength and courage.

Netti's grief was overwhelming, even greater than when she learned of Conrad's passing.

"Waldo was so innocent and pure. There was no hint of meanness in his sweet spirit. How could such an injustice happen?" Netti lamented over and over again. She cried and wrestled with God once again, this time until December.

After Liesel and Felix returned to the safe farm, Netti leaned on Theodor and Elise for strength, as she had little left of her own and couldn't get her usual breakthrough with God. In a sense, one held up her right hand and the other her left, as the battle raged in her mind and spirit. Elise came down from her father's farm for weeks at a time, sometimes even bringing him along. And Theodor stayed at home with Netti as much as he could, barely managing to keep up with his duties at the hospital. They all took turns caring for Helene, Hermine, and Karla.

But on December 9, 1943, Netti's world came back together as quickly as it had fallen apart ten weeks before. As the relentless bombing of Cologne continued, phone service was down much of the time. However, on this fateful afternoon, the phone rang and Netti picked it up.

"Netti, it's Gisela. Sit down if you're standing. It's the greatest news ever. Waldo's alive!"

"Dear, Jesus! Oh my God! Thank you, dear Lord. Somehow I hoped—I knew he had to be alive. Thank you, sweet Jesus! Thank you, Gisela." Netti started laughing through tears of joy, and she even jumped up and down. Her precious Waldo was alive.

"Where is he, Gisela? When can we go see him? How did you find out?"

"Gerda Shultz, a nurse that I know recognized him at a hospital in Hannover. Netti, he had a horrible head injury. It was a gunshot wound. He might never be the same."

"That's what Liesel said. But he's alive and I need to go to him."

"Oh, Netti, they moved him to a sanatorium somewhere south of Hannover."

"What do you mean somewhere?"

"We finally learned they were taking him to a place near Gottingen. But when they arrived, damage from a bombing raid had closed the sanatorium and no one was there. The hospital has no record of where they left Waldo, and we couldn't find him anyplace near there. And no one can find the attendants who drove him, so we don't know where Waldo is."

"We have to find him as soon as possible, Gisela!"

"We will. We won't stop looking until we do."

During 1944, Netti, Gisela, and everyone else they could enlist searched for Waldo. They looked everywhere, but every lead was a disappointing dead end. In their despair, life went on in Germany. The Allies invaded France in June and pushed their way toward the northwestern border of the homeland. Most now accepted that Germany would lose the war; it was only a matter of when. But the propaganda machine in Berlin still pushed out glowing reports of hope, which the true believers gladly accepted.

It was the children of Germany who broke Netti's heart. Most of them knew nothing but what the Hitler Youth fed them. What hurt her most was looking into their eyes; Netti saw no light, no flicker of hope, only dead stares. They were the lost generation of Germany, beyond reach. But lost as they were, they remained recklessly dangerous to anyone who questioned the Reich or got in their way, including mother, father, sister, and brother. Netti wept and prayed for the youth of Germany as she did for Waldo.

As 1944 wore on, rationing tightened with the increased shortages of all goods. Cologne's population continued to shrink as terror bombings pummeled the city again and again.

Theodor spent fewer hours at the hospital. Staffing levels were dangerously low and there was no one to interview or hire. His personnel department needed only a small staff of clerks to keep the records of those left.

Though they dreaded the unknown, Netti and Theodor hoped the Allies would win the war as soon as possible to end the madness. Liesel and Felix had more than one close call in their increasing acts of resistance, which were becoming more aggressive and dangerous. But they were surviving and doing everything they could to disrupt the war effort.

* * *

Bad news came to the Wolf Behrmann family in late June. The Allies killed Gert in Normandy. The news derailed Wolf, who was already at the lowest point of his life. He worked only a few hours a week at the Hohe Strasse Bank, as damage to the building drastically reduced their services. He was drinking heavily and in a deep depression as his life crumbled around him. He regretted what he had done and how his hatred for Jews had hurt so many, even himself. In particular, he was feeling guilty about what he did to Lisbeth and Trudi, two women whom he always liked, apart from his lustful longings.

"How could I have sent them to their deaths?" He thought. Then he downed another shot in hopes of deadening a conscience that was coming to life, something that had been dormant for years.

Gert's body never came home, but Wolf, Elise, and Gisela came together momentarily to plan a funeral service. Netti and Theodor also attended the memorial with a few others at a funeral home conducting one service after the other, day in and day out. Wolf now longed for the love of his wife and her adopted daughter. But it was too late, as they had no feelings left for the shell of a man who had abused them mentally for many years. No, they only honored Gert. Then they returned to their own lives, leaving Wolf standing at the door of the funeral home, a broken man.

A month later, the Wehrmacht informed Wolf that the enemy had severely wounded Erich in France. He was in the understaffed and overcrowded army hospital in Bonn. Wolf begged Elise to go with him to visit Erich. She went for Erich, not Wolf. Elise felt that if there was any chance to redeem her son, she would take it. She loved her sons even though they always went their father's way. By their teenage years, they treated their mother badly. But Elise knew Christ had redeemed her sorry life, and she believed He could do the same for her son.

Shrapnel had ripped through Erich's stomach. He almost bled to death. His life was in the balance for several days, but he survived and was recuperating. Erich was a broken and disillusioned man who was surprised to see his mother and father together.

"Are you together again?" Erich asked."

"No! I only came to see you," Elise said. "To see if I could help you in some way. The trip has upset me; I need to find a bathroom."

After Elise left, Erich shut his eyes and turned his head away from Wolf.

"What? You can't even look your father in the eye anymore?"

"You know why. I'll never forgive you for what you did to mother and me with Mitzi."

"Damnit! Grow up, Erich, that's the way the world is." After telling Erich why he had to leave Germany, Wolf turned and left the ward.

"Where's your father," Elise said after returning from the bathroom.

"He stepped out for a smoke. It wasn't going well."

"You had words?"

"Did you know that he's leaving Germany? He said he's going to try to get to Spain and then on to South America. He admitted to committing serious crimes at the bank and would most likely end up in prison for the rest of his life if Germany lost the war."

"He doesn't tell me anything, Erich. The further away, the better."

"How did you ever put up with him for so long, mother? The abuse, the cheating."

"It still eats at you?"

"What he did to you and me with Mitzi. Yes, it still bothers the hell out of me. But what eats at me most, Mother, is what I did. I don't think I'll ever shake it; never be able to live contently again."

"I don't understand, son. What are you talking about?"

Erich said nothing for a minute, as he replayed in his mind what he did to Trudi. "I need to tell someone what I've done," he thought. "I should tell her how I still love Trudi, but my spite and pride probably sent her to her death."

"What is it, Erich?"

"I did something to someone that I'll regret the rest of my life. For the rest of my pathetic life, it'll haunt me, and it should. I can't tell you any more, Mother."

"What can I do? I love you, Son. I want to help in any way I can."

"I love you too, Mother. But I didn't love you when I should have. I don't deserve your love now, or anything from you."

"Everyone deserves a second chance. Maybe I can't help you, Erich, but I know someone who can. He's made something good out of my worthless, selfish life."

"I know you're religious now, Mother. Maybe someday it's my only hope too. Maybe some time, but not now, though."

"Sometime, Son," Elise said as she leaned over and kissed Erich on the cheek. "After you're released, I want you to come to the farm and live with your grandfather and me."

"I'd like that, Mother."

Erich went to the farm with his mother in August and stayed there until the war ended. Elise's love was a healing balm for Erich's soul. He recovered not only physically but also mentally. He listened to what she told him about Jesus and wanted to embrace Him, but he couldn't get past his guilt and the deep feeling that he was unworthy of forgiveness. His mother didn't push her faith, knowing it would take time for her son to heal and reach out for the free gifts of healing and redemption that her Savior offered.

* * *

On the cold, icy morning of January 28, 1945, Gisela Dressler Behrmann sat in the break room at the hospital. Yesterday's Berlin propaganda rag lay on the table. Officials were still trying to dupe its readers into believing the German counteroffensive would crush the Russian assault from the east and the Allies' advance from the west. Gisela snubbed out her cigarette and took her last sip of coffee, hoping the caffeine would sharpen her senses after yet another restless night of sleep. She stood and brushed ashes off her white uniform while walking to her duty station in the surgical ward on the second floor. Gabi Haupenstahl, one of Gisela's few friends at the Brunswick hospital, beamed with the latest gossip.

"Did you hear the big news?"

"No, Gabi. What news?"

"They brought a famous person to the hospital early this morning."

"Why would anyone famous come here?"

"They brought her in by ambulance. There was a bad auto accident down by Helmstedt. Icy roads."

"Who was the famous person?"

"Oh, what's her name . . . ah . . . Haas, Howe, or something like that. You know, the famous runner who had bad luck with an injury at the Olympics. Remember, in '36? And then she became a big socialite in Berlin who always had her picture in the papers."

Gisela's jaw dropped. "Do you mean Mitzi Hauer?"

"Yes, that's it—Mitzi Hauer. You remember her."

"Sonofabitch! I can't believe it!"

"What is it, Gisela?"

"Where is she, Gabi?"

"Oh, she's in the morgue. She was already dead when they got to the scene of the accident."

A flood of emotions—anger, jealousy, and sadness—bombarded Gisela as she remembered what a vicious and cruel woman Mitzi was. Then her focus returned. "Was a little girl brought in with her?"

"Little girl? I didn't hear anything about a girl."

"Damn it, Gretchen had to be with her!"

"Who's Gretchen?"

"Her daughter. She had to be with her."

"Ask Mary Kramer. She's still down the hall and was there when they brought the woman in."

Gisela turned and walked briskly down the hall, looking for the crusty old nurse. She finally found her in the supply room near the end of the hall.

"I heard about the dead woman they brought in this morning and that you were there."

"I was. Why do you care?"

"Did they bring a girl in with her?"

"They did. How did you know?"

"She's my cousin's daughter. Is she dead?"

"The medics said she should have died; the crash knocked her out, but she regained consciousness before they got her here. Doctor Weiner checked her out and said she was fine except for a large bump on her head and a few minor cuts. They said a truck crushed the driver's side of the automobile, but the passenger's side had little damage—lucky girl."

"Do you know where she is?"

"They released her."

"Released . . . Who took her?"

"Anna Dohman was there and agreed to keep her until they could find her relatives. Everyone thought that was better than taking her to the children's shelter."

"Do you know where Anna lives?"

"They'll give you her address downstairs."

After explaining the matter to her supervisor and asking for the day off, Gisela got Anna Dohman's address and drove the twelve blocks to her home. She told Anna about her relationship with the girl and asked if she could see her.

"She's upstairs in my oldest daughter's bedroom, on the right. She's most likely sleeping by now, but you're welcome to go up."

Gisela went up the stairs and entered the bedroom. She saw Gretchen Behrmann lying peacefully on the bed across the room. As she crossed the room, Gisela recognized the unbelievable coincidence playing out before her eyes. Twenty years ago, she was the little girl lying in the bed with a broken heart after losing her parents. Then it was Elise who came to her, gently kissing her on the forehead, and assuring her that everything would be okay.

Gisela was overcome with emotions. She paused for several minutes to gather herself, wiping away her tears. She thought of how much she loved and missed her mother and father but also how much she loved and appreciated Elise for loving her without reservation under difficult circumstances.

Now, at least temporarily, she would play the role that Elise played those many years ago. She had to be gentle and loving, as Gretchen didn't have the advantage of knowing her the way she knew Elise.

Gisela moved to Gretchen's bedside and knelt down to kiss her forehead. She sat quietly by her bed for several hours until she stirred and woke up. Gisela spent a painful hour telling Gretchen that her mother was gone but she would love and take care of her. She held the frightened and confused child tightly as they both sobbed.

She comforted Gretchen the rest of the day and started to build a bond of lasting trust. With the blessing of Anna Dohman, Gisela took Gretchen home that night. The only items the medics recovered from the mangled automobile, and all Gretchen now had, was a small suitcase with a few clothes and her mother's handbag.

With the help of a neighbor who watched Gretchen during the day, Gisela kept her until she verified with the authorities that the girl was kin. Netti came from Cologne, along with Elise, to testify that she was Gretchen's aunt. Finally, the authorities allowed the family to take permanent custody of the child. And in February, Netti and Elise took Gretchen to Cologne to live with Netti and her girls.

Gisela drove to Cologne every weekend to spend time with Gretchen. In a short time, Gretchen came to depend on Gisela's loving support. Life was hard for the young girl, but with Netti's healing love, Gisela's consistent visits, and the time spent with her cousins, Gretchen slowly adapted to her new life.

News of Mitzi's death shocked Liesel and Stefan, though they didn't shed a tear. They were thankful that Gretchen was safe and living with Netti and the girls. The misfortune weighed on everyone's mind and made them think of Didi. Was he alive? they wondered. Would he ever return home to see his daughter? Gisela was torn and didn't know how she should feel or what she wanted.

Mitzi's parents took her body back to Berlin for burial. They were stunned by her untimely death, and the Gestapo's accusations that Mitzi murdered Alfred Von Koenig, including their thorough search of Mitzi's parents' home. The Gestapo never told Mitzi's parents what they were looking for, but it was obvious it must be something valuable or important to someone with great standing in the Reich.

In the chaos and confusion caused by the Allies moving closer to Cologne, Netti and Theodor decided to move to Meiningen with the girls. For several months Katia wanted them to make the move, and finally Netti realized the time had come to do so. Gisela was leaving her job in Brunswick, and she planned to be in Cologne in March to go with Netti and the girls to Meiningen. She only wanted to be with Gretchen.

Netti and Gisela never gave up their search for Waldo and had identified three more places where he could be. They were all between Cologne and Meiningen, so it was their plan to check each place on their trip east.

On March 2, Netti was gathering items she would take to Meiningen. She paused and looked at Mitzi's handbag in her closet, wondering if it had anything in it worth taking. She had thrown Mitzi's handbag into her auto with Gretchen's suitcase for the trip from Brunswick to Cologne. She didn't know that Gisela had never bothered to look inside the bag, so she threw it aside after arriving home. It seemed heavy as she opened it. At the bottom was a handkerchief wrapped around something. Curious, she pulled it out and removed the handkerchief, revealing the most beautiful and expensive necklace she had ever seen.

"Where did Mitzi get it, and what should I do with it now?" Netti thought. "If it was stolen, it could be dangerous to the family if the authorities find us with it." Netti finally decided to stow it with her few pieces of jewelry, including her mother's green jade wedding ring, in the most secure place in her luggage.

* * *

Dieter Behrmann turned his head back and forth trying to focus and let his eyes adjust to the bright light. His head ached ferociously. He was finally able to concentrate on the person at the foot of his bed: a frail young woman in a white hospital smock.

"You're finally awake," she said in Russian.

Didi's Russian was good enough to understand what she said. He nodded, trying to recall what happened and why he was in a hospital with incredible pain in his head, stomach, and legs. Then, like a dam bursting, it started coming back to him. "Klara! Where's Klara?" he spoke in German before he could catch himself.

The nurse replied in German, "They brought a nun in with you, Father. I'm sorry, but she died."

"No, no! Not Klara!" Didi sobbed.

He bit down on his cheek and clutched his face, but it didn't mask the pain from the words that crushed his heart. Covering his eyes, Didi wept bitterly trying to understand why. "How long will I reap the wrath of God and men for all I've done?" he thought. "Can I ever pay the price for the little Jewish girl's and Kora's lives? Can I ever make it up to Father, Netti, and Gisela?" It was too much; all Didi wanted to do now was turn over and die. But then Galina came to mind. "I have to live for her," he whispered.

"Are you German?" the nurse asked in German.

"Am I in a German hospital?" Didi asked.

"No, Father Pashkin, you're in a Russian military hospital."

"You've seen my papers?"

"We had to identify you and determine your blood type. You've had four transfusions."

"How is it that you speak German so well?"

"That doesn't matter. Were you trying to get to Germany?"

Didi paused for a few seconds. Then he felt a sense of peace about the woman. "Yes, we were going to my home in Cologne. Please don't say anything."

"I won't, Alexey. It is Alexey, right?"

Pausing again, Didi pondered what he should say. "No, it's not. We disguised ourselves to avoid questioning as we worked our way home."

The nurse moved close and whispered, "We're also trying to get back to Germany, so you can trust me. What should I call you? What's your real name?"

"I'm not sure why, but I trust you," Didi said. "My name is Dieter, but my family calls me Didi."

Lili Strobel dropped the metal tray in her hand, and it clanked loudly as it hit the floor. "No, it couldn't be," she thought. "It's impossible for this to be Didi, the son Jürgen has often mentioned. Or is it God's hand miraculously moving on Jürgen's behalf again?" Lili moved closer as tears welled up in her eyes. "This might sound like a strange question, but is your last name Behrmann?"

Didi had a look of astonishment on his face. He couldn't say a word but didn't have to; Lili knew the answer to her question. She turned away quickly as she started to sob. "I'll be back soon," she called out as she ran off.

"How could she know my last name? There's no way she could know," Didi thought. The bewildering twist of fate overshadowed the thought of losing Klara . "Maybe I'm dreaming or delirious," he thought.

Lili ran to Jürgen, tears still in her eyes. "Come with me," she called urgently. "Hurry!"

"What is it, Lili? Why are you crying?"

"Just come and see."

"Okay, I'm almost done here."

Lili fidgeted as she waited for the doctor to finish with his patient.

"Alright, Lili, show me what you're so excited about."

Jürgen, still recovering from a virus, tried to keep up with Lili, who was almost running toward the far end of the hospital tent. Didi turned his head as he heard footsteps. They were both stunned as their eyes met. The pain and suffering he brought to his father's life overwhelmed Didi. He needed his father's love more than anything in the world, but "How could he ever love such a son again?" he thought.

When Jürgen realized his long-lost son was right in front of him, he ran to his bedside, kissed him on the cheek, and pulled him up into his arms. "I love you, son. I love you; thank you, dear God. Praise your name."

Didi held on to his father as hard as he could. "I'm sorry, so sorry, Father! I love you. Please forgive me."

Tears rolled down Lili's cheeks as she witnessed the miraculous reunion ordered somewhere in the halls of heaven. What God would do next never stopped thrilling her, but what she was now seeing was almost beyond belief. The reunion continued for nearly an hour as father and son rejoiced, crying many tears, and hugging often.

But Didi was again devastated by the news of his mother, sister, and aunt's abduction. His father didn't know their whereabouts or if they were still alive. Didi had thought about his mother every day since leaving for the Wehrmacht in 1941. He was comforted by thoughts of her every time he was in trouble. Only she could comfort him.

Dieter Behrmann's body and mind slowly began healing. The bitter loss of Klara started to ease and his burden of guilt over his rebellion against his father was lifting. He saw that God's hand must have moved miraculously to reunite him with his father. And with Lili's testimony of how God changed her life, for the first time Didi opened his heart to the Lord.

No doubt, father and son couldn't resolve all their issues in a day, a week, or a month. But with love and forgiveness flowing, and God's help, they knew one day they could restore the bond they had when Didi was a child. And as Didi recovered, so did his father. Jürgen was finally getting back the strength he lost in fighting off a series of viruses. But Jürgen and Lili were still weak from the long hours of work, low caloric intake, and overall stress of endless surgeries.

Nonetheless, Colonel Dobrynin believed it was time for them to leave the Russian surgical hospital and escape to Germany. The plan was still to have them go to a forward aid station as a medical team. When a request came for aid, Sergey, Jürgen, Lili, and now Didi would leave the hospital in an ambulance headed west to a forward aid station in Germany. At the right place and time, the Germans would leave the ambulance, striking out on their own, hopefully reaching safety in their homeland.

On March 5, 1945, the call came for help from a forward aid station east of the Oder River, fifteen kilometers south of Kustrin, Germany. It was nighttime as Sergey stocked the ambulance with supplies for the forward station and the three escapees. Colonel Dobrynin, now with a tear in his eye, hugged Lili for almost a minute before letting her go.

"Take care of her, Jürgen. Take care of yourself, too. Maybe someday we'll all meet again." To his surprise, the colonel struggled to say good-bye to the young woman he now thought of as a daughter and to the excellent doctor he counted as a friend. Dobrynin knew he would miss them. And Jürgen and Lili would miss the colonel who saved their lives and always treated them graciously. Lili counted on him almost as she did her father. Dobrynin managed to pull together a notable sum of marks, four boxes of chocolate bars, and eight cartons of cigarettes, which would aid the travelers in getting help on their journey home.

It was nearing midnight when the ambulance and its four occupants left the surgical hospital with Sergey at the wheel. They traveled nearly forty kilometers to the town of Golice, which was just 20 kilometers north of Frankfurt an der Oder. It was after one in the morning when Sergey bid his three riders great success as they exited the ambulance. They unloaded their suitcases, a medical bag, and pistols for each. Sergey tenderly kissed Lili. "I'll try to find you after the war," he said.

Lili returned his kiss with more passion. "I hate to leave you now, Sergey! I pray one day we'll find each other again." She quickly turned, and the three Germans disappeared into the cold night.

Jürgen felt strongly that he should flag down the next truck heading south on the road to Frankfurt an der Oder, though it meant taking a chance. Traffic was light, but within five minutes they saw headlights coming their way. Jürgen stepped into the road and motioned for the truck to stop. An elderly Polish man was transporting poultry. Reluctantly, he said if they could squeeze in behind the cages in the back they could ride to his destination.

As the truck stopped north of Frankfurt an der Oder, the three threw down their belongings and jumped out. They hid in a nearby stand of trees until they could decide what to do next. Their hope was to blend in with German citizens who were still frantically evacuating to the west ahead of the brutal Russian advance. The flow of people was slowing down but still able to provide cover until they could get deeper into Germany.

They were warned before leaving the surgical hospital that Germany was desperate, forcing males from twelve to sixty to join the fight to protect the homeland. Jürgen and Didi knew they had to be careful to avoid being captured and forced back into the army.

It upset Lili when Jürgen decided against going to Berlin because of the impending danger there. She desperately wanted to find her parents. But Jürgen felt strongly that God was leading them to Leipzig. Knowing that God was faithful to lead Jürgen, Lili submitted to his direction.

None of the three were in good shape to be traveling on foot in the cold and damp conditions, particularly Jürgen. They continued slowly and cautiously and as they did, Jürgen's health declined rapidly. His lungs were failing with another onslaught of pneumonia.

They had several close calls on the exhausting three-week journey, arriving in Leipzig on March 29. The university hospital was still open with limited staff and supplies. They admitted Jürgen on March 30. His condition was bordering on critical, and his life would hang in the balance if the treatment he needed wasn't successful.

Leipzig was in shambles, as was most of Germany. None of the three, who had been out of the country for almost four years, could grasp the ruination of their beloved homeland. As the air assaults continued and the Allies advanced, communications were hit and miss. It was difficult to make contact by telephone or telegraph. While Jürgen recovered, Didi and Lili stayed with the one remaining man at the hospital whom he knew.

They all waited in fear, believing the Allies would capture the city soon. Within a few weeks, the U.S. Second and Sixty-Ninth

Infantry Divisions invaded Leipzig with all their might. For two days the fighting was fierce from block to block and building to building. But the weakened and outmanned defenders of the city were no match for their invaders, and soon all residents were under the control of the Americans. Didi and Lili stayed in Jürgen's hospital room until the fighting was over. Fortunately, the hospital sustained only minor damage in the battle, and there were no casualties.

Pneumonia and an undetermined virus had Jürgen near death for three weeks. He lost another twenty pounds. Several times Didi and Lili almost gave up, thinking he wouldn't make it through the night. But Jürgen turned the corner in late April, but took another three weeks to recover his strength.

On May 10, Jürgen tried to contact his family. With communications in shambles, he couldn't reach anyone in Cologne or Meiningen for days. Didi was still hesitant about contacting the family. He still felt guilty, not knowing how they would react or if they would even want to see him. He didn't have the courage to tell his father about the little Jewish girl and doubted he ever would. Jürgen was hesitant to fully explain to Didi how he ended up with the Russian army.

On May 22, Jürgen finally got a telegram through to Katia in Meiningen. Her brief but joyful response told him the family in Cologne had recently moved to Meiningen, and they were all safe. Later, Jürgen sent two telegrams to Netti. The last one, on June 13, detailed his intent to arrive in Meiningen by train on June 17. After sending that telegram, something happened on June 14 and 16 that shocked Jürgen and Didi to the core.

* * *

March 2 was the date that Netti, Theodor, Gisela, and the four girls planned to leave Cologne. Gisela was torn between staying with Elise or Gretchen. She was concerned for the safety of her mother but couldn't separate herself from the girl she had come to love.

The day before they were to depart, Elise had made the now dangerous drive down from the farm through the bombed-out streets of Cologne. She wanted to see them all one more time and talk to Netti about Erich. She arrived by late morning and pitched in to help them prepare for the trip. After lunch, Elise asked Netti to join her on a walk near the woods.

"I'll miss all of you, Netti."

"Thanks, Elise. You've been like a mother to me. I'd like you to come for a long visit if we stay in Meiningen after the war is over. I wish you could come with us now."

"I do too, but Father thinks we'll be safe on the farm when the Americans get here. It looks like that could happen in a few weeks."

"What about Wolf? Is he going to ride it out in Cologne?"

"We're not sure, but from what we know it looks like he's gone. He said he was going to Spain and then to South America. But Erich is who I wanted to talk to you about in private."

"Not my favorite subject. How's he feeling?"

"He's doing better. His physical pain is nearly gone, and he's getting around well. What I need to tell you concerns his mental and spiritual health. He didn't tell me what horrible things he did, but I know he directed some of them at you and Trudi. He's sorry for all he did. He's been guilt-ridden for a long time. But, Netti, the great news is, after talking to him for weeks, he's repented and has now taken Jesus as his Lord."

"Praise God, Elise! I'm so happy for him and you. What great news!"

"I asked him to come with me today, but he said he's not ready to face you."

"I understand."

"But he asked me to pass on a request. I know you and your brothers and sisters had a special pact of the heart where you made binding promises to one another. And Erich told me that you let him join your pact years ago."

"We did, and it's still binding."

"That's good because he wants to use his one special request for you and Trudi. He said you promised to honor it."

"He's right. We have to do what he asks as long as it isn't illegal or immoral. But I can speak only for myself, Elise. We don't know if we'll ever see Trudi again. What does he want to ask of us?"

"He requests that you both forgive him for what he did to you. He hopes that because Jesus forgave him, you will too."

Netti's lips started to quiver and tears formed in her eyes. She took Elise in her arms. "Of course I forgive him. Please tell him that I did a long time ago. Let Erich know that I love him and want only the best for him."

"I will. Thanks for being sensitive and caring." Elise squeezed Netti even tighter. "I treasure you so much, Netti. Now we better get back so that I can get home before dark."

The following morning, Theodor's and Gisela's automobiles wound their way south from Cologne. The bridges crossing the Rhine were no longer usable, so they had to go to Bonn before going east. Tears came to Netti's eyes as she looked back at the shell of the beautiful city she had come to love. "How could such madness happen," she wondered? "Such destruction, horror, and waste." Netti turned back to the road ahead, looking to her future in Meiningen and hoping somehow they would find Waldo. With the war getting closer, they knew it could be a dangerous trip.

They planned to stop at the three places where Waldo could be and arrive in Meiningen before dark. Gretchen and Hermine rode with Gisela in her auto. The girls were now close and enjoyed each other's company. Theodor was driving his auto. Netti was next to him, and Karla and Helene were in the back seat. Netti left her auto at the farm with Elise.

They drove to Bonn and then headed east, making their first stop at a nursing home in Limburg. Netti shook as she and Theodor entered the shabby, run-down, one-story building. But to her great dismay, Waldo Behrmann wasn't there.

They were soon off to Kirchheim, where Netti hoped they would finally find Waldo. But again she experienced bitter disappointment. Now there was only one more chance to find her brother. Exasperated, Netti begged God: "We have to find Waldo here, Lord! If we don't, he's lost to us forever." Then she told Theodor, "I'm scared. It's almost four. Are we still on schedule to make it to Meiningen by dark?"

"We're still on schedule, dear. We might only be here for a few minutes, I'm afraid, unless we find Waldo." The two autos stopped at the Saint Josef Home for the Insane south of Eisenach. With apprehension, Netti and Theodor entered the pleasant-looking, well-kept, two-story building. There was no attendant at the reception station, so Netti went on by, walking down a long hall.

As she walked, her right eye teared up. She paused, feeling a tingly sensation, and then it happened. Wafting down the hall came the sweet sound of a slightly out of tune violin playing "Netti's Song." Netti screamed out, "Waldo, Waldo!" She ran down the hall with tears of joy. Netti opened three doors without finding her brother. But as she opened the fourth door, she saw a man sitting in a chair on the far side of the dimly lit room. He was playing a violin. It had to be Waldo.

Netti ran to his side and pulled his head to her chest as he finished the piece. "Waldo! Thank Jesus we've finally found you." She hugged him tightly as tears flowed from her face onto her dress. But there was no response from Waldo. He sat motionless as Netti held him.

Then she moved back to kiss his cheek. As he turned toward the light Netti saw the horrible scarring and disfigurement to the right side of his face. Horrified, she had never seen such deformity. Waldo's eyes stared forward, not moving left, right, up, or down. Netti began wailing in anguish at the awful sight of her beloved Waldo, knowing that most of who he was might be gone forever.

When Theodor put his arm around Netti to comfort her, he noticed an attendant sitting by the window on the other side of the room. The middle-aged man caught his eye and came over.

"Is he family?"

"Yes, he's my brother and we've been looking for him for a long time."

"Glad someone finally found him; he's been here for six months."

"He's just staring! Does he ever say anything?" Netti asked.

"No. Hasn't said a word since he's been here, and the doctors say he never will. The only thing he does is come down here every afternoon and play that catchy tune. What I don't understand, though, is that he always plays the song around four o'clock."

Chills went down both Netti's and Theodor's spines, knowing that's when Waldo had always played "Netti's Song."

Netti got on her knees in front of Waldo and looked directly into his eyes. "Waldo!" she said loudly, "It's your Netti." His eyes blinked several times and then a smile came over his face.

Encouraged, Netti moved to the left and his eyes followed her. Then she moved back to the right and again Waldo's eyes followed her.

"That's never happened before, Frau. We need to tell Doctor Von Rensing right away," the man said.

"Can you bring the doctor here?" Netti asked.

"I'll try to find him; he should be somewhere down the hall."

As Netti waited for the doctor, she elicited more reactions from Waldo, to her and Theodor's delight. She was crying tears of joy, thinking there was hope for her brother after all. Within minutes, Doctor Von Rensing entered the room with the attendant. For twenty minutes he discussed Waldo's condition with Netti and Theodor. He thought his prognosis was hopeless, but after seeing Waldo's reactions to Netti, he said there might be a glimmer of hope.

After sending Theodor outside to tell Gisela the great news, Netti went with the doctor to confirm that Waldo was her brother. They also talked about the possibility of taking Waldo home in the future. He didn't give her much hope but didn't rule out the possibility either.

Netti and the doctor both feared that Waldo would regress when she left, so she vowed to return as often as possible. She told him it was only sixty kilometers to her new home. With joy and hope now in their hearts, Netti and the others had a peaceful and safe trip to Meiningen.

Katia and Lukas were ecstatic about finding Waldo but sad to learn of his condition. Though worn out, Netti talked to Katia deep into the night, catching up with all the happenings in Meiningen and Cologne. It didn't surprise Katia that her brother had fled Germany to save his skin. She was glad Erich had come to God and that Elise was such a strong woman in Netti's life.

Katia said that it was hard on her father when Netti's grandmother died the year before. "But at least the heart attack took her quickly," she mused. Even in his grief, Doctor Lukas Behrmann, at seventy-six, continued practicing medicine part-time while Katia was still in charge of the Meiningen Public Library.

Ralph and Rudi were both thriving in America and wanted Katia to immigrate there as soon as possible after the war ended. Katia hated the idea of leaving her father alone, but she knew she had to join her husband and son. Netti said she would stay with her grandfather if no one else could.

After many years, the big Behrmann house in Meiningen was full again and, even better for Lukas and Katia, full of vibrant children. No one knew the exact timing, or what would eventually happen, but they all knew the war would end soon and their lives would change, hopefully for the better. Most important, they knew that Liesel and Stefan were safe and that Waldo might come home one day. What they didn't know was the fate of Jürgen, Lisbeth, Sophie, Trudi, and Didi. And they couldn't help worrying about them until they all came home.

9

ARRIVAL

etti Behrmann stirred when she felt someone jostling her shoulder.

"Netti, wake up!"

Netti looked up drowsily to see Katia standing over her.

"Oh, Katia, you're here. What time is it?" Netti twisted her body and pushed herself up to a sitting position on the bench.

"It's after seven. Now they're saying the train will be here within the hour."

"It's about time," Netti said as she stretched her stiff body.

"The man at the ticketing counter said the Americans commandeered the original train from Leipzig to move their troops. Another train wasn't available for three hours. And that train waited on a siding for over two hours while higher priority trains passed."

"With all the chaos, we should be thankful if it gets here by midnight."

"I'm sorry that I didn't get here sooner. There was a problem in closing the library, which held me up for several hours."

"It's okay, Aunt Katia. I'm sure glad you woke me, though."

"Why Netti? Were you having a bad dream?"

"A horrible dream. Father wasn't on the train when it arrived. A very evil looking man wearing an undertaker's suit approached me. With a smirk, he said, 'No one is ever coming home; they're all dead.' That's when you woke me up. June 17, 1945, is becoming the longest day of my life. I only hope it ends with the happiness we're all looking for."

Netti and Katia's conversation woke the girls, who had been sleeping on the bench across from Netti. Two of them sat up.

"I'm hungry, Auntie Netti. Can we go home?"

"You don't have to, Helene. I brought streusel and dates for everyone," Katia said.

"Yippee, Aunt Katia," exclaimed Karla. "Is it in your sack?"

"It is. Wake Gretchen and Hermine gently, and we'll take a look."

The girls munched on their treats and laughed, enjoying the moment after having a good nap. All four girls were close, though Gretchen had been with them only a few months. They chattered on, having fun the way six- and seven-year-old girls do. And the old gentleman next to them, Anton Bader, enjoyed their youthful enthusiasm.

"I'm sorry that you had to bring the girls with you, Netti. I hope it wasn't a problem."

"No, Auntie, they've behaved well and napped a lot."

"I would have taken time off to stay with them, but we're already so short staffed. And who would have thought your grandfather would come down with a bug on the day we needed him to babysit?"

"It worked out well, and the children are so excited to see Father."

Herr Bader's son still hadn't arrived, and it concerned him that his train wouldn't get in that night. Netti asked him where the young woman, Anika Dunkle, was. "Oh, her father's train came in a little after six. She said quick goodbyes and rushed out to meet him. Your friend thought it best not to wake you. I'm sorry you missed saying goodbye to her."

"I am too. I hope everything works out for them."

As Theodor and Gisela were returning from who knows where, the Americans were making another security sweep through the train station. This time Netti wasn't in the best of moods, still trying to wake up and shake off the fearful effects of her bad dream. To Theodor's surprise, she wasn't hospitable to the two young Americans, very much out of character for her.

"Are you okay, dear?" Theodor asked.

"I'm sorry. I've been here too long, and I'm finding it hard to deal with the anxiety about Father."

"I know how hard it is, but it won't be long now. I'm as tired of waiting as you are, Netti. And I wish the damned Americans would stop checking and rechecking our papers. I mean, what the hell, they've seen us sitting here or walking around the station all day."

"Looks like Netti's not the only one on edge," Gisela said.

"You should talk, Gisela. You've been pacing around here like a caged lion."

"Oh, hell, Theodor; we're all frazzled, but it won't do any good to keep getting on each other's nerves."

"Gisela's right, Theodor; we need to sit down and take some deep breaths and be thankful the train will be here soon."

Katia came back from the lavatory to join Netti, Gisela, and Theodor, who were sitting quietly on their bench across from the girls, who were chattering and poking at each other. Katia sat down and stretched out, hoping the train might get in early. Netti once again pulled out the crumpled telegram from her father. She stared at it intensely, as though it would say something different or tell her who was coming on the train with her father. But it didn't, so she put it back in her purse.

Netti's mind drifted as she considered the possibilities of who could be with her father. Then suddenly the necklace came to mind. She never told anyone what she found in Mitzi's purse, and it still surprised her that Gisela, usually the curious one, hadn't searched it. "Knowing Mitzi," she pondered again, "she probably stole it." She had thought about throwing the necklace in a trash barrel and forgetting all about it. But she thought better of that idea, finally deciding to tell her father about it in the next few days. Netti also looked forward to giving him her mother's imperial jade wedding ring, which was hidden with Mitzi's necklace. She had held it for her mother or father since the day Lisbeth gave it to Liesel before fleeing the barn. Above all, though, Netti hoped against hope that one day soon her mother would be wearing the ring again.

It was ten to eight and Netti was playing on the floor with Karla and Hermine. Seeing her joy, Theodor spoke to Gisela just loud enough for Netti to hear. "Such is the world of Netti Behrmann."

Netti bristled as she always did when hearing Theodor's tedious expression. "I heard that, Theodor. Are you purposely trying to annoy me or just trying to make me laugh?"

"Neither one, dear. Just commenting on all the wonderful blessings in your world."

"Well, stop it, please."

"I guess that's your pat response too."

"Ohh," Netti slurred, almost laughing. "You win, Theodor."

Just as Netti got up from the floor, the announcement finally came: "Train from Leipzig now arriving on platform four."

Netti started shaking, unable to calm herself. The moment she had waited so long for was finally here. And she found it difficult to control her emotions. Fear and uncertainty buffeted great joy and hope. The others only looked forward to seeing Jürgen. None of them had expectations beyond that.

Theodor and the seven members of the Behrmann family made their way out the side door of the terminal and walked briskly to platform four. It was a cool June evening, and the sun had almost set. They didn't know that much of the south end of platform four was under construction to repair damage from the February bombing raid. The trains stopped well south of where they normally would, because that debarking zone was unusable. Also, the train station had blocked off some access to the south with large curtains to seal off a potentially dangerous construction site.

Anton Bader also accompanied Netti to platform four, thinking his son could be on the train from Leipzig. He said he had never received specific instructions about what train his son was taking, only that he would arrive sometime on the seventeenth. He also said Netti had talked of her father in such glowing terms that he would like to meet him.

Soon they all heard the sound of a train clacking slowly down the track as it entered the station. Two shrill whistle blasts signaled its arrival, exciting the whole family and many others on the platform. The train slipped further down the track and finally stopped. Most of the passenger cars were to the south of the construction curtains.

Suspense built as the family looked for Jürgen's appearance through the four-meter corridor between the edge of the platform and the construction curtains. There were now over a hundred people waiting on platform four to greet their loved ones and friends. All were restricted to a site ten meters north of the construction curtains.

Netti saw her father first. Her heart jumped when she recognized him. Strangely, as he passed the curtains, he turned back and raised his right hand, as if to say stop, then he turned back and continued walking toward them. A moment later the others saw him, and Katia yelled out, "There he is, everyone!" She immediately started to quiver as tears filled her eyes. They were all shocked as Jürgen approached. He was so pale and thin, not the same man who left the Cologne train station four years ago.

Then Gisela yelled, "That can't be; is that Trudi with Uncle Jürgen?"

"My God, it is!" said Netti, now breaking down as she stared in disbelief at the gaunt woman she hardly recognized as her sister.

"Who's the woman holding Jürgen's arm?" Theodor asked.

"I don't know, but it looks like she's with them," Katia said.

Theodor yelled as loud as he could, "Jürgen, Jürgen, over here, Jürgen!"

Jürgen heard his good friend's voice, and as he turned toward them, he saw his precious Netti first in the sea of waiting faces. He stumbled as he was overcome with emotion, but Lili steadied him. Jürgen wanted to run to Netti and Theodor as fast as he could, but he lacked the strength to do so.

Netti crowded to the front of those waiting and jumped into her father's arms as he reached the receiving platform. He kissed her cheek and held her as tightly as his frail body would allow. Netti was crying all over his suit jacket. "Father, father, father, I needed you!"

"I missed you so much, sweetheart. I always felt your prayers—felt like you were always close."

"I sensed your closeness too, father, but I needed your comforting touch. So much has happened. I don't know where to begin."

"It's been four years, sweetie. We'll have to catch up, but not now—maybe tomorrow."

"Of course. I'm just glad to have you home again." Jürgen hugged Netti again as she turned her head to see the others approaching.

Then Jürgen took Katia in his arms and kissed her tear-drenched cheek. "Dear Katia, how are you, darling?"

"We're okay. My God, Jürgen, what kind of hell have you been through?"

Theodor and Gisela moved close and put their arms around Jürgen and Katia. They were appalled at how emaciated he looked, with dark circles under his sunken eyes. They told him how much they missed him and how glad they were that he was now safely home.

As they were reminiscing, Netti and Trudi embraced tenderly, holding each other and not saying a word. Trudi soaked up all the strength she could from Netti, something she missed and craved. "You're a mess, sister, but we'll fix that with lots of tender love and care."

"Oh, God, Netti, it's so good to be home—with my family."

Just then Trudi felt a tug on the back of her jacket. "Mommy, is it you, Mommy?"

Trudi hadn't seen her girls who had been hidden among the grown-ups. She thought maybe they left them at home. Trudi turned quickly. To her amazement, she saw a beautiful girl she hardly recognized. Trudi took Helene in her arms and showered her with kisses. She rocked her back and forth. "I love you, sweetheart. Mommy missed you so very much." All Helene could do was cry and clutch her mother tightly.

It had been nearly four years since Trudi last saw her daughters. Helene had been four and now she was a week away from her eighth birthday. "You're so big, darling, so preciously beautiful." Trudi's heart sang out as she looked around for Hermine. Then she saw a little girl, holding Gisela's hand, with a puzzled look on her face. Trudi knew it was her Hermine. "Thank you, God! What a wonderful sight." She had been only two and a half when she left her in that barn, promising to come back, and now she had. Trudi's heart ached for Hermine. "She probably doesn't remember who I am," she thought.

Trudi slowly walked to her little girl and knelt beside her. "Hi, darling; do you remember me?"

Hermine backed up closer to Gisela's right hip and said, "Mommy?"

"Yes, precious one, I'm your mommy." Trudi tried to choke back the tears, which she thought would upset her girl, who looked so fragile. "Do you have a hug for mommy?"

"Yesssss," she said shyly as she slowly came to Trudi with open arms. Trudi kissed her on the cheek and gently took her in her arms. She looked up at Netti with tears rolling down her face.

Lili faded into the background, allowing Jürgen to freely enjoy the reunion he had looked forward to for so long. Then Netti asked her father about the young woman with him.

"Lili," Jürgen said, as he turned to see where she was. "Come here, dear; I want you to meet my family. This is Netti, whom you know all about. And this is my sister Katia. This is my niece Gisela. I can't believe it, but these are my granddaughters, Helene and Hermine. Netti, this can't be Karla?"

"It is, Father." Tears came to Jürgen's eyes, knowing the loss of Kurt had crushed his daughter. Netti sensed what her father was thinking. "It still hurts, Father, but it gets a little easier each day." He didn't say a word but just tenderly hugged his girl again.

"Who is this little girl, Gisela?"

"It'll shock you, Uncle Jürgen. It's your granddaughter, Gretchen."

"Dear God, how? How is she here, and where's her mother?"

"It's complicated, Father. We'll fill you in later," Netti answered.

Jürgen understood that they didn't want to say any more about it in front of Gretchen.

"Come here, darlings." Jürgen knelt gingerly to embrace both Karla and Gretchen as they slowly came to him. Getting up, he said to Lili, "And this is my best friend, Theodor."

Lili shook all their hands as he introduced them. Then Jürgen said, "This is Lili Strobel, a new addition to our family."

"What do you mean, Jürgen?" Katia asked.

"Lili's been with me through hell these last two and a half years. But God's been with us the whole time. We've seen Him move in ways that's hard to explain. I wouldn't be here without Lili, and I've come to love her as a daughter. She got horrible news last month. Her mother and father died last year during a bombing raid in Berlin. And both of her brothers died in Russia. Her family is gone, so I made her part of ours."

Jürgen put his arm around Lili, affirming his proclamation and love for her. She cried as she looked at those who loved Jürgen and thought of her own family who she would never see again. Lili hoped they were as wonderful as Jürgen said and would accept and love her. But it was too hard for her to think about a new life with new people right then. Lili held Jürgen's eyes for a second;

both knew it might be a long time, if ever, before they could share where they'd been and what they did. First, they would have to justify what they did in their own minds, if they could.

Netti was ecstatic that her father was finally home, and to see Trudi was both a joyous blessing and a shock. But the question that Netti had been afraid to ask concerned the fate of her mother and Sophie. "They were with Trudi, but now where are they?" she thought. "Are Trudi and Lili the only *we* that Father referred to in his telegram?" she wondered. "Where is Mother?" Netti asked, as she looked at her father with pleading eyes.

Jürgen looked sadly at his daughter. "I'm sorry, darling."

Netti knew for a long time—deep in her spirit—that her mother was gone. Now she had to face the finality of it. Netti let her father comfort her. She was all cried out, so only a tear fell from her eye.

As Jürgen released her, Trudi hugged Netti again. "Mother asked me to tell you how much she loved you, and how sorry she was for not treating you right. She desperately wanted to come home to make everything right with you and father."

"Thanks, Trudi. Those words mean everything to me." Both of them wept again.

"You would have been so proud of the woman mother became under such horrible conditions. Through great suffering, she came to the end of herself and learned how to love in a deep and meaningful way. She loved two little girls in our apartment with all her heart. Mother was sorry that she hadn't shown the same love to us, Netti."

"Dear God, you don't know how much I wanted that love, Trudi. I'm sorry that she didn't get her wish to make it home. Thanks, Sis. It blesses me to know how she felt at the end."

"Everyone came to love mother in a new way. We were all close those last months. We found God, Netti. I don't discount your Jesus, but I've returned to my heritage, the Jewish faith. It's a long story, but through the agony of it all, I met and married a wonderful Jewish man. Johann and his father went to the gas chambers with others we knew." Trudi was trembling as she spoke of her husband, choking back more tears.

"Dear God, that breaks my heart, Trudi."

"But he gave me back something no one will ever take from me, Netti."

"I'm so thankful that you found your God."

"Sophie also returned to her heritage before it was too late. She doubted and scoffed most of the time, always saying that if God were real, He would never allow such horror. But she finally relented and made her peace with Him."

"Sophie's gone, too?" Netti asked.

Jürgen and Trudi looked at each other with sad but puzzled faces. Both then looked back toward the construction curtains. "No, darling, your Aunt Sophie is with us. She was taking care of something but should be along soon," Jürgen said.

"Thank you, dear Jesus. I don't know what I'd do if I lost mother and Sophie, too," Netti said.

Jürgen took Netti in his arms again. "My heart breaks for your loss, sweetheart. I don't know what to say. I never thought this war would do such damage and take so many lives here at home. Everyone knew we would be in danger, but we couldn't fathom what was happening here."

"They were at the church, Father, that's what upsets me even more. It's been over three years, but the hurt never goes away."

"I know, sweetheart, I know. At the right time, Netti, seeds are put in the ground so new life can bloom. And sometimes He reserves blessings for His perfect time. He's a miraculous Savior who has something special for you, darling. God's faithful to keep all of His promises."

"It's special to have all of you back, Father. That's enough for me."

As Netti turned, wiping tears from her eyes, she saw three people approaching. To her astonishment, it was Didi and a woman helping Sophie as she walked feebly toward them. Netti had a hard time sorting out all that was happening. "How could Didi, Trudi, and Sophie all be with Father?" she thought. "It doesn't make sense. It must be God. He's the only one who orchestrates the impossible."

Didi purposely held back, hesitant about the reunion that was seconds away. He had made peace with his father and knew he forgave him for acting like a fool before the war. Jürgen assured him again that he wasn't at fault for Kora's death. Didi knew in his heart that his father was just grateful to have his son back. But he wasn't as sure about how the rest of the family would feel. He hadn't seen Netti for months before he left for the Wehrmacht. He knew that she could hardly stand to be in the same room with him. And Aunt Katia's scorn continually haunted him. How could he face her? He wanted to turn and run, but it was too late. "But maybe it'll be okay," he thought. "After all, Trudi seemed happy to see me. And Sophie never blamed me for anything. She just hugged me. God please help me."

Netti held back as Didi and Sophie drew near. Didi immediately caught Katia's eyes looking directly at him. He dreaded confronting her. Then as he looked down to Katia's left, it happened again to his bewilderment. There she was, the little girl who looked like Kora. It was the girl who led him out of the death trench near Rovno, who pointed to shelter along the stream, and came to him near the village of Valeuka. Didi believed she wasn't real, but here she was again. Why was she appearing to him now?

The little girl smiled at Didi, something she had never done before. Then she looked up into Katia's eyes with a broad smile, matching Katia's smile as she looked down.

"Does she see her?" Didi thought, now more in awe of what was happening. Then the little girl looked back at him with the same smile. She reached out both arms, signaling him to come. Then she put down her left arm and waved goodbye with her right hand before disappearing. As Katia looked back at Didi, she raised her arms toward him with a broad smile and tears in her eyes. Now he understood it all, as he ran to Katia's arms. They embraced tearfully before either spoke.

"What did you see when you looked down, Aunt Katia?"

"See? Nothing, Didi. But I had the strangest feeling. I don't know if I can explain it. It was a warm sensation coming up on my right side. When I turned to look, I felt total peace, Didi! It's crazy, but I know Kora was assuring me that she's okay and wants all of us to be free. So now I need to forgive you, Didi. I never did in my heart. I need to forgive Jürgen and myself too."

"You forgave me when you raised your arms, motioning me to come. For the first time I felt it, Aunt Katia, the warmth, the love, the forgiveness. And now finally—once and for all—I can forgive myself."

After eighteen years, they both knew it was alright. Didi's guilt lifted, as he felt true forgiveness. And Katia received the total peace that had been so elusive.

Katia's hugging Didi broke the ice. Soon Netti and the others, except Gisela, were welcoming him home and showering him with hugs and kisses. Emotion overwhelmed Didi, as he soaked up the love that was a healing balm to his soul. He felt like he could breathe again, could live again.

Then Didi saw Gisela, beautiful but sad. He had forgiven her years ago for what he knew was a minor offense. But he hadn't forgiven himself for his stupidity, the horrible mistake of marrying Mitzi and all that happened after that. He doubted she would ever forgive him. Then his focus went from Gisela to the girl standing in front of her. Her pretty face, which looked so much like Mitzi, stunned Didi. It had to be Gretchen, the daughter he only hoped to see again. "She was only two when I left her behind, and now she must be almost seven," Didi thought. He bit down softly on his cheek as he approached her. Gretchen looked puzzled as everyone around watched intently. Sadly, they all realized that Gretchen didn't know who her father was. Gisela knelt down beside her. "This is your daddy, darling." Gretchen turned from Didi and hid her face in Gisela's chest.

"Don't rush it, Didi; it's a shock for her," Gisela said. Didi pulled back, just thankful to see his girl again. But at that moment he couldn't help but think of his other daughter. "Is Galina safe? How long will it be before I can go to Minsk and get her?" As Didi looked at Gisela, grief over the loss of Klara rushed back in.

"How did she get here? Is Mitzi here, too?"

Gisela stood up and said, "No, Didi; she died in an auto accident earlier this year. Thank God Gretchen was okay, and we found her."

"It must be God. He's the only one who could bring us all back to this place," Didi said. "I know it's not right, but I feel only sad about my life with Mitzi. Hearing that she's dead doesn't make me any sadder."

"No, none of us feel bad, except for the sadness of a wasted life and a lost soul," Netti said. "It's going to be okay, Didi. In time Gretchen will know that you're her daddy, and we'll all help you in any way we can."

"Thanks, Netti. That means everything to me now." Didi took his sister in his arms and rocked her gently, letting her love spark new life and hope in his heart. Netti's eyes watered again as she knew her brother, who once was lost was now found.

Sophie was having a difficult time standing, so Isabell propped her up. Netti kissed Sophie's cheek. "Do you need to sit down, Auntie?"

"No, dear, I'm fine."

"Is this someone who made the journey home with you and Trudi?" Netti asked.

"Yes, Netti, this is Isabell Riese. She lived with us in Lodz, and we went to Auschwitz together," Sophie said. "We call her Issy and love her as a sister. Your father adopted Lili into the family, and we adopted Issy. Sadly, she finds herself in the same position as Lili; her family is gone. She recently learned that her father died in Dachau and her mother perished in Warsaw."

"I'm sorry, Isabell. I know the pain you must be feeling, but we'll love you like our own," Netti said.

"From the love I've received from Trudi and Sophie, I know you will."

Netti and Isabell embraced tenderly, knowing each suffered horribly because of the whims of a madman and those who foolishly followed him. "I can't believe that mother, Trudi, and Sophie went to a Polish ghetto and then to a death camp," Netti thought. "How terrible that must have been."

As they did for Lili, everyone graciously welcomed Isabell to the Behrmann family. She felt their love and acceptance immediately and asked them all to call her Issy.

Sophie was hesitant to say anything about what happened to them. Trudi had told Jürgen and now Netti that they almost lost Sophie several times, but she always bounced back. She said so much happened in Poland and on their journey home that it would take hours to tell the incredible story. But Trudi did tell everyone that she knew it wouldn't be long until the old Sophie was back. "In fact," she said with a broad smile, "I'm sure one day soon you'll all be laughing and saying, 'There goes Sophie again.'"

It puzzled Netti as to how Didi, Sophie, and Trudi found her father; and why he didn't tell her about them in his telegram. "How did this all happen, Father?"

"Didi's been with me for a few months. It's a long story that I'll tell you about later, sweetheart. He asked me not to say anything, worrying about everyone's reaction when they found out he was coming home. As for Sophie and Trudi, by a pure miracle of God they found us three days ago, after I sent my last telegram. It's also a story for later."

"But what about you and Lili, Father? Where were you all that time?"

"Not now, Netti. It's a long and complicated story. I'm not ready to go into it tonight."

"I understand. But I'd like to know all about it soon."

Most of the people waiting on the platform were gone, as Anton Bader came over to meet Jürgen. He had stayed back, watching the joyous family reunion. Netti caught Herr Bader out of the corner of her eye and walked over to introduce him to her father. But as he approached Jürgen, Bader suddenly stopped and reached inside his jacket. He quickly pulled out a small pistol and pointed it at Jürgen.

Netti and the others froze in shock, but not Jürgen.

"You know who I am?"

"Yes, I recognize you, Heinz Wagner."

The turn of events stunned Theodor and Netti. They had politely conversed for hours with the man who wanted to kill Jürgen.

"I've been waiting many years to get my revenge," Wagner said.

The sound of two shots rang across the train station and Jürgen slumped to the platform. One shot grazed his shoulder and the other one hit him in the chest. Chaos reigned as Netti, Theodor, and others ran to Jürgen. As they did, Heinz Wagner put the pistol barrel in his mouth and fired another round. Gisela and Trudi quickly grabbed the girls and sheltered their eyes from the gruesome scene. Wagner writhed on the platform for a few seconds and then he was still, as Netti and Theodor knelt next to Jürgen.

"No, God! How could this be?" Netti screamed in her mind. "How could God let this happen after Father went through hell to get home. How could He allow such a cruel twist?"

Those now gathered around Jürgen were screaming or crying in disbelief. Then Theodor put his hands under Jürgen's limp body and lifted him. Devastated, no one else knew what to do. Suddenly, Jürgen opened his eyes and shook his head back and forth. Netti screamed out, "Thank you, dear Jesus! Praise your name." She looked at Theodor, and both knew at that moment what had saved him.

Theodor reached under Jürgen's jacket and pulled out the shredded New Testament and cigarette case from his shirt pocket. There was a hole in each, but the bullet hadn't made it completely through the backside of the heavy cigarette case. As Theodor ripped open Jürgen's shirt, they saw a red mark on his chest, with a trickle of blood. The force of the bullet had just broken the skin, and the impact had only stunned Jürgen for a minute. He felt pain where the second bullet grazed his shoulder. After getting his jacket and shirt off, they found a flesh wound with little blood on his left shoulder.

An American medic arrived with a first-aid kit and helped Gisela patch Jürgen up. The military police covered Heinz Wagner's body and then questioned everyone about what happened. The family was still trying to gather themselves from this latest blow, which almost resulted in another gut-wrenching loss.

A disturbing thought ran through Netti's mind: "What if Father would have obeyed my deepest wish for him to quit smoking?" She could hardly bear thinking about what would have happened if only the New Testament were in his shirt pocket. But, at the same time, Netti and her father knew it was only God's provision that saved him, once again. They both knew His plans might take years to complete, but He's never early or late.

After bandaging Jürgen, Theodor and Didi helped him to his feet. Everyone, including Theodor, knew that God had interceded once more in their lives, for which they gave Him great thanks. In pain, Jürgen went to the girls to assure them he was okay, wiping away their tears and kissing each on the cheek.

As Jürgen sat back down on a bench, with Netti on one side and Katia on the other, he suddenly remembered something. "Netti, go down south past the construction curtains; someone wants to see you."

"Who wants to see me, Father?"

"Just go, sweetheart; you'll see."

Not having any idea about what her father was talking about Netti slowly walked south to the construction curtains. As she went down to where the passengers had left the train, she saw only two American soldiers and a train conductor. By now she was feeling dizzy with all the excitement and not having much to eat. Netti sat down on a bench to steady herself and rest for a minute. She was so thankful that her father had survived yet again. Netti was also grateful that the "we" in his telegram included so many loved ones that she thought she'd never see again. She bowed her head to thank her heavenly Father for being so gracious to all of them.

"Netti," a voice called.

Netti stirred from deep thought, thinking she heard a familiar voice calling her name.

"Netti."

This time the call got her attention. She raised her head and opened her eyes. As Netti looked up, she thought she was dreaming or hallucinating. "Too much stress," she thought.

"Netti, are you okay?"

Netti's heart jumped and skipped several beats as she realized it was no hallucination.

"But how could this be?" she thought. "Of all the miracles in my life, this is the greatest one of all!"

Netti sprang to her feet and leaped into the waiting arms of the gaunt man with sunken but loving eyes. "Conrad, Conrad! How can it be you, Conrad?"

"Just hold me, Netti. I'll explain later, but now I just need to feel your warmth and love."

Netti looked into Conrad's eyes and moved closer to him. They kissed gently. Netti broke down in Conrad's arms. It was all too much for her. She sobbed deeply, pressing her head against his chest and holding him as tightly as she could. He stroked her hair, saying how much he loved her and how he had dreamed of this day when he could hold her again.

"Your father told me about Mose and your son. It breaks my heart, Netti. I'm sorry."

"It gets better as time passes, but it'll always hurt. But now I know healing can finally come to all our lives. Tell me what happened, Conrad. The authorities told us that you died of a stroke at Buchenwald. They even sent us your wallet and watch."

"I'm sorry for that, sweetheart. I've worried for a long time that our trick would hurt you. I could kick myself."

"What do you mean, Conrad? What trick?"

"We always did things to confuse the guards. The last trick we played was switching identities. I took Kurt's shirts and he took mine. They identified us by the number sown on our shirts, just above the inverted red triangle. I managed to hide my pocket watch and wallet the whole time we were in prison. I gave them to Kurt and he gave me his ring that he had hidden. It was a foolish idea that we didn't think through. Dear God, that's one stunt I wish we'd never pulled. We had no idea what would happen."

"What did happen?"

"Something horrible. A prisoner went crazy and killed a guard with his bare hands. In retribution, the commandant ordered the immediate execution of five prisoners. The most brutal person in the camp, Major Alfred Von Buskirk, walked up and down the line of prisoners, shooting five in the head. Kurt was the last one he shot. It took a year before I began to recover. You know how much I loved him."

"Conrad, dear Jesus, will the accounts of senseless carnage ever stop?"

"I'm sorry that I hurt you, Netti."

"You couldn't know what would happen, and now you're here, darling. That's all I care about. I'm rejoicing beyond belief, but at the same time, I'm feeling bad about Kurt. Tell me, though, you were there all that time, Conrad, eight years?"

"I was in prison all that time. They sent me from Cologne to Buchenwald in 1937. Then they sent me to three other camps before the Americans freed me."

"But how did you get to Leipzig?"

"That's a long story; it would take me all day to tell you about it. Now I only want to hold you, if that's okay?"

"That's all I want you to do, darling."

"Just know that God saved me many times. What He did will thrill you."

"I'm already far beyond amazed at what's happened today. But why didn't you come to me right away with father and the others?"

"I wanted you to enjoy the reunion with him and your family, first. And I was also selfish, wanting to enjoy this moment alone with you."

"It wasn't selfish at all, darling. It was perfect, and I'm all yours now. I just hope nobody pinches me and I wake up. Father hinted that something special was in store when he comforted me about losing Mose and Kurt. Tell me Conrad, how did you ever find father in Leipzig?"

"I didn't find him. I saw Didi yesterday when I went to the train station to buy my ticket to Meiningen. Most people would say it was an incredible coincidence, but we know better."

"Why would you come here, and not Cologne?"

"I just knew you were here, sweetheart. I tried but couldn't reach you in Cologne."

"So you weren't with father and the others when he sent his last telegram?"

"That's right. Since we were leaving the next day, we decided not to send another one."

"It's okay. The way it worked out was precious. Are you upset that I married Mose?"

"No, it seemed like the best choice you could make. I knew that Mose loved you from the start."

"You kidded me about it all the time."

"I'm sorry that you had to experience those losses, Netti."

"It was hard, as hard as losing you, Conrad. But now I see the whole picture. I know it's time to move on from grief and embrace what God has given back to me."

"It's time for all of us to move on from this hell and begin our lives anew. Are you ready to join the others?"

"Yes, they'll be so thrilled and shocked to see you. Did you hear the commotion, the gunshots earlier?"

"Gunshots! No, what happened?"

"Another miracle involving father. You'll hear all the details soon."

The sight of Conrad walking toward them arm in arm with Netti dumbfounded Katia, Gisela, and Theodor. Everyone rejoiced with them, hardly able to fathom all that was playing out on platform four of the Meiningen train station. The area was now empty except for an American soldier, two train station workers, and the Behrmann family.

It was nearing nine o'clock and only a few dim lights held back the closing darkness. Everyone agreed it was time to go home and wind down from what had proved to be an exhausting day for all. But it was obvious, with eleven adults and four children, that two autos couldn't take everyone home. Netti, Conrad, Trudi, and Theodor insisted the others needed to go home and rest. Gisela could drive Theodor's auto and they would wait for Katia to return for them.

As the others left for the parking lot with their belongings, Netti, Conrad, Theodor, and Trudi went back inside the train station. They sat down in the deserted station on benches facing each other.

"How is father really doing, Trudi, after learning that mother is gone?" Netti asked.

"When Sophie told him, three days ago, it crushed him, Netti. He went in the other room alone for over an hour. His eyes were red when he came back. He cried the whole time. Then he tried to be brave about it. But a few times since, I've seen the tears well up in his eyes. He's hurting badly, Netti. We need to comfort him in any way we can."

"We all will. I feel so sad for him. I need to ask you something else, Trudi."

"What, Sis?"

"First, I need to tell you that Gert lost his life in France and Erich was badly wounded."

"How sad. I'm sorry that I never got close to Gert, but it's still terrible news. What about Erich, is he okay?"

"He is, partially at least. Physically he's almost all the way back, but he has a way to go, otherwise."

"Has he changed at all, Netti—you know?"

"Yes, he's given his life to God, and he's sincerely sorry for what he did to you and me. That's what I wanted to talk to you about, for him."

"I think I know, but go ahead, Netti."

"Erich is using his one promise of the heart to ask for your forgiveness."

"I have no choice but to forgive him, and I do. I don't even know what happened for sure, Netti, do you?"

"No, I don't. Erich never said if he was the one who told Wolf, though the guilt he felt was great for whatever part he played in your misery. But his Lord has forgiven him, and now all he wants is to make it right with everyone he hurt. You know he'll always love you, Trudi. But it might take a long time before he's able to face you again."

"I don't think I'm ready to see him for a while, either. I forgive him, but the pain will be with me for a long time. I just don't understand Erich. If he were older, I could have loved him back when he kissed me. He was such a sweet boy; then he let his hate hurt so many people."

"I know, Trudi. I could never understand Erich, but now I feel good about how his life is going."

"Is he at home with Wolf and Elise?"

"No, Erich and Elise are at the farm with his grandfather."

"What about Wolf? I almost hope he got what he deserved."

"Nobody knows for sure. He planned to flee Germany to avoid capture for crimes he had committed. Then one day he was gone. We think he was going to Spain and then on to South America."

"Good riddance! What about my brother and sister, Netti?"

"Liesel's fine. She's now back in Cologne with her husband, Felix. They'll live in my place until we get back."

"My little sister's married?"

"A lot has happened since you've been gone, Trudi."

"And Waldo?"

Netti stared at the floor and then looked up at Trudi, not being able to hide the hole in her heart. "It's not good, Sis."

"God, no! He's gone, too?"

"No, he's not dead, but he has a severe head injury. We can go see him tomorrow. Please don't ask me anything more. Wait till you see him, and you'll understand. I can't explain it any further; it hurts too much."

"That scares the hell out of me, Netti. I need to see and hold my brother as soon as I can."

"You will, dear."

"What about Stefan? Is he back in Cologne now?"

"He's with Liesel and Felix. Fortunately, he came through the war unscathed."

"I'm thankful for some good news," Trudi sighed.

"The other problem is Wilhelm. He's continually asked Katia about you since your abduction by the Gestapo. She says he still loves you, probably more than he did when they took you."

"Darling Wilhelm. How do I deal with that now, Netti? I'm still hurting so much for what they did to my husband. Johann was the most gentle and wonderful man; he loved and protected me with everything he had."

"You need to grieve for as long as it takes. My heart still hurts for Mose, but now I know I can go on with Conrad. Someday you might feel the same about Wilhelm."

"Maybe. I know I'll have to see him, but right now I can't think about it."

Netti reached across and took Trudi's hands. "Of course you can't, sweetie. He'll understand once he knows what happened."

"Does Father know about Waldo and his brother?" Trudi asked.

"I'm sure he'll ask Katia or Gisela about them before we see him later."

"I'm worried about his condition, Netti. Hearing about Waldo won't help."

"I know. At least we can all start to heal, even Waldo. But now we have to concentrate on the move back to Cologne. We have to get out of here before the Russians take charge in July. Trying to get something for the family home and arranging to pick up Waldo so that he can go with us, won't be easy."

"I can't think about that now, Netti, maybe tomorrow?"

"Tomorrow's fine. After all that's happened, each one of us needs a good night's sleep."

Jürgen was stricken when Katia told him about their mother and Waldo. Doubts about his decision surfaced again. After Katia left to pick up the others at the train station, he asked Sophie one more time if they made the right decision in honoring Markus' request. It was the same question he asked her after she told him of Lisbeth's passing. Neither could fully accept the fact that, even though they did all they could to honor Markus' request to protect his children, Waldo and Trudi still had to go through hell. And Lisbeth would most likely be alive, and Sophie would have avoided her own hell if they had never moved to Cologne.

Sophie reminded Jürgen that he felt strongly at the time it was God's will for him to honor Markus' request. "Who knows what would have happened if we didn't honor his request," Sophie said. "All three of his children might have gone to the gas chambers." She pleaded with Jürgen to have faith that God led him, and He was in the decision they made those many years ago. Even so, both knew it would take time to find the peace they sought about the decision that changed the course of so many lives.

Jürgen took Sophie in his arms. "I can't tell you how glad I am to have you in my life again, little Sis. Dear God, I missed you so much. Every day I thought of you. I thought often of the first day we met. How you won me over with your winning ways and those dazzling magic tricks. Then there was the day you scared us half to death, coming out of the bushes and saying, 'Boo.'"

"And you put me in a headlock and scrubbed the top of my head. Then I asked you if I could be your blood sister. You said you already took me as your sister the first day we met. I played those scenes in my mind a million times over the last three years. They kept me going, and I'll always be thankful for your love, Jürgen."

Jürgen and Lili weren't ready to tell the family about where they were and what they did. They still felt it was God's leading for them to help the Russian soldiers, but they had little peace about telling anyone about it. Didi knew only part of their story, and they knew only part of his. They all agreed to say nothing until everyone was comfortable with sharing the details. However, all three knew God's hand was on them in a special way, as shown by the trail of miracles and fulfillment of promises that led them home. They might always have the shadow of sorrow in their hearts, but they would also have the peace and strength to look forward and embrace the loved ones surrounding them.

A trip to Minsk was already on Didi's mind. He had to bring Galina home to meet her sister and the rest of the family. He hoped, deep down, that God would heal the pain of losing Klara and maybe one day allow him to make everything right with Gisela. He had no wish to rekindle their relationship; he only wanted Gisela to forgive him for his mistakes.

It was almost ten when Katia got back to the train station. She let Netti and Trudi know that she had told their father about Waldo, his mother, Wolf, Liesel, and Stefan. "The news of Waldo and his mother crushed him again, but he was happy for Liesel and Stefan and almost indifferent about his brother."

"We're all overwhelmed with what we've learned today. There's still so much we don't know," Netti said.

"We all have our stories to tell, Netti. I'm not sure if Sophie and I will ever be able to tell you everything that happened to us. I'm not sure if I want to remember most of it. And from what little Didi has told me, his story could be as bad as, or worse, than ours. I know he doesn't want to talk about it. And even father has been almost secretive about where he and Lili have been."

"Each of them has a lot to tell us; maybe tomorrow, Trudi?"

"Let's go home," said Katia.

Everyone wearily picked up their belongings and started walking to Katia's auto. Theodor trailed behind, hearing the clacking of heels on the cobblestone. His mind was spinning in amazement at the happenings of the day. He now knew for sure that God had moved incredibly on behalf of the family. "I've seen too much, God," Theodor thought. "I can't put it off any longer. Tonight Netti has to tell me how I can open my heart and receive the gift she's always offering. I need to know you, God, the way she does."

At that moment he felt privileged to be a small part of what was happening. But most of all, he was happy for Netti, the young woman he loved. He was able to rejoice that Conrad was alive and with her again. As he trailed the others, Theodor whispered in reverence so no one would hear, "Such is the world of Netti Behrmann."